WORDS THAT WILL TAKE YOU TO THE TOP OF THE WORLD . . .

"The last of the lonely places is the sky, a trackless void where nothing lives or grows, and above it, space itself. Man may have been destined to walk upon ice and sand, or climb the mountains or take a craft upon the sea. But surely he was never meant to fly? But he does, and finding out how to do it was his last great adventure. . . ."

—Frederick Forsyth

"I alighted gently in my own home meadow at Devizes, after such a journey as no mortal upon earth has ever yet taken and lived to tell the tale. I have seen the beauty and I have seen the horror of the heights—and greater beauty or greater horror than that is not within the ken of man. . . ."

—Sir Arthur Conan Doyle

"They took Peter from the wreckage with scarcely a scar except his twisted leg. Death had smoothed out some of the age in him, and left his face much as I remembered it long ago. It was from *Pilgrim's Progress* I read next morning, when I stood in the soft spring rain beside his grave: 'So he passed over, and all the trumpets sounded for him on the other side.'"

—John Buchan

EDITED AND INTRODUCED BY

FREDERICK FORSYTH

GREAT FLYING STORIES

POCKET BOOKS

New York   London   Toronto   Sydney   Tokyo   Singapore

This book is a work of fiction. Names, characters, places and incidents are products of the author's imagination or are used fictitiously. Any resemblance to actual events or locales or persons, living or dead, is entirely coincidental.

POCKET BOOKS, a division of Simon & Schuster Inc.
1230 Avenue of the Americas, New York, NY 10020

Copyright © 1991 by Frederick Forsyth

Published by arrangement with W.W. Norton & Company, Inc.

All rights reserved, including the right to reproduce this book or portions thereof in any form whatsoever. For information address W.W. Norton & Company, Inc., 500 Fifth Avenue, New York, NY 10110

ISBN: 0-671-00062-4

First Pocket Books printing August 1997

10 9 8 7 6 5 4 3 2 1

POCKET and colophon are registered trademarks of Simon & Schuster Inc.

Cover photo © Philip Makanna/Ghosts

Printed in the U.S.A.

Contents

Contents

Acknowledgements

Grateful acknowledgement is made to the following for permission to reprint the material in this volume:

My First Aeroplane and *The Argonauts of the Air* by H. G. Wells reproduced by permission of A. P. Watt Ltd. on behalf of the Literary Executors of the Estate of H. G. Wells.

Spads and Spandaus by Captain W. E. Johns reproduced by permisson of A. P. Watt on behalf of W. E. Johns (Publications) Ltd.

To Penguin Books as publishers of *Over to You* by Roald Dahl, the volume in which the story *They Shall Not Grow Old* appears.

Winter's Morning from *Declarations of War* by Len Deighton by permission of Jonathan Cape Ltd.

My Dream of Flying to Wake Island is from the collection *Low-Flying Aircraft* published by Jonathan Cape, London. © 1976 by J. G. Ballard. Reproduced by permission of the author and his agent Margaret Hanbury.

Richard Bach for kind permission to reproduce *Cat*.

The Greatest People in the World and *How Sleep the Brave* by H. E. Bates (Flying Officer X) © Estate of H. E. Bates.

Whilst all reasonable attempts have been made to contact the original copyright holders, the Publishers would be happy to hear from those they have been unable to trace, and due acknowledgement will be made in future editions.

Preface

In an earlier venture among this series of books, a volume called *Great Racing Stories,* it was announced that the introduction to the next, *Great Flying Stories,* would be written by none other than Group Captain Leonard Cheshire VC, now Lord Cheshire.

Almost at the last moment he wrote to me asking, due to pressure of work on himself, if I would take over in his stead. I protested that the reader would be ill-served by the substitution for a bomber ace and war hero of some dilettante with a blink-and-you-miss-it flying career.

He was insistent and I conceded. I still think the reader has drawn a bit of a short straw. Anyway, here goes . . .

Introduction

There are, I believe, five truly lonely places in the world. These are places so wild and barren, so vast in their spread and so awesome in their solitude that they attract few visitors and even then only of a certain type. Moreover, by the power of the influence they exercise upon those who go there, they leave those visitors slightly changed in themselves.

I never knew one of those who had travelled in the lonely places who did not have a proper respect for the power of the Almighty and the Infinite nor lacked an awareness of the inconsequential frailty of Man. Arrogance is for those who live in cities and, as Nansen remarked, rub against each other like pebbles until they become smooth and round.

One of these places is the mountains. Those who have stood, alone, high in the Himalayas or the Andes or even our European Alps, and looked across at the vista of bleak white giants have told me of the sense of utter frailty that consumes the traveller amid this booming silence.

A second place must be the Artic wastes. Man is a warm-blooded creature and few can escape a *frisson* at the contemplation of endless, freezing, merciless, empty cold. Like the ice deserts, the sand deserts also count among the five. These I have seen; here too the vastness, the emptiness and the silence impress upon the traveller a proper sense of his own frailty, a labouring flea who could so easily vanish in that wilderness and none would be the wiser.

The fourth, of course, is the sea, in its way perhaps even more frightening because it moves, constantly and with enormous power. Not for nothing are sailors God-fearing people, for they have seen His fist. On occasion, fishing in the Indian or Atlantic Oceans, I have watched walls of green water higher than houses moving towards the boat, comforted myself that my charter skipper knew what he was doing but still, down in a deep green trough surrounded by moving mountains or peering out from the crest across a wild plain of tossing white-caps, have known the fear inspired by the sheer power of this brutish phenomenon.

The last of the lonely places is the sky, a trackless void where nothing lives or grows, and above it, space itself. Man may have been destined to walk upon ice or sand, or climb the mountains or take a craft upon the sea. But surely he was never meant to fly? But he does, and finding out how to do it was his last great adventure.

Today most of us can fly; that is, we can sit in an armchair with a glass of wine, confident that Mr. Boeing will keep us up there and Messrs. Rolls and Royce will push us along to our holiday destination. Peering through a porthole we prefer not to think that the temperature out there in the stratosphere is seventy-six below zero, the pressure a lethal tenth of an atmosphere, the oxygen content almost zero and all around us is thirty-five thousand feet of screaming rushing air.

But it was not always so, the safety and the comfort, the warmth and the company. The sky can be a wild and lonely place, and thus it was for the pioneers and the fighting men in their frail, creaking contraptions, aware (as we are not) of the fragile line of skill and courage that marked the border between life and the long tumbling fall to death far below.

Still, I have chosen to start this collection of flying stories with humour, H. G. Wells' "My First Aeroplane," a hilarious evocation of the days when a flying machine was a proper toy for a young gentleman, could be parked in the courtyard, take off behind the vicar's orchard and, if Fate willed, crash into a farmer's midden with no harm done.

Introduction

"The Unparalleled Adventures of One Hans Pfaall" by Edgar Allan Poe is quite different, a weird fantasy that seems to draw elements from Baron Münchhausen and Rip Van Winkle. But fun, all the same.

Sir Arthur Conan Doyle's "The Horror of the Heights" is strange too, but in a quite different way. Another tale from the very earliest days of flying, it describes a man who wanted to fly high, very high, as high as our airliners today, to discover what lived above forty thousand feet. So he flew up there, not as we would in a comfortable cocoon, but in an open single-seater with a stuttering engine, wrapped against the freezing cold and sucking on an oxygen bottle to stay alive. And there discovered . . . but I won't spoil the story. All nonsense, of course, as we now know, but one of the first tales to underline how frightening the sky can be.

Wherever Man goes, he seems to find a new element in which to fight, and the First World War turned the amusing, entertaining flying machine into a killer. It also threw up some amazing fighter aces: Richthofen, Boelcke and Immelman for the Germans; Fonck Nungesser and Guynemer for the French; Bishop, Ball, McCudden, Mannock and Hawker for the Commonwealth and Luke and Rickenbacker for the Americans. Many great stories of skill and heroism in the air came out of the Great War, or hark back to it, and I have chosen five.

The first is a little cameo by Capt. W. E. Johns, whom as a boy I read avidly because of his "Biggles" stories. "Spads and Spandaus" describes a baptism of fire for a newly-arrived American Spad squadron at the hands of the fearsome Richthofen Circus. The language may sound a bit *Boy's Own Paper* (did they really say "Oh gosh" when the windscreen disintegrated?—I fear in 1957 we'd have said something a lot less printable) but there was nothing sissy about the risks they ran, those young men of Flanders. The single-skin petrol tanks were fire-hazards, the doped canvas frames went up in flames like tinder, the engines cut out, the guns jammed, the wing-struts snapped and fell apart, and they had no parachutes. The life-expectancy of a new pilot on a line-squadron was twenty days, and that was the average; most were dead in ten. And as for psychiatric stress-counselling . . . !

Introduction

With "The Greatest People in the World" I have jumped
to the Second World War and one of the greatest writers of
flying stories ever—H. E. Bates. I was an early fan because
my parents were lifelong friends of H. E. and Madge Bates
and I was almost brought up with their sons Richard and
Jonathan, in the fields of Kent—*The Darling Buds of May*
countryside.

Although not a flier himself, H. E. Bates was a super
writer with an acute observation and a genuine love of
people. Early in the war, already an established novelist but
of romantic and bucolic fiction, he volunteered for service
and was sent to the Royal Air Force, given the rank of Flying
Officer and told to write morale-boosting stories. Living on
a Stirling bomber station, he just watched the young men
who took off into the dusk each night on bombing missions
over Germany, to come back (some of them) in the pre-
dawn. Out of this came a series of pastiches and cameos that
formed a small anthology, *The Greatest People in the World*
by "Flying Officer X"—his pseudonym. Personally, I rate it
as a classic, a gem, and I have chosen the title story for this
volume.

I have also included later in the book a second, and longer
story by Bates, "How Sleep the Brave," about a Stirling
crew shot down over the North Sea and their struggle to
survive in a pitching dinghy. Although he was never a pilot,
navigator or bomb-aimer, and was never shot down, H. E.
Bates' portrayal of the men who were is one of the most
perceptive descriptions I have read of those strange people
who insist on taking to the air.

Roald Dahl, who died recently, was best known for his
stories for children. But in "They Shall Not Grow Old" he
produced one of the oddest, weirdest stories ever written
with a flying background. Even now I find it hard to decide
whether it is about the supernatural, reincarnation or
premonition. But it haunts; one remembers it.

"Winter's Morning," which follows, is another gem, this
time by Len Deighton. Set back in the First World War, it
seems at first prosaic enough, a cameo of fighter pilots going
off on a morning patrol above Flanders, but ends with a
lovely sting in the tail which sets all the reader's preconcep-
tions on their heads.

Introduction

J. G. Ballard's "My Dream of Flying to Wake Island" is another haunting, enigmatic story in the mood of Roald Dahl. It is the only story from the space age, yet it is not about space. It concerns an astronaut (only a passing reference to space) who, brain-injured in some hinted-at accident, recuperates alone by the seashore. He unearths the carcass of a Second World War bomber in the sand, develops an oblique and unspoken love for a lady aviator who befriends him but, more importantly, also develops an impossible obsession for flying the sand-encrusted wreck to Wake Island in the Pacific. A strange tale.

Richard Bach is better known for *Jonathan Livingston Seagull* (also a story about wings and flight) but in "Cat" he also evokes another characteristic of flying people—superstition. Fliers seem to share this with sailors and boxers; they believe in good and bad luck, and often in mascots to bring the first and avoid the second. In "Cat" Mr. Bach enters the world of a USAF squadron of F-84 Thunderstreaks based somewhere in Europe in the mid-1950s, and of a strange Persian cat who sits near the runway watching them take off and land. Does the cat really, by its presence or absence, affect whether they live or die?

With H. G. Wells' second contribution "The Argonauts of the Air," we go back to the very embryo-days of flying, of hare-brained schemes, crazy inventions, mad designs and lunatic risks. Unlike "My First Aeroplane" there is nothing hilarious about Monson's Flying Machine; it is just a very deadly contraption. But there were many in those days, as amateurs, engineers and enthusiasts tried to build something that would actually leave terra firma and fly. Usually, like Mr. Monson, they got it wrong.

"How Sleep the Brave," which I have already mentioned, precedes a very short story by an author quite forgotten today, F. Britten Austin. It was published in the long-dead *Strand Magazine* in 1914. I have used it because it recalls what those string-and-wire planes were originally sent to Flanders to do: not fight but observe enemy ground movements and report back. "The Air Scout" tells of such a mission and of the pilot's desperate attempts to return home to his own lines and drop his message-bag before the avenging German fighters could close with him. They were amazingly brave men, those air scouts. I once clambered aboard a 1914 Boxkite at an air show—it seemed to be made of varnished garden canes, doped bedsheet and piano wire. The thought of being shot at by ground artillery while flying one at two thousand feet was enough to put me right off lunch. Death may be more spectacular in a fast-flying jet, but it is just as certain when falling from two thousand feet at eight miles an hour.

I do not apologize for concluding the collection with another story from the First World War on the same theme, because John Buchan was another author I consumed as a boy, and Mr. Standfast was a wonderful character. Buchan, of course, was more famous for his stories of Richard Hannay, perhaps our first fictional secret agent and a world removed from George Smiley. But Buchan, like W. E. Johns, also came through the First World War, saw action and went on to write about it. "The Summons Comes for Mr. Standfast" is actually the last chapter of the book about Peter Pienaar, a South African clearly based on a friend of Buchan. But it stands up as a story in its own right. Buchan describes it from the point of view of an infantry officer staring upwards as six German spotter planes realize how weak the British division really is and gleefully head home with the news—news that would doom the British troops to immediate attack and destruction. Five German planes are intercepted and brought down. Only one remains, clearly flown by the ace Lensch. Can nobody stop him? Enter "Mr. Standfast," the nickname of Pienaar, in an obsolete old crate called a Gladas, which is no match for the German. There's not a dry eye in the dug-out!

I also include it because it contains the best last line ever written. Buchan did not invent it; he quoted Bunyan's *Pilgrim's Progress*. But what last lines . . .

Frederick Forsyth
Hertford, July 1991

GREAT FLYING STORIES

My First Aeroplane

(Alauda Magna)

H. G. Wells

My first aeroplane! What vivid memories of youth that recalls!

Far back it was, in the spring of 1912, that I acquired "Alauda Magna," the Great Lark, for so I christened her; and I was then a slender young man of four-and-twenty, with hair—beautiful blond hair—all over my adventurous young head. I was a dashing young fellow enough, in spite of the slight visual defect that obliged me to wear spectacles on my prominent, aquiline, but by no means shapeless nose—the typical flyer's nose. I was a good runner and swimmer, a vegetarian as ever, an all-wooler, and an ardent advocate of the extremest views in every direction about everything. Precious little in the way of a movement got started that I wasn't in. I owned two motor-bicycles, and an enlarged photograph of me at that remote date, in leather skull-cap, goggles, and gauntlets, still adorns my study fireplace. I was also a great flyer of war-kites, and a voluntary scout-master of high repute. From the first beginnings of the boom in flying, therefore, I was naturally eager for the fray.

I chafed against the tears of my widowed mother for a time, and at last told her I could endure it no longer.

1

"If I'm not the first to fly in Mintonchester," I said, "I leave Mintonchester. I'm your own son, Mummy, and that's *me!*"

And it didn't take me a week to place my order when she agreed.

I found one of the old price-lists the other day in a drawer, full of queer woodcuts of still queerer contrivances. What a time that was! An incredulous world had at last consented to believe that it could fly, and in addition to the motor-car people and the bicycle people, and so on, a hundred new, unheard-of firms were turning out aeroplanes of every size and pattern to meet the demand. Amazing prices they got for them too—three hundred and fifty was cheap for the things! I find four hundred and fifty, five hundred, five hundred *guineas* in this list of mine; and many as capable of flight as oak trees! They were sold, too, without any sort of guarantee, and with the merest apology for instruction. Some of the early aeroplane companies paid nearly 200 per cent on their ordinary shares in those early years.

How well I remember the dreams I had—and the doubts!

The dreams were all of wonder in the air. I saw myself rising gracefully from my mother's paddock, clearing the hedge at the end, circling up to get over the vicar's pear trees, and away between the church steeple and the rise of Withycombe, towards the market-place. Lord! how they would stare to see me! "Young Mr. Betts again!" they would say. "We *knew* he'd do it."

I would circle and perhaps wave a handkerchief, and then I meant to go over Lupton's gardens to the grounds of Sir Digby Foster. There a certain fair denizen might glance from the window . . .

Ah, youth! Youth!

My doubts were all of the make I should adopt, the character of the engines I should choose . . .

I remember my wild rush on my motor-bike to London to see the things and give my order, the day of muddy-traffic dodging as I went from one shop to another, my growing exasperation at hearing everywhere the same refrain, "Sold out! Can't undertake to deliver before the beginning of April."

Not me!

My First Aeroplane

I got "Alauda Magna" at last at a little place in Blackfriars Road. She was an order thrown on the firm's hands at the eleventh hour by the death of the purchaser through another maker, and I ran my modest bank account into an overdraft to get her—to this day I won't confess the price I paid for her. Poor little Mumsey! Within a week she was in my mother's paddock, being put together after transport by a couple of not-too-intelligent mechanics.

The joy of it! And a sort of adventurous tremulousness. I'd had no lessons—all the qualified teachers were booked up at stupendous fees for months ahead; but it wasn't in my quality to stick at a thing like that! I couldn't have endured three days' delay. I assured my mother I had had lessons, for her peace of mind—it is a poor son who will not tell a lie to keep his parent happy.

I remember the exultant turmoil of walking round the thing as it grew into a credible shape, with the consciousness of half Mintonchester peering at me through the hedge, and only deterred by our new trespass-board and the disagreeable expression of Snape, our trusted gardener, who was partly mowing the grass and partly on sentry-go with his scythe, from swarming into the meadow. I lit a cigarette and watched the workmen sagely, and we engaged an elderly unemployed named Snorticombe to keep watch all night to save the thing from meddlers. In those days, you must understand, an aeroplane was a sign and a wonder.

"Alauda Magna" was a darling for her time, though nowadays I suppose she would be received with derisive laughter by every schoolboy in the land. She was a monoplane, and, roughly speaking, a Blériot, and she had the dearest, neatest seven-cylinder forty-horse-power GKC engine, with its GBS flywheel, that you can possibly imagine. I spent an hour or so tuning her up—she had a deafening purr, rather like a machine-gun in action—until the vicar sent round to say that he was writing a sermon upon "Peace" and was unable to concentrate his mind on that topic until I desisted. I took his objection in good part, and, after a culminating volley and one last lingering look, started for a stroll round the town.

In spite of every endeavour to be modest I could not but feel myself the cynosure of every eye. I had rather carelessly forgotten to change my leggings and breeches I had bought for the occasion, and I was also wearing my leather skull-cap with ear-flaps carelessly adjusted, so that I could hear what people were saying. I should think I had half the population under fifteen at my heels before I was half-way down the High Street.

"You going to fly, Mr. Betts?" says one cheeky youngster.

"Like a bird!" I said.

"Don't you fly till we comes out of school," says another.

It was a sort of Royal progress that evening for me. I visited old Lupton, the horticulturist, and he could hardly conceal what a great honour he thought it. He took me over his new greenhouse—he had now got, he said, three acres of surface under glass—and showed me all sorts of clever dodges he was adopting in the way of intensive culture, and afterwards we went down to the end of his old flower-garden and looked at his bees. When I came out my retinue of kids was still waiting for me, reinforced. Then I went round by Paramors and dropped into the Bull and Horses, just as if there wasn't anything particular up, for a lemon squash. Everybody was talking about my aeroplane. They just shut up for a moment when I came in, and then burst out with questions. It's odd nowadays to remember all that excitement. I answered what they had to ask me and refrained from putting on any side, and afterwards Miss Flyteman and I went into the commercial-room and turned over the pages of various illustrated journals and compared the pictures with my machine in a quiet, unassuming sort of way. Everybody encouraged me to go up—everybody.

I lay stress on that because, as I was soon to discover, the tides and ebbs of popular favour are among the most inexplicable and inconsistent things in the world.

I particularly remember old Cheeseman, the pork-butcher, whose pigs I killed, saying over and over again, in a tone of perfect satisfaction, "You won't 'ave any difficulty in going *up*, you won't. There won't be any difficulty 'bout going *up*." And winking and nodding to the other eminent tradesmen there assembled.

I *hadn't* much difficulty in going up. "Alauda Magna" was a cheerful lifter, and the roar and spin of her engine had hardly begun behind me before she was off her wheels—

snap, snap, they came up above the ski gliders—and swaying swiftly across the meadows towards the vicarage hedge. She had a sort of onward roll to her, rather like the movement of a corpulent but very buoyant woman.

I had just a glimpse of brave little Mother, trying not to cry, and full of pride in me, on the veranda, with both the maids and old Snape beside her, and then I had to give all my attention to the steering-wheel if I didn't want to barge into the vicar's pear trees.

I'd felt the faintest of tugs just as I came up, and fancied I heard a resounding whack on our new Trespassers Will Be Prosecuted board, and I saw the crowd of people in the lane running this way and that from my loud humming approach; but it was only after the flight was all over that I realized what that fool Snorticombe had been up to. It would seem he had thought the monster needed tethering— I won't attempt to explain the mysteries of his mind—and he had tied about a dozen yards of rope to the end of either wing and fixed them firmly to a couple of iron guy-posts that belonged properly to the Badminton net. Up they came at the tug of "Alauda," and now they were trailing and dancing and leaping along behind me, and taking the most vicious dives and lunges at everything that came within range of them. Poor old Templecom got it hottest in the lane, I'm told—a frightful whack on his bald head; and then we ripped up the vicar's cucumber frames, killed and scattered his parrot, smashed the upper pane of his study window, and just missed the housemaid as she stuck her head out of the upper bedroom window. I didn't, of course, know anything of this at the time—it was on a lower plane altogether from my proceedings. I was steering past his vicarage—a narrow miss—and trying to come round to clear the pear trees at the end of the garden—which I did with a graze—and the trailers behind me sent leaves and branches flying this way and that. I had reason to thank Heaven for my sturdy little GKC.

Then I was fairly up for a time.

I found it much more confusing than I had expected; the engine made such an infernal whir-r-row for one thing, and the steering tugged and struggled like a thing alive. But I got her heading over the market-place all right. We buzzed over

Stunt's the greengrocer, and my trailers hopped up his back premises and made a sanguinary mess of the tiles on his roof, and sent an avalanche of broken chimney-pot into the crowded street below. Then the thing dipped—I suppose one of the guy-posts tried to anchor for a second in Stunt's rafters—and I had the hardest job to clear the Bull and Horses' stables. I didn't, as a matter of fact, completely clear them. The ski-like alighting runners touched the ridge for a moment and the left wing bent against the top of the chimney-stack and floundered over it in an awkward, destructive manner.

I'm told that my trailers whirled about the crowded market-place in the most diabolical fashion as I dipped and recovered, but I'm inclined to think all this part of the story has been greatly exaggerated. Nobody was killed, and it couldn't have been half a minute from the time I appeared over Stunt's to the time when I slid off the stable roof and in among Lupton's glass. If people had taken reasonable care of themselves instead of gaping at me, they wouldn't have got hurt. I had enough to do without pointing out to people that they were likely to be hit by an iron guy-post which had seen fit to follow me. If anyone ought to have warned them it was that fool Snorticombe. Indeed, what with the incalculable damage done to the left wing and one of the cylinders getting out of rhythm and making an ominous catch in the whirr, I was busy enough for anything on my own private personal account.

I suppose I am in a manner of speaking responsible for knocking old Dudney off the station bus, but I don't see that I can be held answerable for the subsequent evolutions of the bus, which ended after a charge among the market stalls in Cheeseman's shop-window, nor do I see that I am to blame because an idle and ill-disciplined crowd chose to stampede across a stock of carelessly distributed earthenware and overturned a butter stall. I was a mere excuse for all this misbehaviour.

I didn't exactly fall into Lupton's glass, and I didn't exactly drive over it. I think ricochetting describes my passage across his premises as well as any single word can.

It was the queerest sensation, being carried along by this big, buoyant thing, which had, as it were, bolted with me, and feeling myself alternately lifted up and then dropped with a scrunch upon a fresh greenhouse-roof, in spite of all my efforts to get control. And the infinite relief when at last, at the fifth or sixth pounce, I rose—and kept on rising!

I seemed to forget everything disagreeable instantly. The doubt whether after all "Alauda Magna" was good for flying vanished. She was evidently very good. We whirred over the wall at the end, with my trailers still bumping behind, and beyond one of them hitting a cow, which died next day, I don't think I did the slightest damage to anything or anybody all across the breadth of Cheeseman's meadow. Then I began to rise, steadily but surely, and, getting the thing well in hand, came swooping round over his piggeries to give Mintonchester a second taste of my quality.

I meant to go up in a spiral until I was clear of all the trees and things and circle about the church spire. Hitherto I had been so concentrated on the plunges and tugs of the monster I was driving, and so deafened by the uproar of my engine, that I had noticed little of the things that were going on below; but now I could make out a little lot of people, headed by Lupton with a garden fork, rushing obliquely across the corner of Cheeseman's meadow. It puzzled me for a second to imagine what they could think they were after.

Up I went, whirring and swaying, and presently got a glimpse down the High Street of the awful tangle everything had got into in the market-place. I didn't at the time connect that extraordinary smash-up with my transit.

It was the jar of my whack against the weathercock that really stopped my engines. I've never been able to make out quite how it was I hit the unfortunate vane; perhaps the twist I had given my left wing on Stunt's roof spoilt my steering; but, anyhow, I hit the gaudy thing and bent it, and for a lengthy couple of seconds I wasn't by any means sure whether I wasn't going to dive straight down into the market-place. I got her right by a supreme effort—I think the people I didn't smash might have squeezed out one drop of gratitude for that—drove pitching at the tree-tops of Withycombe, got round, and realized the engines were stopping. There wasn't any time to survey the country and arrange for a suitable landing place; there wasn't any chance

7

of clearing the course. It wasn't my fault if a quarter of the population of Mintonchester was swarming out over Cheeseman's meadow. It was the only chance I had to land without a smash, and I took it. Down I came, a steep glide, doing the best I could for myself.

Perhaps I did bowl a few people over; but progress is progress.

And I had to kill his pigs. It was a case of either dropping among the pigs and breaking my rush, or going full tilt into the corrugated-iron piggeries beyond. I might have been cut to ribbons. And pigs are born to die.

I stopped, and stood up stiffly upon the framework and looked behind me. It didn't take me a moment to realize that Mintonchester meant to take my poor efforts to give it an Aviation Day all to itself in a spirit of ferocious ingratitude.

The air was full of the squealing of the two pigs I had pinned under my machine and the bawling of the nearer spectators. Lupton occupied the middle distance with a garden fork, with the evident intention of jabbing it into my stomach. I am always pretty cool and quick-witted in an emergency. I dropped off poor "Alauda Magna" like a shot, dodged through the piggery, went up by Frobisher's orchard, nipped over the yard wall of Hink's cottages, and was into the police-station by the back way before anyone could get within fifty feet of me.

"Halloa!" said Inspector Nenton; "smashed the thing?"

"No," I said; "but people seem to have got something the matter with them. I want to be locked in a cell."

For a fortnight, do you know, I wasn't allowed to come near my own machine. I went home from the police-station as soon as the first excitement had blown over a little, going round by Love Lane and the Chart so as not to arouse any febrile symptoms. I found Mother frightfully indignant, you can be sure, at the way I had been treated. And there, as I say, was I, standing a sort of siege in the upstairs rooms, and sturdy little "Alauda Magna," away in Cheeseman's fields, being walked round and stared at by everybody in the world but me. Cheeseman's theory was that he had seized her. There came a gale one night, and the dear thing was blown clean over the hedge among Lupton's greenhouses again, and then Lupton sent round a silly note to say that if we didn't remove her she would be sold to defray expenses, going off into a long tirade about damages and his solicitor. So Mother posted off to Clamps', the furniture removers at Upnorton Corner, and they got hold of a timber-waggon, and popular feeling had allayed sufficiently before that arrived for me to go in person to superintend the removal. There she lay like a great moth above the *débris* of some cultural projects of Lupton's, scarcely damaged herself except for a hole or so and some bent rods and stays in the left wing and a smashed skid. But she was bespattered with pigs' blood and pretty dirty.

I went at once by instinct for the engines, and had them in perfect going order before the timber-waggon arrived.

A sort of popularity returned to me with that procession home. With the help of a swarm of men we got "Alauda Magna" poised on the waggon, and then I took my seat to see she balanced properly, and a miscellaneous team of seven horses started to tow her home. It was nearly one o'clock when we got to that, and all the children turned out to shout and jeer. We couldn't go by Pook's Land and the vicarage, because the walls are too high and narrow, and so we headed across Cheeseman's meadow for Stokes' Waste and the Common, to get round by that *détour*.

I was silly, of course, to do what I did—I see that now—but sitting up there on my triumphal car with all the multitude about me excited me. I got a kind of glory on. I really only meant to let the propellers spin as a sort of hurrahing, but I was carried away. Whuz-z-z-z! It was like something blowing up, and behold! I was sailing and plunging away from my wain across the Common for a second flight.

"Lord!" I said.

I fully meant to run up the air a little way, come about, and take her home to our paddock, but those early aeroplanes were very uncertain things.

After all, it wasn't such a very bad shot to land in the vicarage garden, and that practically is what I did. And I don't see that it was my fault that all the vicarage and a lot of friends should be having lunch on the lawn. They were doing that, of course, so as to be on the spot without having

9

to rush out of the house when "Alauda Magna" came home again. Quiet exultation—that was their game. They wanted to gloat over every particular of my ignominious return. You can see that from the way they had arranged the table. I can't help it if Fate decided that my return wasn't to be so ignominious as all that, and swooped me down on the lot of them.

They were having their soup. They had calculated on me for the dessert, I suppose.

To this day I can't understand how it is I didn't kill the vicar. The forward edge of the left wing got him just under the chin and carried him back a dozen yards. He must have had neck vertebrae like steel; and even then I was amazed his head didn't come off. Perhaps he was holding on underneath; but I can't imagine where. If it hadn't been for the fascination of his staring face I think I could have avoided the veranda, but, as it was, that took me by surprise. That was a fair crumple up. The wood must have just rotted away under its green paint; but, anyhow, it and the climbing roses and the shingles above and everything snapped and came down like stage scenery, and I and the engines and the middle part drove clean through the French windows on to the drawing-room floor. It was jolly lucky for me, I think, that the French windows weren't shut. There's no unpleasanter way of getting hurt in the world than flying suddenly through thin window-glass; and I think I ought to know. There was a frightful jawbation, but the vicar was out of action, that was one good thing. Those deep, sonorous sentences! But perhaps they would have calmed things . . .

That was the end of "Alauda Magna," my first aeroplane. I never even troubled to take her away. I hadn't the heart to . . .

And then the storm burst.

The idea seems to have been to make Mother and me pay for everything that had ever tumbled down or got broken in Mintonchester since the beginning of things. Oh! and for any animal that had ever died a sudden death in the memory of the oldest inhabitant. The tariff ruled high, too. Cows were twenty-five to thirty pounds and upward; pigs about a pound each, with no reduction for killing a quantity; verandas—verandas were steady at forty-five guineas.

Dinner services, too, were up, and so were tiling and all branches of the building trade. It seemed to certain persons in Mintonchester, I believe, that an era of unexampled prosperity had dawned upon the place—only limited, in fact, by the solvency of me and Mother. The vicar tried the old "sold to defray expenses" racket, but I told him he might sell.

I pleaded defective machinery and the hand of God, did my best to shift the responsibility on to the firm in Blackfriars Road, and, as an additional precaution, filed my petition in bankruptcy. I really hadn't any property in the world, thanks to Mother's goodness, except my two motor-bicycles, which the brutes took, my photographic dark-room, and a lot of bound books on aeronautics and progress generally. Mother, of course, wasn't responsible. She hadn't lifted a wing.

Well, for all that, disagreeables piled up so heavily on me, what with being shouted after by a rag-tag and bobtail of schoolboys and golf caddies and hobbledehoys when I went out of doors, threatened with personal violence by stupid people like old Lupton, who wouldn't understand that a man can't pay what he hasn't got, pestered by the wives of various gentlemen who saw fit to become out-of-work on the strength of alleged injuries, and served with all sorts of silly summonses for all sorts of fancy offences, such as mischie-vous mischief and manslaughter and wilful damage and trespass, that I simply had to go away from Mintonchester to Italy, and leave poor little Mother to manage them in her own solid, undemonstrative way. Which she did, I must admit, like a Brick.

They didn't get much out of her, anyhow, but she had to break up our little home at Mintonchester and join me at Arosa, in spite of her dislike of Italian cooking. She found me already a bit of a celebrity because I had made a record, so it seemed, by falling down three separate crevasses on three successive days. But that's another story altogether.

From start to finish I reckon that first aeroplane cost my mother over nine hundred pounds. If I hadn't put my foot down, and she had stuck to her original intention of paying all the damage, it would have cost her three thousand . . . But it was worth it. It was worth it. I wish I could live it all

H. G. Wells

over again; and many an old codger like me sits at home now and deplores those happy, vanished, adventurous times, when any lad of spirit was free to fly—and go anywhere—and smash anything—and discuss the question afterwards of just what the damages amounted to and what his legal liability might be.

The Unparalleled Adventure of One Hans Pfaall

Edgar Allan Poe

With a heart of furious fancies,
  Whereof I am commander,
With a burning spear *and a horse of air,*
To the wilderness I wander.
        —*Tom O'Bedlam's Song.*

By late accounts from Rotterdam, that city seems to be in a high state of philosophical excitement. Indeed, phenomena have there occurred of a nature so completely unexpected— so entirely novel—so utterly at variance with preconceived opinions—as to leave no doubt on my mind that long ere this all Europe is in an uproar, all physics in a ferment, all reason and astronomy together by the ears.

It appears that on the _____ day of _____ (I am not positive about the date) a vast crowd of people, for purposes not specifically mentioned, were assembled in the great square of the Exchange in the well-conditioned city of Rotterdam. The day was warm—unusually so for the season—there was hardly a breath of air stirring; and the multitude were in no bad humour at being now and then besprinkled with friendly showers of momentary duration, that fell from large white masses of cloud profusely distributed about the blue vault of the firmament. Nevertheless, about noon, a slight but remarkable agitation became apparent in the assembly: the clattering of ten thousand tongues succeeded; and, in an instant afterward, ten thousand faces were upturned toward the heavens, ten thousand pipes descended simultaneously from the corners of ten thousand mouths, and a shout, which could be compared to nothing but the roaring of Niagara, resounded long, loudly, and furiously, through all the city and through all the environs of Rotterdam.

The origin of this hubbub soon became sufficiently evident. From behind the huge bulk of one of those sharply defined masses of cloud already mentioned, was seen slowly to emerge into an open area of blue space, a queer, heterogeneous, but apparently solid substance, so oddly shaped, so whimsically put together, as not to be in any manner comprehended, and never to be sufficiently admired, by the host of sturdy burghers who stood open-mouthed below. What could it be? In the name of all the devils in Rotterdam, what could it possibly portend? No one knew; no one could imagine; no one—not even the burgomaster Mynheer Superbus Von Underduk—had the slightest clue by which to unravel the mystery; so, as nothing more reasonable could be done, every one to a man replaced his pipe carefully in the corner of his mouth, and maintaining an eye steadily upon the phenomenon, puffed, paused, waddled about, and grunted significantly—then waddled back, grunted, paused, and finally—puffed again.

In the meantime, however, lower and still lower toward the goodly city, came the object of so much curiosity, and the cause of so much smoke. In a very few minutes it arrived near enough to be accurately discerned. It appeared to be—yes! it *was* undoubtedly a species of balloon; but surely no *such* balloon had ever been seen in Rotterdam before. For who, let me ask, ever heard of a balloon manufactured entirely of dirty newspapers? No man in Holland certainly; yet here, under the very noses of the people, or rather at some distance *above* their noses was the identical thing in question, and composed, I have it on the best authority, of the precise material which no one had ever before known to be used for a similar purpose. It was an egregious insult to the good sense of the burghers of Rotterdam. As to the shape of the phenomenon, it was even still more reprehensible. Being little or nothing better than an huge fool's-cap turned upside down. And this similitude was regarded as by no means lessened when, upon nearer inspection, the crowd saw a large tassel depending from its apex, and around, the upper rim or base of the cone, a circle of little instruments, resembling sheep-bells, which kept up a continual tinkling to the tune of "Betty Martin." But still worse.—Suspended by blue ribbons to the end of this fantastic machine, there hung, by way of car, an enormous drab beaver hat, with a brim superlatively broad, and a hemispherical crown with a black band and a silver buckle. It is, however, somewhat remarkable that many citizens of Rotterdam swore to having seen the same hat repeatedly before; and indeed the whole assembly seemed to regard it with eyes of familiarity; while the vrow Grettel Pfaall, upon sight of it, uttered an exclamation of joyful surprise, and declared it to be the identical hat of her good man himself. Now this was a circumstance the more to be observed, as Pfaall, with three companions, had actually disappeared from Rotterdam about five years before, in a very sudden and unaccountable manner, and up to the date of this narrative all attempts at obtaining intelligence concerning them had failed. To be sure, some bones which were thought to be human, mixed up with a quantity of odd-looking rubbish, had been lately discovered in a retired situation to the east of the city; and some people went so far as to imagine that in this spot a foul murder had been committed, and that the sufferers were in all probability Hans Pfaall and his associates. But to return.

The balloon (for such no doubt it was) had now descended to within a hundred feet of the earth, allowing the crowd below a sufficiently distinct view of the person of its occupant. This was in truth a very singular somebody. He could not have been more than two feet in height; but this altitude, little as it was, would have been sufficient to destroy his *equilibrium*, and tilt him over the edge of his tiny car, but for the intervention of a circular rim reaching as high as the breast, and rigged on to the cords of the balloon. The body of the little man was more than proportionally broad, giving to his entire figure a rotundity highly absurd. His feet, of course, could not be seen at all. His hands were enormously large. His hair was gray, and collected into a *queue* behind. His nose was prodigiously long, crooked, and inflammatory; his eyes full, brilliant, and acute; his chin and cheeks, although wrinkled with age, were broad, puffy, and double; but of ears of any kind there was not a semblance to be discovered upon any portion of his head. This odd little gentleman was dressed in a loose surtout of sky-blue satin, with tight breeches to match, fastened with silver buckles at the knees. His vest was of some bright yellow material; a white taffety cap was set jauntily on one side of his head; and, to complete his equipment, a blood-red silk handkerchief enveloped his throat, and fell down, in a dainty manner, upon his bosom, in a fantastic bow-knot of super-eminent dimensions.

Having descended, as I said before, to above one hundred feet from the surface of the earth, the little old gentleman was suddenly seized with a fit of trepidation, and appeared disinclined to make any nearer approach to *terra firma*. Throwing out, therefore, a quantity of sand from a canvas bag, which he lifted with great difficulty, he became stationary in an instant. He then proceeded, in a hurried and agitated manner, to extract from a side-pocket in his surtout a large morocco pocket-book. This he poised suspiciously in his hand, then eyed it with an air of extreme surprise, and was evidently astonished at its weight. He at length opened it, and drawing therefrom a huge letter sealed with red sealing-wax and tied carefully with red tape, let it fall precisely at the feet of the burgomaster, Superbus Von Underduk. His Excellency stooped to take it up. But the aëronaut, still greatly discomposed, and having apparently no further business to detain him in Rotterdam, began at this moment to make busy preparations for departure; and it being necessary to discharge a portion of ballast to enable him to reascend, the half dozen bags which he threw out, one after another, without taking the trouble to empty their contents, tumbled, every one of them, most unfortunately upon the back of the burgomaster, and rolled him over and over no less than half a dozen times, in the face of every individual in Rotterdam. It is not to be supposed, however, that the great Underduk suffered this impertinence on the part of the little old man to pass off with impunity. It is said, on the contrary, that during each of his half dozen circumvolutions he emitted no less than half a dozen distinct and furious whiffs from his pipe, to which he held fast the whole time with all his might, and to which he intends holding fast (God willing) until the day of his decease.

In the meantime the balloon arose like a lark, and, soaring far away above the city, at length drifted quietly behind a cloud similar to that from which it had so oddly emerged, and was thus lost forever to the wondering eyes of the good citizens of Rotterdam. All attention was now directed to the letter, the descent of which, and the consequences attending thereupon, had proved so fatally subversive of both person and personal dignity to his Excellency, Von Underduk. That functionary, however, had not failed, during his circumgyratory movements, to bestow a thought upon the important object of securing the epistle, which was seen, upon inspection, to have fallen into the most proper hands, being actually addressed to himself and Professor Rubadub, in their official capacities of President and Vice-President of the Rotterdam College of Astronomy. It was accordingly opened by those dignitaries upon the spot, and found to contain the following extraordinary, and indeed very serious, communication:

"To their Excellencies Von Underduk and Rubadub, President and Vice-President of the States' College of Astronomers, in the city of Rotterdam.

"Your Excellencies may perhaps be able to remember an humble artizan, by name Hans Pfaall, and by occupation a mender of bellows, who, with three others, disappeared from Rotterdam, about five years ago, in a manner which must have been considered unaccountable. If, however, it so please your Excellencies, I, the writer of this communication, am the identical Hans Pfaall himself. It is well known to most of my fellow-citizens, that for the period of forty years I continued to occupy the little square brick building, at the head of the alley called Sauerkraut, in which I resided at the time of my disappearance. My ancestors have also resided therein time out of mind—they, as well as myself, steadily following the respectable and indeed lucrative profession of mending of bellows: for, to speak the truth, until of late years, that the heads of all the people have been set agog with politics, no better business than my own could an honest citizen of Rotterdam either desire or deserve. Credit was good, employment was never wanting, and there was no lack of either money or good-will. But, as I was saying, we soon began to feel the effects of liberty and long speeches, and radicalism, and all that sort of thing. People who were formerly the best customers in the world, had now not a moment of time to think of us at all. They had as much as they could do to read about the revolutions, and keep up with the march of intellect and the spirit of the age. If a fire wanted fanning, it could readily be fanned with a newspaper; and as the government grew weaker, I have no doubt that leather and iron acquired durability in proportion—for, in a very short time, there was not a pair of bellows in all Rotterdam that ever stood in need of a stitch or required the assistance of a hammer. This was a state of things not to be endured. I soon grew as poor as a rat, and, having a wife and children to provide for, my burdens at length became intolerable, and I spent hour after hour in reflecting upon the most convenient method of putting an end to my life. Duns, in the meantime, left me little leisure for contemplation. My house was literally besieged from morning till night. There were three fellows in particular who worried me beyond endurance, keeping watch continually about my door, and threatening me with the law. Upon these three I vowed the bitterest revenge, if ever I should be so happy as to get them within my clutches; and I believe nothing in the world but the pleasure of this anticipation prevented me from putting my plan of suicide into immediate execution, by blowing my brains out with a blunderbuss. I thought it best, however, to dissemble my wrath, and to treat them with promises and fair words, until, by some good turn of fate, an opportunity of vengeance should be afforded me.

"One day, having given them the slip, and feeling more than usually dejected, I continued for a long time to wander about the most obscure streets without object, until at length I chanced to stumble against the corner of a bookseller's stall. Seeing a chair close at hand, for the use of customers, I threw myself doggedly into it, and, hardly knowing why, opened the pages of the first volume which came within my reach. It proved to be a small pamphlet treatise on Speculative Astronomy, written either by Professor Encke of Berlin or by a Frenchman of somewhat similar name. I had some little tincture of information on matters of this nature, and soon became more and more absorbed in the contents of the book—reading it actually through twice before I awoke to a recollection of what was passing around me. By this time it began to grow dark, and I directed my steps toward home. But the treatise (in conjunction with a discovery in pneumatics, lately communicated to me as an important secret, by a cousin from Nantz) had made an indelible impression on my mind, and, as I sauntered along the dusky streets, I revolved carefully over in my memory the wild and sometimes unintelligible reasonings of the writer. There are some particular passages which affected my imagination in an extraordinary manner. The longer I meditated upon these, the more intense grew the interest which had been excited within me. The limited nature of my education in general, and more especially my ignorance on subjects connected with natural philosophy, so far from rendering me diffident of my own ability to comprehend what I had read, or inducing me to mistrust the many vague notions which had arisen in consequence, merely served as a farther stimulus to imagination; and I was vain enough, or perhaps reasonable enough, to doubt whether those crude ideas which, by arising in ill-regulated minds, have all the appearance, may not often in effect possess all the force, the reality, and other inherent properties, of instinct or intuition.

"It was late when I reached home, and went immediately to bed. My mind, however, was too much occupied to sleep, and I lay the whole night buried in meditation. Arising early in the morning, I repaired eagerly to the bookseller's stall, and laid out what little ready money I possessed, in the purchase of some volumes of Mechanics and Practical Astronomy. Having arrived at home safely with these, I devoted every spare moment to their perusal, and soon made such proficiency in studies of this nature as I thought sufficient for the execution of a certain design with which either the Devil or my better genius had inspired me. In the intervals of this period, I made every endeavour to conciliate the three creditors who had given me so much annoyance. In this I finally succeeded—partly by selling enough of my household furniture to satisfy a moiety of their claim, and partly by a promise of paying the balance upon completion of a little project which I told them I had in view, and for assistance in which I solicited their services. By these means (for they were ignorant men) I found little difficulty in gaining them over to my purpose.

"Matters being this arranged, I contrived, by the aid of my wife and with the greatest secrecy and caution, to dispose of what property I had remaining, and to borrow, in small sums, under various pretences, and without giving any attention (I am ashamed to say) to my future means of repayment, no inconsiderable quantity of ready money. With the means thus accruing I proceeded to procure at intervals, cambric muslin, very fine, in pieces of twelve yards each; twine; a lot of the varnish of caoutchouc; a large and deep basket of wicker-work, made to order; and several other articles necessary in the construction and equipment of a balloon of extraordinary dimensions. This I directed my wife to make up as soon as possible, and gave her all requisite information as to the particular method of proceeding. In the meantime I worked up the twine into network of sufficient dimensions; rigged it with a hoop and the necessary cords; and made purchase of numerous instruments and materials for experiment in the upper regions of the upper atmosphere. I then took opportunities of conveying by night, to a retired situation east of Rotterdam, five iron-bound casks, to contain about fifty gallons each, and one of a larger size; six tin tubes, three inches in diameter, properly shaped, and ten feet in length; a quantity of a

particular metallic substance, or semi-metal, which I shall
not name, and a dozen demijohns of *a very common acid.*
The gas to be formed from these latter materials is a gas
never yet generated by any other person than myself—or at
least never applied to any similar purpose. I can only
venture to say here, that it is *a constituent of azote,* so long
considered irreducible, and that its density is about 37.4
times *less than that of hydrogen.* It is tasteless, but not
odourless; burns, when pure, with a greenish flame; and is
instantaneously fatal to animal life. Its full secret I would
make no difficulty in disclosing, but that it of right belongs
(as I have before hinted) to a citizen of Nantz, in France, by
whom it was conditionally communicated to myself. The
same individual submitted to me, without being at all aware
of my intentions, a method of constructing balloons from
the membrane of a certain animal, through which substance
any escape of gas was nearly an impossibility. I found it
however altogether too expensive, and was not sure, upon
the whole, whether cambric muslin with a coating of gum
caoutchouc, was not equally as good. I mention this circumstance, because I think it probable that hereafter the individual in question may attempt a balloon ascension with
the novel gas and material I have spoken of, and I do not
wish to deprive him of the honour of a very singular
invention.

"On the spot which I intended each of the smaller casks
to occupy respectively during the inflation of the balloon, I
privately dug a small hole; the holes forming in this manner
a circle twenty-five feet in diameter. In the centre of this
circle, being the station designed for the large cask, I also
dug a hole of greater depth. In each of the five smaller holes,
I deposited a canister containing fifty pounds, and in the
larger one a keg holding one hundred and fifty pounds, of
cannon powder. These—the keg and canisters—I connected in a proper manner with covered trains; and having
let into one of the canisters the end of about four feet of
slow-match, I covered up the hole, and placed the cask over
it, leaving the other end of the match protruding about an
inch, and barely visible beyond the cask. I then filled up the
remaining holes, and placed the barrels over them in their
destined situation!

21

"Besides the articles above enumerated, I conveyed to the *dépôt,* and there secreted, one of M. Grimm's improvements upon the apparatus for condensation of the atmospheric air. I found this machine, however, to require considerable alteration before it could be adapted to the purposes to which I intended making it applicable. But, with severe labour and unremitting perseverance, I at length met with entire success in all my preparations. My balloon was soon completed. It would contain more than forty thousand cubic feet of gas; would take me up easily, I calculated, with all my implements, and, if I managed rightly, with one hundred and seventy-five pounds of ballast into the bargain. It had received three coats of varnish, and I found the cambric muslin to answer all the purposes of silk itself, being quite as strong and a good deal less expensive.

"Every thing being now ready, I exacted from my wife an oath of secrecy in relation to all my actions from the day of my first visit to the bookseller's stall; and promising, on my part, to return as soon as circumstances would permit, I gave her what little money I had left, and bade her farewell. Indeed I had no fear on her account. She was what people call a notable woman, and could manage matters in the world without my assistance. I believe, to tell the truth, she always looked upon me as an idle body— a mere make-weight—good for nothing but building castles in the air—and was rather glad to get rid of me. It was a dark night when I bade her good-bye, and taking with me, as *aides-de-camp,* the three creditors who had given me so much trouble, we carried the balloon, with the car and accoutrements, by a roundabout way, to the station where the other articles were deposited. We there found them all unmolested, and I proceeded immediately to business.

"It was the first of April. The night, as I said before, was dark; there was not a star to be seen; and a drizzling rain, falling at intervals, rendered us very uncomfortable. But my chief anxiety was concerning the balloon, which, in spite of the varnish with which it was defended, began to grow rather heavy with the moisture; the powder also was liable to damage. I therefore kept my three duns working with great diligence, pounding down ice around the central cask, and stirring the acid in the others. They did not cease, however, importuning me with questions as to what I intended to do with all this apparatus, and expressed much dissatisfaction at the terrible labour I made them undergo. They could not perceive (so they said) what good was likely to result from their getting wet to the skin, merely to take a part in such horrible incantations. I began to get uneasy, and worked away with all my might, for I verily believe the idiots supposed that I had entered into a compact with the Devil, and that, in short, what I was now doing was nothing better than it should be. I was, therefore, in great fear of their leaving me altogether. I contrived, however, to pacify them by promises of payment of all scores in full, as soon as I could bring the present business to a termination. To these speeches they gave, of course, their own interpretation; fancying, no doubt, that at all events I should come into possession of vast quantities of ready money; and provided I paid them all I owed, and a trifle more, in consideration of their services, I dare say they cared very little what became of either my soul or my carcass.

"In about four hours and a half I found the balloon sufficiently inflated. I attached the car, therefore, and put all my implements in it: a telescope; a barometer, with some important modifications; a thermometer; an electrometer; a compass; a magnetic needle; a seconds watch; a bell; a speaking-trumpet, etc., etc., etc.; also a globe of glass, exhausted of air, and carefully closed with a stopper—not forgetting the condensing apparatus, some unslacked lime, a stick of sealing-wax, a copious supply of water, and a large quantity of provisions, such as pemmican, in which much nutriment is contained in comparatively little bulk. I also secured in the car a pair of pigeons and a cat.

"It was now nearly daybreak, and I thought it high time to take my departure. Dropping a lighted cigar on the ground, as if by accident, I took the opportunity, in stooping to pick it up, of igniting privately the piece of slow-match, the end of which as I said before, protruded a little beyond the lower rim of one of the smaller casks. This manœuvre was totally unperceived on the part of the three duns; and, jumping into the car, I immediately cut the single cord which held me to the earth, and was pleased to find that I shot upward with inconceivable rapidity, carrying with all ease one hundred and seventy-five pounds of leaden ballast, and able to have carried up as many more. As I left the earth, the barometer stood at thirty inches, and the centigrade thermometer at 19°.

"Scarcely, however, had I attained the height of fifty yards, when, roaring and rumbling up after me in the most tumultuous and terrible manner, came so dense a hurricane of fire, and gravel, and burning wood, and blazing metal, and mangled limbs, that my very heart sunk within me, and I fell down in the bottom of the car, trembling with terror. Indeed, I now perceived that I had entirely overdone the business, and that the main consequences of the shock were yet to be experienced. Accordingly, in less than a second, I felt all the blood in my body rushing to my temples, and immediately thereupon, a concussion, which I shall never forget, burst abruptly through the night, and seemed to rip the very firmament asunder. When I afterward had time for reflection, I did not fail to attribute the extreme violence of the explosion, as regarded myself, to its proper cause—my situation directly above it, and in the line of its greatest power. But at the time, I thought only of preserving my life. The balloon at first collapsed, then furiously expanded, then whirled round and round with sickening velocity, and finally, reeling and staggering like a drunken man, hurled me over the rim of the car, and left me dangling, at a terrific height, with my head downward, and my face outward, by a piece of slender cord about three feet in length, which hung accidentally through a crevice near the bottom of the wicker-work, and in which, as I fell, my left foot became most providentially entangled. It is impossible—utterly impossible—to form any adequate idea of the horror of my situation. I gasped convulsively for breath—a shudder resembling a fit of the ague agitated every nerve and muscle in my frame—I felt my eyes starting from their sockets—a horrible nausea overwhelmed me—and at length I lost all consciousness in a swoon.

The Unparalleled Adventure of One Hans Pfaall

"How long I remained in this state it is impossible to say. It must, however, have been no inconsiderable time, for when I partially recovered the sense of existence, I found the day breaking, the balloon at a prodigious height over a wilderness of ocean, and not a trace of land to be discovered far and wide within the limits of the vast horizon. My sensations, however, upon this recovering, were by no means so replete with agony as might have been anticipated. Indeed, there was much of madness in the calm survey which I began to take of my situation. I drew up to my eyes each of my hands, one after the other, and wondered what occurrence could have given rise to the swelling of the veins, and the horrible blackness of the finger-nails. I afterward carefully examined my head, shaking it repeatedly, and feeling it with minute attention, until I succeeded in satisfying myself that it was not, as I had more than half suspected, larger than my balloon. Then, in a knowing manner, I felt in both my breeches pockets, and, missing therefrom a set of tablets and a tooth-pick case, endeavoured to account for their disappearance, and not being able to do so, felt inexpressibly chagrined. It now occurred to me that I suffered great uneasiness in the joint of my left ankle, and a dim consciousness of my situation began to glimmer through my mind. But, strange to say! I was neither astonished nor horror-stricken. If I felt any emotion at all, it was a kind of chuckling satisfaction at the cleverness I was about to display in extricating myself from this dilemma; and never, for a moment, did I look upon my ultimate safety as a question susceptible of doubt. For a few minutes I remained wrapped in the profoundest meditation. I have a distinct recollection of frequently compressing my lips, putting my fore-finger to the side of my nose, and making use of other gesticulations and grimaces common to men who, at ease in their arm-chairs, meditate upon matters of intricacy or importance. Having, as I thought, sufficiently collected my ideas, I now, with great caution and deliberation, put my hands behind my back, and unfastened the large iron buckle which belonged to the waistband of my pantaloons. This buckle had three teeth, which, being somewhat rusty, turned with great difficulty on their axis. I brought them, however, after some trouble, at right angles to the body of the buckle, and was glad to find them remain firm in that position. Holding within my teeth the instrument thus obtained, I now proceeded to untie the knot of my cravat. I had to rest several times before I could accomplish this manœuvre; but it was at length accomplished. To one end of the cravat I then made fast the buckle, and the other end I tied, for greater security, tightly around my wrist. Drawing now my body upward, with a prodigious exertion of muscular force, I succeeded, at the very first trial, in throwing the buckle over the car, and entangling it, as I had anticipated, in the circular rim of the wicker-work.

"My body was now inclined toward the side of the car, at an angle of about forty-five degrees; but it must not be understood that I was therefore only forty-five degrees below the perpendicular. So far from it, I still lay nearly level with the plane of the horizon; for the change of situation which I had acquired, had forced the bottom of the car considerably outward from my position, which was accordingly one of the most imminent peril. It should be remembered, however, that when I fell, in the first instance, from the car, if I had fallen with my face turned toward the balloon, instead of turned outwardly from it, as it actually was; or if, in the second place, the cord by which I was suspended had chanced to hang over the upper edge, instead of through a crevice near the bottom of the car—I say it may readily be conceived that, in either of these supposed cases, I should have been unable to accomplish even as much as I had now accomplished, and the disclosures now made would have been utterly lost to posterity. I had therefore every reason to be grateful; although, in point of fact, I was still too stupid to be any thing at all, and hung for, perhaps, a quarter of an hour, in that extraordinary manner, without making the slightest farther exertion, and in a singularly tranquil state of idiotic enjoyment. But this feeling did not fail to die rapidly away, and thereunto succeeded horror, and dismay, and a sense of utter helplessness and ruin. In fact, the blood so long accumulating in the vessels of my head and throat, and which had hitherto buoyed up my spirits with delirium, had now begun to retire within their proper channels, and the distinctness which

was thus added to my perception of the danger, merely
served to deprive me of the self-possession and courage to
encounter it. But this weakness was, luckily for me, of no
very long duration. In good time came to my rescue the
spirit of despair, and, with frantic cries and struggles, I
jerked my way bodily upward, till at length, clutching with a
vicelike grip the long-desired rim, I writhed my person over
it, and fell headlong and shuddering within the car.

"It was not until some time afterward that I recovered
myself sufficiently to attend to the ordinary cares of the
balloon. I then, however, examined it with attention, and
found it, to my great relief, uninjured. My implements were
all safe, and, fortunately, I had lost neither ballast nor
provisions. Indeed, I had so well secured them in their
places, that such an accident was entirely out of the question. Looking at my watch, I found it six o'clock, I was still
rapidly ascending, and the barometer gave a present altitude of three and three-quarter miles. Immediately beneath
me in the ocean, lay a small black object, slightly oblong in
shape, seemingly about the size of a domino, and in every
respect bearing a great resemblance to one of those toys.
Bringing my telescope to bear upon it, I plainly discerned it
to be a British ninety-four-gun ship, close-hauled, and
pitching heavily in the sea with her head to the WSW.
Besides this ship, I saw nothing but the ocean and the sky,
and the sun, which had long arisen.

"It is now high time that I should explain to your
Excellencies the object of my voyage. Your Excellencies will
bear in mind that distressed circumstances in Rotterdam
had at length driven me to the resolution of committing
suicide. It was not, however, that to life itself I had any
positive disgust, but that I was harnessed beyond endurance
by the adventitious miseries attending my situation. In this
state of mind, wishing to live, yet wearied with life, the
treatise at the stall of the bookseller, backed by the oppor-
tune discovery of my cousin of Nantz, opened a resource to
my imagination. I then finally made up my mind. I determined to depart, yet live—to leave the world, yet continue
to exist—in short, to drop enigmas, I resolved, let what
would ensue, to force a passage, if I could, *to the moon*.
Now, lest I should be supposed more of a madman than I

actually am, I will detail, as well as I am able, the considerations which led me to believe that an achievement of this nature, although without doubt difficult, and full of danger, was not absolutely, to a bold spirit, beyond the confines of the possible.

"The moon's actual distance from the earth was the first thing to be attended to. Now, the mean or average interval between the *centres* of the two planets is 59.9643 of the earth's equatorial *radii,* or only about 237,000 miles. I say the mean or average interval; but it must be borne in mind that the form of the moon's orbit being an ellipse of eccentricity amounting to no less than 0.05484 of the major semi-axis of the ellipse itself, and the earth's centre being situated in its focus, if I could, in any manner, contrive to meet the moon in its perigee, the above-mentioned distance would be materially diminished. But, to say nothing at present of this possibility, it was very certain that, at all events, from the 237,000 miles I would have to deduct the *radius* of the earth, say 4000, and the radius of the moon, say 1080, in all 5080, leaving an actual interval to be traversed, under average circumstances, of 231,920 miles. Now this, I reflected, was no very extraordinary distance. Travelling on the land has been repeatedly accomplished at the rate of sixty miles per hour; and indeed a much greater speed may be anticipated. But even at this velocity, it would take me no more than 161 days to reach the surface of the moon. There were, however, many particulars inducing me to believe that my average rate of travelling might possibly very much exceed that of sixty miles per hour, and as these considerations did not fail to make a deep impression upon my mind, I will mention them more fully hereafter.

"The next point to be regarded was one of far greater importance. From indications afforded by the barometer, we find that, in ascensions from the surface of the earth we have, at the height of 1000 feet, left below us about one thirtieth of the entire mass of atmospheric air; that at 10,600 we have ascended through nearly one third; and that at 18,000 which is not far from the elevation of Cotopaxi, we have surmounted one half the material, or, at all events, one half the *ponderable,* body of air incumbent upon our globe. It is also calculated that at an altitude not exceeding the hundredth part of the earth's diameter—that is, not exceeding eighty miles—the rarefaction would be so excessive that animal life could in no manner be sustained, and, moreover, that the most delicate means we possess of ascertaining the presence of the atmosphere would be inadequate to assure us of its existence. But I did not fail to perceive that these latter calculations are founded altogether on our experimental knowledge of the properties of air, and the mechanical laws regulating its dilation and compression, in what may be called, comparatively speaking, *the immediate vicinity* of the earth itself; and, at the same time, it is taken for granted that animal life is and must be essentially *incapable of modification* at any given unattainable distance from the surface. Now, all such reasoning and from such *data* must, of course, be simply analogical. The greatest height ever reached by man was that of 25,000 feet, attained in the aëronautic expedition of Messieurs Gay-Lussac and Biot. This is a moderate altitude, even when compared with the eighty miles in question; and I could not help thinking that the subject admitted room for doubt and great latitude for speculation.

"But, in point of fact, an ascension being made to any given altitude, the ponderable quantity of air surmounted in any *farther* ascension is by no means in proportion to the additional height ascended (as may be plainly seen from what has been stated before), but in a *ratio* constantly decreasing. It is therefore evident that, ascend as high as we may, we cannot, literally speaking, arrive at a limit beyond which *no* atmosphere is to be found. It *must exist,* I argued; although it *may* exist in a state of infinite rarefaction.

"On the other hand, I was aware that arguments have not been wanting to prove the existence of a real and definite limit to the atmosphere, beyond which there is absolutely no air whatsoever. But a circumstance which has been left out of view by those who contend for such a limit, seemed to me, although no positive refutation of their creed, still a point worth very serious investigation. On comparing the intervals between the successive arrivals of Encke's comet at its perihelion, after giving credit, in the most exact manner, for all the disturbances due to the attractions of the planets, it appears that the periods are gradually diminishing; that is to say, the major axis of the comet's ellipse is growing shorter, in a slow but perfectly regular decrease. Now, this is precisely what ought to be the case, if we suppose a resistance experienced from the comet from an extremely *rare ethereal medium* pervading the regions of its orbit. For it is evident that such a medium must, in retarding the comet's velocity, increase its centripetal, by weakening its centrifugal, force. In other words, the sun's attraction would be constantly attaining greater power, and the comet would be drawn nearer at every revolution. Indeed, there is no other way of accounting for the variation in question. But again: the real diameter of the same comet's nebulosity is observed to contract rapidly as it approaches the sun, and dilate with equal rapidity in its departure toward its aphelion. Was I not justifiable in supposing, with M. Valz, that this apparent condensation of volume has its origin in the compression of the same ethereal medium I have spoken of before, and which is dense in proportion to its vicinity to the sun? The lenticular-shaped phenomenon, also called the zodiacal light, was a matter worthy of attention. This radiance, so apparent in the tropics, and which cannot be mistaken for any meteoric lustre, extends from the horizon obliquely upward, and follows generally the direction of the sun's equator. It appeared to me evidently in the nature of a rare atmosphere extending from the sun outward, beyond the orbit of Venus at least, and I believed indefinitely farther.* Indeed, this medium I could not suppose confined to the path of the comet's ellipse, or to the immediate neighbourhood of the sun. It was easy, on the contrary, to imagine it pervading the entire regions of our planetary system, condensed into what we call atmosphere at the planets themselves, and perhaps at some of them modified by considerations purely geological; that is to say, modified, or varied in its proportions (or absolute nature) by matters volatilized from the respective orbs.

"Having adopted this view of the subject, I had little

---

*The zodiacal light is probably what the ancients called Trabes. *Emicant Trabes quos docos vocant.*—Pliny lib. 2, p. 26.

farther hesitation. Granting that on my passage I should meet with atmosphere *essentially* the same as at the surface of the earth, I conceived that, by means of the very ingenious apparatus of M. Grimm, I should readily be enabled to condense it in sufficient quantity for the purposes of respiration. This would remove the chief obstacle in a journey to the moon. I had indeed spent some money and great labour in adapting the apparatus to the object intended, and confidently looked forward to its successful application, if I could manage to complete the voyage within any reasonable period. This brings me back to the *rate* at which it would be possible to travel.

"It is true that balloons, in the first stage of their ascensions from the earth, are known to rise with a velocity comparatively moderate. Now, the power of elevation lies altogether in the superior gravity of the atmospheric air compared with the gas in the balloon; and, at first sight, it does not appear probable that, as the balloon acquires altitude, and consequently arrives successively in atmosphere *strata* of densities rapidly diminishing—I say, it does not appear at all reasonable that, in this its progress upward, the original velocity should be accelerated. On the other hand, I was not aware that, in any recorded ascension, a *diminution* had been proved to be apparent in the absolute rate of ascent; although such should have been the case, if on account of nothing else, on account of the escape of gas through balloons ill-constructed, and varnished with no better material than the ordinary varnish. It seemed, therefore, that the effect of such escape was only sufficient to counterbalance the effect of the acceleration attained in the diminishing of the balloon's distance from the gravitating centre. I now considered that, provided in my passage I found the *medium* I had imagined, and provided that it should prove to be *essentially* what we denominate atmospheric air, it could make comparatively little difference at what extreme state of rarefaction I should discover it—that is to say, in regard to my power of ascending—for the gas in the balloon would not only be itself subject to similar rarefaction (in proportion to the occurrence of which, I could suffer an escape of so much as would be requisite to prevent explosion), but, *being what it was,* would, at all events, continue specifically lighter than any compound whatever of mere nitrogen and oxygen. Thus there was a chance—in fact there was a strong probability—that, *at no epoch of my ascent, I should reach a point where the united weights of my immense balloon, the inconceivably rare gas within it, the car, and its contents, should equal the weight of the mass of the surrounding atmosphere displaced;* and this will be readily understood as the sole condition upon which my upward flight would be arrested. But, if this point were even attained, I could dispense with ballast and other weight to the amount of nearly three hundred pounds. In the meantime, the force of gravitation would be constantly diminishing, in proportion to the squares of the distances, and so, with a velocity prodigiously accelerating, I should at length arrive in those distant regions where the force of the earth's attraction would be superseded by that of the moon.

"There was another difficulty, however, which occasioned me some little disquietude. It has been observed, that, in balloon ascensions to any considerable height, besides the pain attending respiration, great uneasiness is experienced about the head and body, often accompanied with bleeding at the nose, and other symptoms of an alarming kind, and growing more and more inconvenient in proportion to the altitude attained.* This was a reflection of a nature somewhat startling. Was it not probable that these symptoms would increase until terminated by death itself? I finally thought not. Their origin was to be looked for in the progressive removal of the *customary* atmospheric pressure upon the surface of the body, and consequent distention of the superficial blood-vessels—not in any positive disorganization of the animal system, as in the case of difficulty in breathing, where the atmospheric density is *chemically insufficient* for the due renovation of blood in a ventricle of

---

*Since the original publication of Hans Pfaall, I find that Mr. Green, of Nassau-balloon notoriety, and other late aëronauts, deny the assertions of Humboldt, in this respect, and speak of a *decreasing* inconvenience—precisely in accordance with the theory here urged.

the heart. Unless for default of this renovation, I could see no reason, therefore, why life could not be sustained even in a *vacuum;* for the expansion and compression of chest, commonly called breathing, is action purely muscular, and the *cause,* not the *effect,* of respiration. In a word, I conceived that, as the body should become habituated to the want of atmospheric pressure, the sensations of pain would gradually diminish—and to endure them while they continued, I relied with confidence upon the iron hardihood of my constitution.

"Thus, may it please your Excellencies, I have detailed some, though by no means all, the considerations which led me to form the project of a lunar voyage. I shall now proceed to lay before you the result of an attempt so apparently audacious in conception, and, at all events, so utterly unparalleled in the annals of mankind.

"Having attained the altitude before mentioned—that is to say three miles and three-quarters—I threw out from the car a quantity of feathers, and found that I still ascended with sufficient rapidity; there was, therefore, no necessity for discharging any ballast. I was glad of this, for I wished to retain with me as much weight as I could carry, for the obvious reason that I could not be *positive* either about the gravitation or the atmospheric density of the moon. I as yet suffered no bodily inconvenience, breathing with great freedom, and feeling no pain whatever in the head. The cat was lying very demurely upon my coat, which I had taken off, and eyeing the pigeons with an air of *nonchalance.* These latter being tied by the leg, to prevent their escape, were busily employed in picking up some grains of rice scattered for them in the bottom of the car.

"At twenty minutes past six o'clock, the barometer showed an elevation of 26,400 feet, or five miles to a fraction. The prospect seemed unbounded. Indeed, it is very easily calculated by means of spherical geometry, how great an extent of the earth's area I beheld. The convex surface of any segment of a sphere is, to the entire surface of the sphere itself, as the versed sine of the segment to the diameter of the sphere. Now, in my case, the versed sine—that is to say, the *thickness* of the segment beneath me—was about equal to my elevation, or the elevation of the point of

33

sight above the surface. 'As five miles, then, to eight thousand,' would express the proportion of the earth's area seen by me. In other words, I beheld as much as a sixteen-hundredth part of the whole surface of the globe. The sea appeared unruffled as a mirror, although, by means of the telescope, I could perceive it to be in a state of violent agitation. The ship was no longer visible, having drifted away, apparently to the eastward. I now began to experience, at intervals, severe pain in the head, especially about the ears—still, however, breathing with tolerable freedom. The cat and pigeons seemed to suffer no inconvenience whatsoever.

"At twenty minutes before seven, the balloon entered a long series of dense cloud, which put me to great trouble, by damaging my condensing apparatus, and wetting me to the skin; this was, to be sure, a singular *recontre,* for I had not believed it possible that a cloud of this nature could be sustained at so great an elevation. I thought it best, however, to throw out two five-pound pieces of ballast, reserving still a weight of one hundred and sixty-five pounds. Upon so doing, I soon rose above the difficulty, and perceived immediately, that I had obtained a great increase in my rate of ascent. In a few seconds after my leaving the cloud, a flash of vivid lightning shot from one end of it to the other, and caused it to kindle up, throughout its vast extent, like a mass of ignited charcoal. This, it must be remembered, was in the broad light of day. No fancy may picture the sublimity which might have been exhibited by a similar phenomenon taking place amid the darkness of the night. Hell itself might have been found a fitting image. Even as it was, my hair stood on end, while I gazed afar down within the yawning abysses, letting imagination descend, and stalk about in the strange vaulted halls, and ruddy gulfs, and red ghastly chasms of the hideous and unfathomable fire. I had indeed made a narrow escape. Had the balloon remained a very short while longer within the cloud—that is to say, had not the inconvenience of getting wet, determined me to discharge the ballast—my destruction might, and probably would, have been the consequence. Such perils, although little considered, are perhaps the greatest which must be encountered in balloons. I had by this time, however, attained too great an elevation to be any longer uneasy on this head.

"I was now rising rapidly, and by seven o'clock the barometer indicated an altitude of no less than nine miles and a half. I began to find great difficulty in drawing my breath. My head, too, was excessively painful; and, having felt for some time a moisture about my cheeks, I at length discovered it to be blood, which was oozing quite fast from the drums of my ears. My eyes, also, gave me great uneasiness. Upon passing the hand over them they seemed to have protruded from their sockets in no inconsiderable degree; and all objects in the car, and even the balloon itself, appeared distorted to my vision. These symptoms were more than I had expected, and occasioned me some alarm. At this juncture, very imprudently, and without consideration, I threw out from the car three five-pound pieces of ballast. The accelerated rate of ascent thus obtained, carried me too rapidly, and without sufficient gradation, into a highly rarefied *stratum* of the atmosphere, and the result had nearly proved fatal to my expedition and to myself. I was suddenly seized with a spasm which lasted for more than five minutes, and even when this, in a measure, ceased, I could catch my breath only at long intervals, and in a gasping manner—bleeding all the while copiously at the nose and ears, and even slightly at the eyes. The pigeons appeared distressed in the extreme, and struggled to escape; while the cat mewed piteously, and, with her tongue hanging out of her mouth, staggered to and fro in the car as if under the influence of poison. I now too late discovered the great rashness of which I had been guilty in discharging the ballast, and my agitation was excessive. I anticipated nothing less than death, and death in a few minutes. The physical suffering I underwent contributed also to render me nearly incapable of making any exertion for the preservation of my life. I had, indeed, little power of reflection left, and the violence of the pain in my head seemed to be greatly on the increase. Thus I found that my senses would shortly give way altogether, and I had already clutched one of the valve ropes with the view of attempting a descent, when the recollection of the trick I had played the three creditors, and the possible consequences to myself, should I return, operated to deter me for the moment. I lay down in the bottom of the car, and endeavoured to collect my faculties. In this I so far succeeded as to determine upon the experiment of losing blood. Having no lancet, however, I was constrained to perform the operation in the best manner I was able, and finally succeeded in opening a vein in my left arm, with the blade of my penknife. The blood had hardly commenced flowing when I experienced a sensible relief, and by the time I had lost about half a moderate basin-full, most of the worst symptoms had abandoned me entirely. I nevertheless did not think it expedient to attempt getting on my feet immediately; but, having tied up my arm as well as I could, I lay still for about a quarter of an hour. At the end of this time I arose, and found myself freer from absolute *pain* of any kind than I had been during the last hour and a quarter of my ascension. The difficulty of breathing, however, was diminished in a very slight degree, and I found that it would soon be positively necessary to make use of my condenser. In the meantime, looking toward the cat, who was again snugly stowed away upon my coat, I discovered to my infinite surprise, that she had taken the opportunity of my indisposition to bring into light a litter of three little kittens. This was an addition to the number of passengers on my part altogether unexpected; but I was pleased at the occurrence. It would afford me a chance of bringing to a kind of test the truth of a surmise, which, more than anything else, had influenced me in attempting this ascension. I had imagined that the *habitual* endurance of the atmospheric pressure at the surface of the earth was the cause, or nearly so, of the pain attending animal existence at a distance above the surface. Should the kittens be found to suffer uneasiness *in an equal degree with their mother*, I must consider my theory in fault, but a failure to do so I should look upon as a strong confirmation of my idea.

"By eight o'clock I had actually attained an elevation of seventeen miles above the surface of the earth. Thus it seemed to me evident that my rate of ascent was not only on the increase, but that the progression would have been apparent in a slight degree even had I not discharged the ballast which I did. The pains in my head and ears returned, at intervals, with violence, and I still continued to bleed occasionally at the nose; but, upon the whole, I suffered much less than might have been expected. I breathed, however, at every moment, with more and more difficulty, and each inhalation was attended with a troublesome spasmodic action of the chest. I now unpacked the condensing apparatus, and got it ready for immediate use.

"The view of the earth, at this period of my ascension, was beautiful indeed. To the westward, the northward, and the southward, as far as I could see, lay a boundless sheet of apparently unruffled ocean, which every moment gained a deeper and deeper tint of blue. At a vast distance to the eastward, although perfectly discernible, extended the islands of Great Britain, the entire Atlantic coasts of France and Spain, with a small portion of the northern part of the continent of Africa. Of individual edifices not a trace could be discovered, and the proudest cities of mankind had utterly faded away from the face of the earth.

"What mainly astonished me, in the appearance of things below, was the seeming concavity of the surface of the globe. I had, thoughtlessly enough, expected to see its real *convexity* become evident as I ascended; but a very little reflection suffices to explain the discrepancy. A line, dropped from my position perpendicularly to the earth, would have formed the perpendicular of a right-angled triangle, of which the base would have extended from the right-angle to the horizon, and the hypotenuse from the horizon to my position. But my height was little or nothing in comparison with my prospect. In other words, the base and hypotenuse of the supposed triangle would, in my case, have been so long, when compared to the perpendicular, that the two former might have been regarded as nearly parallel. In this manner the horizon of the aëronaut appears always to be *upon a level* with the car. But as the point immediately beneath him seems, and is, at a great distance below him, it seems, of course, also at a great distance below the horizon. Hence the impression of concavity; and this impression must remain, until the elevation shall bear so great a proportion to the prospect, that the apparent parallelism of the base and hypotenuse disappears.

"The pigeons about this time seeming to undergo much

suffering, I determined upon giving them their liberty. I first untied one of them, a beautifully grey-mottled pigeon, and placed him upon the rim of the wicker-work. He appeared extremely uneasy, looking anxiously around him, fluttering his wings, and making a loud cooing noise, but could not be persuaded to trust himself from the car. I took him up at last, and threw him to about half a dozen yards from the balloon. He made, however, no attempt to descend as I had expected, but struggled with great vehemence to get back, uttering at the same time very shrill and piercing cries. He at length succeeded in regaining his former station on the rim, but had hardly done so when his head dropped upon his breast, and he fell dead within the car. The other one did not prove so unfortunate. To prevent his following the example of his companion, and accomplishing a return, I threw him downward with all my force, and was pleased to find him continue his descent, with great velocity, making use of his wings with ease, and in a perfectly natural manner. In a very short time he was out of sight, and I have no doubt he reached home in safety. Puss, who seemed in a great measure recovered from her illness, now made a hearty meal of the dead bird, and then went to sleep with much apparent satisfaction. Her kittens were quite lively, and so far envinced not the slightest sign of any uneasiness.

"At a quarter past eight, being able no longer to draw breath without the most intolerable pain, I proceeded forthwith to adjust around the car the apparatus belonging to the condenser. This apparatus will require some little explanation, and your Excellencies will please to bear in mind that my object, in the first place, was to surround myself and the car entirely with a barricade against the highly rarefied atmosphere in which I was existing, with the intention of introducing within this barricade, by means of my condenser, a quantity of this same atmosphere sufficiently condensed for the purposes of respiration. With this object in view I had prepared a very strong, perfectly airtight, but flexible gum-elastic bag. In this bag, which was of sufficient dimensions, the entire car was in a manner placed. That is to say, it (the bag) was drawn over the whole bottom of the car, up its sides, and so on, along the outside of the ropes, to the upper rim or hoop where the net-work is attached. Having pulled the bag up in this way, and formed a complete enclosure on all sides, and at bottom, it was now necessary to fasten up its top or mouth, by passing its material over the hoop of the net-work—in other words, between the net-work and the hoop. But if the net-work were separated from the hoop to admit this passage, what was to sustain the car in the meantime? Now the net-work was not permanently fastened to the hoop, but attached by a series of running loops or nooses. I therefore undid only a few of these loops at one time, leaving the car suspended by the remainder. Having thus inserted a portion of the cloth forming the upper part of the bag, I refastened the loops—not to the hoop, for that would have been impossible, since the cloth now intervened—but to a series of large buttons, affixed to the cloth itself, about three feet below the mouth of the bag; the intervals between the buttons having been made to correspond to the intervals between the loops. This done, a few more of the loops were unfastened from the rim, a farther portion of the cloth introduced, and the disengaged loops then connected with their proper buttons. In this way it was possible to insert the whole upper part of the bag between the net-work and the hoop. It is evident that the hoop would not drop down within the car, while the whole weight of the car itself, with all its contents, would be held up merely by the strength of the buttons. This, at first sight, would seem an inadequate dependence; but it was by no means so, for the buttons were not only very strong in themselves, but so close together that a very slight portion of the whole weight was supported by any one of them. Indeed, had the car and contents been three times heavier than they were, I should not have been at all uneasy. I now raised up the hoop again within the covering of gum-elastic, and propped it at nearly its former height by means of three light poles prepared for the occasion. This was done, of course, to keep the bag distended at the top, and to preserve the lower part of the net-work in its proper situation. All that now remained was to fasten up the mouth of the enclosure; and this was readily accomplished by gathering the folds of the material together, and twisting them up very tightly on the inside by means of a kind of stationary *tourniquet.*

"In the sides of the covering thus adjusted round the car, had been inserted three circular panes of thick but clear glass, through which I could see without difficulty around me in every horizontal direction. In that portion of the cloth forming the bottom, was likewise a fourth window, of the same kind, and corresponding with a small aperture in the floor of the car itself. This enabled me to see perpendicularly down, but having found it impossible to place any similar contrivance overhead, on account of the peculiar manner of closing up the opening there, and the consequent wrinkles in the cloth, I could expect to see no objects situated directly in my zenith. This, of course, was a matter of little consequence; for, had I even been able to place a window at top, the balloon itself would have prevented my making any use of it.

"About a foot below one of the side windows was a circular opening, three inches in diameter, and fitted with a brass rim adapted in its inner edge to the windings of a screw. In this rim was screwed the large tube of the condenser, the body of the machine being, of course, within the chamber of gum-elastic. Through this tube a quantity of the rare atmosphere circumjacent being drawn by means of a *vacuum* created in the body of the machine, was thence discharged, in a state of condensation, to mingle with the thin air already in the chamber. This operation being repeated several times, at length filled the chamber with atmosphere proper for all the purposes of respiration; but in so confined a space it would, in a short time, necessarily become foul, and unfit for use from frequent contact with the lungs. It was then ejected by a small valve at the bottom of the car—the dense air readily sinking into the thinner atmosphere below. To avoid the inconvenience of making a total *vacuum* at any moment with the chamber, this purification was never accomplished all at once, but in a gradual manner—the valve being opened only for a few seconds, then closed again, until one or two strokes from the pump of the condenser had supplied the place of the atmosphere ejected. For the sake of experiment I had put the cat and kittens in a small basket, and suspended it outside the car to a button at the bottom, close by the valve, through which I could feed them at any moment when necessary. I did this at some little risk, and before closing the mouth of the chamber, by reaching under the car with one of the poles before mentioned to which a hook had been attached. As soon as dense air was admitted in the chamber, the hoop and poles became unnecessary; the expansion of the enclosed atmosphere powerfully distending the gum-elastic.

"By the time I had fully completed these arrangements and filled the chamber as explained, it wanted only ten minutes of nine o'clock. During the whole period of my being thus employed, I endured the most terrible distress from difficulty of respiration, and bitterly did I repent the negligence or rather fool-hardiness, of which I had been guilty, of putting off to the last moment a matter of so much importance. But having at length accomplished it, I soon began to reap the benefit of my invention. Once again I breathed with perfect freedom and ease—and indeed why should I not? I was also agreeably surprised to find myself, in a great measure, relieved from the violent pains which had hitherto tormented me. A slight headache, accompanied with a sensation of fullness or distension about the wrists, the ankles, and the throat, was nearly all of which I had now to complain. Thus it seemed evident that a greater part of the uneasiness attending the removal of atmospheric pressure had actually *worn off,* as I had expected, and that much of the pain endured for the last two hours should have been attributed altogether to the effects of a deficient respiration.

"At twenty minutes before nine o'clock—that is to say, a short time prior to my closing up the mouth of the chamber, the mercury attained its limit, or ran down, in the barometer, which, as I mentioned before, was one of an extended construction. It then indicated an altitude on my part of 132,000 feet, or five-and-twenty miles, and I consequently surveyed at that time an extent of the earth's area amounting to no less than the three-hundred-and-twentieth part of its entire superficies. At nine o'clock I had again lost sight of land to the eastward, but not before I became aware that the balloon was drifting rapidly to the NNW. The ocean beneath me still retained its apparent concavity, although my view was often interrupted by the masses of cloud which floated to and fro.

"At half past nine I tried the experiment of throwing out a handful of feathers through the valve. They did not float as I had expected; but dropped down perpendicularly, like a bullet, *en masse,* and with the greatest velocity—being out of sight in a very few seconds. I did not at first know what to make of this extraordinary phenomenon; not being able to believe that my rate of ascent had, of a sudden, met with so prodigious an acceleration. But it soon occurred to me that the atmosphere was now far too rare to sustain even the feathers; that they actually fell, as they appeared to do, with great rapidity; and that I had been surprised by the united velocities of their descent and my own elevation.

"By ten o'clock I found that I had very little to occupy my immediate attention. Affairs went on swimmingly, and I believed the balloon to be going upward with a speed increasing momently although I had no longer any means of ascertaining the progression of the increase. I suffered no pain or uneasiness of any kind, and enjoyed better spirits than I had at any period since my departure from Rotterdam; busying myself now in examining the state of my various apparatus, and now in regenerating the atmosphere within the chamber. This latter point I determined to attend to at regular intervals of forty minutes, more on account of the preservation of my health, than from so frequent a renovation being absolutely necessary. In the meanwhile I could not help making anticipations. Fancy revelled in the wild and dreamy regions of the moon. Imagination, feeling herself for once unshackled, roamed at will among the ever-changing wonders of a shadowy and unstable land. Now there were hoary and time-honoured forests, and craggy precipices, and waterfalls tumbling with a loud noise into abysses without a bottom. Then I came suddenly into still noonday solitudes, where no wind of heaven ever intruded, and where vast meadows of poppies, and slender, lily-looking flowers spread themselves out a weary distance, all silent and motionless for ever. Then again I journeyed far down away into another country where it was all one dim and vague lake, with a boundary line of clouds. But fancies such as these were not the sole possessors of my brain. Horrors of a nature most stern and most appalling would too frequently obtrude themselves upon my mind, and shake the innermost depths of my soul with the bare supposition of their possibility. Yet I would not suffer my thoughts for any length of time to dwell upon these latter speculations, rightly judging the real and palpable dangers of the voyage sufficient for my undivided attention.

"At five o'clock, P.M., being engaged in regenerating the atmosphere within the chamber, I took that opportunity of observing the cat and kittens through the valve. The cat herself appeared to suffer again very much, and I had no hesitation in attributing her uneasiness chiefly to a difficulty in breathing; but my experiment with the kittens had resulted very strangely. I had expected, of course, to see them betray a sense of pain, although in a less degree than their mother; and this would have been sufficient to confirm my opinion concerning the habitual endurance of atmospheric pressure. But I was not prepared to find them, upon close examination, evidently enjoying a high degree of health, breathing with the greatest ease and perfect regularity, and evincing not the slightest sign of any uneasiness. I could only account for all this by extending my theory, and supposing that the highly rarefied atmosphere around might perhaps not be, as I had taken for granted, chemically insufficient for the purposes of life, and that a person born in such a *medium* might, possibly, be unaware of any inconvenience attending its inhalation, while, upon removal to the denser *strata* near the earth, he might endure tortures of a similar nature to those I had so lately experienced. It has since been to me a matter of deep regret that an awkward accident, at this time, occasioned me the loss of my little family of cats, and deprived me of the insight into this matter which a continued experiment might have afforded. In passing my hand through the valve, with a cup of water for the old puss, the sleeve of my shirt became entangled in the loop, which sustained the basket, and thus, in a moment, loosened it from the button. Had the whole actually vanished into air, it could not have shot from my sight in a more abrupt and instantaneous manner. Positively, there could not have intervened the tenth part of a second between the disengagement of the basket and its absolute disappearance with all that it contained. My good wishes followed it to the earth, but of course, I had no hope that either cat or kittens would ever live to tell the tale of their misfortune.

"At six o'clock, I perceived a great portion of the earth's visible area to the eastward involved in thick shadow, which continued to advance with great rapidity, until, at five minutes before seven, the whole surface in view was enveloped in the darkness of night. It was not, however, until long after this time that the rays of the setting sun ceased to illumine the balloon; and this circumstance, although of course fully anticipated, did not fail to give me an infinite deal of pleasure. It was evident that, in the morning, I should behold the rising luminary many hours at least before the citizens of Rotterdam, in spite of their situation so much farther to the eastward, and thus, day after day, in proportion to the height ascended, would I enjoy the light of the sun for a longer and a longer period. I now determined to keep a journal of my passage, reckoning the days from one to twenty-four hours continuously, without taking into consideration the intervals of darkness.

"At ten o'clock, feeling sleepy, I determined to lie down for the rest of the night; but here a difficulty presented itself, which, obvious as it may appear, had escaped my attention up to the very moment of which I am now speaking. If I went to sleep as I proposed, how could the atmosphere in the chamber be regenerated in the *interim?* To breathe it for more than an hour, at the farthest, would be a matter of impossibility; or, if even this term could be extended to an hour and a quarter, the most ruinous consequences might ensue. The consideration of this dilemma gave me no little disquietude; and it will hardly be believed, that, after the dangers I had undergone, I should look upon this business in so serious a light, as to give up all hope of accomplishing my ultimate design, and finally make up my mind to the necessity of a descent. But this hesitation was only momentary. I reflected that man is the veriest slave of custom, and that many points in the routine of his existence are deemed *essentially* important, which are only so *at all* by his having rendered them habitual. It was very certain that I could not do without sleep; but I might easily bring myself to feel no inconvenience from being awakened at intervals of an hour during the whole period of my repose. It would require but five minutes at most to regenerate the atmosphere in the fullest manner—and the only real difficulty was to contrive a method of arousing myself at the proper moment for so doing. But this was a question which, I am willing to confess, occasioned me no little trouble in its solution. To be sure, I had heard of the student who, to prevent his falling asleep over his books, held in one hand a ball of copper, the din of whose descent into a basin of the same metal on the floor beside his chair, served effectually to startle him up, if, at any moment, he should be overcome with drowsiness. My own case, however, was very different indeed, and left me no room for any similar idea; for I did not wish to keep awake, but to be aroused from slumber at regular intervals of time. I at length hit upon the following expedient, which, simple as it may seem, was hailed by me, at the moment of discovery, as an invention fully equal to that of the telescope, the steam-engine, or the art of printing itself.

"It is necessary to premise, that the balloon, at the elevation now attained, continued its course upward with an even and undeviating ascent, and the car consequently followed with a steadiness so perfect that it would have been impossible to detect in it the slightest vacillation. This circumstance favoured me greatly in the project I now determined to adopt. My supply of water had been put on board in kegs containing five gallons each, and ranged very securely around the interior of the car. I unfastened one of these, and taking two ropes, tied them tightly across the rim of the wicker-work from one side to the other; placing them about a foot apart and parallel, so as to form a kind of shelf, upon which I placed the keg, and steadied it in a horizontal position. About eight inches immediately below these ropes, and four feet from the bottom of the car I fastened another shelf—but made of thin plank, being the only similar piece of wood I had. Upon this latter shelf, and exactly beneath one of the rims of the keg, a small earthen pitcher was deposited. I now bored a hole in the end of the keg over the pitcher, and fitted in a plug of soft wood, cut in a tapering or conical shape. This plug I pushed in or pulled out, as might happen, until, after a few experiments, it arrived at that exact degree of tightness, at which the water, oozing from the hole, and falling into the pitcher below, would fill the latter to the brim in the period of sixty minutes. This, of course, was a matter briefly and easily ascertained, by noticing the proportion of the pitcher filled in any given time. Having arranged all this, the rest of the plan is obvious. My bed was so contrived upon the floor of the car, as to bring my head, in lying down, immediately below the mouth of the pitcher. It was evident, that, at the expiration of an hour, the pitcher, getting full, would be forced to run over, and to run over at the mouth, which was somewhat lower than the rim. It was also evident, that the water thus falling from a height of more than four feet, could not do otherwise than fall upon my face, and that the sure consequence would be, to waken me up instantaneously, even from the soundest slumber in the world.

"It was fully eleven by the time I had completed these arrangements, and I immediately betook myself to bed, with full confidence in the efficiency of my invention. Nor in this matter was I disappointed. Punctually every sixty minutes was I aroused by my trusty chronometer, when, having emptied the pitcher into the bung-hole of the keg, and performed the duties of the condenser, I retired again to bed. These regular interruptions to my slumber caused me even less discomfort than I had anticipated; and when I finally arose for the day, it was seven o'clock, and the sun had attained many degrees above the line of my horizon.

"*April 3rd.* I found the balloon at an immense height indeed, and the earth's convexity had now become strikingly manifest. Below me in the ocean lay a cluster of black specks, which undoubtedly were islands. Overhead, the sky was of a jetty black, and the stars were brilliantly visible; indeed they had been so constantly since the first day of ascent. Far away to the northward I perceived a thin, white, and exceedingly brilliant line, or streak, on the edge of the horizon, and I had no hesitation in supposing it to be the southern disc of the ices of the Polar Sea. My curiosity was greatly excited, for I had hopes of passing on much farther to the north, and might possibly, at some period, find myself placed directly above the Pole itself. I now lamented that my great elevation would, in this case, prevent my taking as accurate a survey as I could wish. Much, however, might be ascertained.

"Nothing else of an extraordinary nature occurred during the day. My apparatus all continued in good order, and the balloon still ascended without any perceptible vacillation. The cold was intense, and obliged me to wrap up closely in an overcoat. When darkness came over the earth, I betook myself to bed, although it was for many hours afterward broad daylight all around my immediate situation. The water-clock was punctual in its duty, and I slept until next morning soundly, with the exception of the periodical interruption.

"*April 4th.* Arose in good health and spirits, and was astonished at the singular change which had taken place in the appearance of the sea. It had lost, in a great measure, the deep tint of blue it had hitherto worn, being now of a greyish-white, and of a lustre dazzling to the eye. The convexity of the ocean had become so evident, that the entire mass of the distant water seemed to be tumbling headlong over the abyss of the horizon, and I found myself listening on tiptoe for the echoes of the mighty cataract. The islands were no longer visible; whether they had passed down the horizon to the southeast, or whether my increasing elevation had left them out of sight, it is impossible to say. I was inclined, however, to the latter opinion. The rim of ice to the northward was growing more and more apparent. Cold by no means so intense. Nothing of importance occurred, and I passed the day in reading, having taken care to supply myself with books.

"*April 5th.* Beheld the singular phenomenon of the sun rising while nearly the whole visible surface of the earth continued to be involved in darkness. In time, however, the light spread itself over all, and I again saw the line of ice to the northward. It was now very distinct, and appeared of a much darker hue than the waters of the ocean. I was evidently approaching it, and with great rapidity. Fancied I could again distinguish a strip of land to the eastward, and one also to the westward, but could not be certain. Weather moderate. Nothing of any consequence happened during the day. Went early to bed.

"*April 6th.* Was surprised at finding the rim of ice at a very moderate distance, and an immense field of the same material stretching away off to the horizon in the north. It was evident that if the balloon held its present course, it would soon arrive above the Frozen Ocean, and I had now little doubt of ultimately seeing the Pole. During the whole of the day I continued to near the ice. Toward night the limits of my horizon very suddenly and materially increased, owing undoubtedly to the earth's form being that of an oblate spheroid, and my arriving above the flattened regions in the vicinity of the Arctic circle. When darkness at length overtook me, I went to bed in great anxiety, fearing to pass over the object of so much curiosity when I should have no opportunity of observing it.

"*April 7th.* Arose early, and, to my great joy, at length beheld what there could be no hesitation in supposing the northern Pole itself. It was there, beyond a doubt, and immediately beneath my feet; but alas! I had now ascended to so vast a distance, that nothing could with accuracy be discerned. Indeed, to judge from the progression of the numbers indicating my various altitudes, respectively, at different periods, between six A.M. on the second of April, and twenty minutes before nine A.M. of the same day (at which time the barometer ran down), it might be fairly inferred that the balloon had now, at four o'clock in the morning of April the seventh, reached a height of *not less,* certainly, than 7254 miles above the surface of the sea. This elevation may appear immense, but the estimate upon which it is calculated gave a result in all probability far inferior to the truth. At all events I undoubtedly beheld the whole of the earth's major diameter; the entire northern hemisphere lay beneath me like a chart orthographically projected: and the great circle of the equator itself formed the boundary line of my horizon. Your Excellencies may, however, readily imagine that the confined regions hitherto unexplored within the limits of the Arctic circle, although situated directly beneath me, and therefore, seen without any appearance of being foreshortened, were still, in themselves, comparatively too diminutive, and at too great a distance from the point of sight, to admit of any very accurate examination. Nevertheless, what could be seen was of a nature singular and exciting. Northwardly from that huge rim before mentioned, and which, with slight qualification, may be called the limit of human discovery in these regions, one unbroken, or nearly unbroken, sheet of ice continues to extend. In the first few degrees of this its progress, its surface is very sensibly flattened, farther on depressed into a plane, and finally, becoming *not a little concave,* it terminates, at the Pole itself, in a circular centre, sharply defined, whose apparent diameter subtended at the balloon an angle of about sixty-five seconds, and whose dusky hue, varying in intensity, was, at all times, darker than any other spot upon the visible hemisphere, and occasionally deepened into the most absolute blackness. Farther than this, little could be ascertained. By twelve o'clock the circular centre had materially decreased in circumference, and by seven P.M. I lost sight of it entirely; the balloon passing over the western limb of the ice, and floating away rapidly in the direction of the equator.

"*April 8th.* Found a sensible diminution in the earth's apparent diameter, besides a material alteration in its general colour and appearance. The whole visible area partook in different degrees of a tint of pale yellow, and in some portions had acquired a brilliancy even painful to the eye. My view downward was also considerably impeded by the dense atmosphere in the vicinity of the surface being loaded with clouds, between whose masses I could only now and then obtain a glimpse of the earth itself. This difficulty of direct vision had troubled me more or less for the last forty-eight hours; but my present enormous elevation brought closer together, as it were, the floating bodies of vapour, and the inconvenience became, of course, more and more palpable in proportion to my ascent. Nevertheless, I could easily perceive that the balloon now hovered above the range of great lakes in the continent of North America, and was holding a course, due south, which would soon bring me to the tropics. This circumstance did not fail to give me the most heart-felt satisfaction, and I hailed it as a happy omen of ultimate success. Indeed, the direction I had hitherto taken, had filled me with uneasiness; for it was evident that, had I continued it much longer, there would have been no possibility of my arriving at the moon at all, whose orbit is inclined to the ecliptic at only the small angle of 5° 8' 48". Strange as it may seem, it was only at this late period that I began to understand the great error I had committed, in not taking my departure from earth at the same point *in the plane of the lunar ellipse*.

"*April 9th.* Today the earth's diameter was greatly diminished, and the colour of the surface assumed hourly a deeper tint of yellow. The balloon kept steadily on her course to the southward, and arrived, at nine P.M., over the northern edge of the Mexican Gulf.

"*April 10th.* I was suddenly aroused from slumber, about five o'clock this morning, by a loud, crackling, and terrific sound, for which I could in no manner account. It was of very brief duration, but, while it lasted, resembled nothing in the world of which I had any previous experience. It is needless to say that I became excessively alarmed, having, in the first instance, attributed the noise to the bursting of the balloon. I examined all my apparatus, however, with great attention, and could discover nothing out of order. Spent a great part of the day in meditating upon an occurrence so extraordinary, but could find no means whatever of accounting for it. Went to bed dissatisfied, and in a state of great anxiety and agitation.

"*April 11th.* Found a startling diminution in the apparent diameter of the earth, and a considerable increase, now observable for the first time, in that of the moon itself, which wanted only a few days of being full. It now required long and excessive labour to condense within the chamber sufficient atmospheric air for the sustenance of life.

"*April 12th.* A singular alteration took place in regard to the direction of the balloon, and although fully anticipated, afforded me the most unequivocal delight. Having reached, in its former course, about the twentieth parallel of southern latitude, it turned off suddenly, at an acute angle, to the eastward, and thus proceeded throughout the day, keeping nearly, if not altogether, *in the exact plane of the lunar ellipse.* What was worthy of remark, a very perceptible vacillation in the car was a consequence of this change of route—a vacillation which prevailed, in a more or less degree, for a period of many hours.

The Unparalleled Adventure of One Hans Pfaall

"*April 13th*. Was again very much alarmed by a repetition of the loud crackling noise which terrified me on the tenth. Thought long upon the subject, but was unable to form any satisfactory conclusion. Great decrease in the earth's apparent diameter, which now subtended from the balloon an angle of very little more than twenty-five degrees. The moon could not be seen at all, being nearly in my zenith. I still continued in the plane of the ellipse, but made little progress to the eastward.

"*April 14th*. Extremely rapid decrease in the diameter of the earth. Today I became strongly impressed with the idea, that the balloon was now actually running up the line of apsides to the point of perigee—in other words, holding the direct course which would bring it immediately to the moon in that part of its orbit the nearest to the earth. The moon itself was directly overhead, and consequently hidden from my view. Great and long-continued labour necessary for the condensation of the atmosphere.

"*April 15th*. Not even the outlines of continents and seas could now be traced upon the earth with distinctness. About twelve o'clock I became aware, for the third time, of that appalling sound which had so astonished me before. It now, however, continued for some moments, and gathered intensity as it continued. At length, while, stupefied and terror-stricken, I stood in expectation of I knew not what hideous destruction, the car vibrated with excessive violence, and a gigantic and flaming mass of some material which I could not distinguish, came with a voice of a thousand thunders, roaring and booming by the balloon. When my fears and astonishment had in some degree subsided, I had little difficulty in supposing it to be some mighty volcanic fragment ejected from that world to which I was so rapidly approaching, and, in all probability, one of that singular class of substances occasionally picked up on the earth, and termed meteoric stones for want of a better appellation.

"*April 16th*. Today, looking upward as well as I could, through each of the side windows alternately, I beheld, to my great delight, a very small portion of the moon's disc protruding, as it were, on all sides beyond the huge circumference of the balloon. My agitation was extreme; for I had now little doubt of soon reaching the end of my perilous voyage. Indeed, the labour now required by the condenser, had increased to a most oppressive degree, and allowed me scarcely any respite from exertion. Sleep was a matter nearly out of the question. I became quite ill, and my frame trembled with exhaustion. It was impossible that human nature could endure this state of intense suffering much longer. During the now brief interval of darkness a meteoric stone again passed in my vicinity, and the frequency of those phenomena began to occasion me much apprehension.

"*April 17th.* This morning proved an epoch in my voyage. It will be remembered that, on the thirteenth, the earth subtended an angular breadth of twenty-five degrees. On the fourteenth this had greatly diminished; on the fifteenth a still more remarkable decrease was observable; and, on retiring on the night of the sixteenth, I had noticed an angle of no more than about seven degrees and fifteen minutes. What, therefore, must have been my amazement, on awakening from a brief and disturbed slumber, on the morning of this day, the seventeenth, at finding the surface beneath me so suddenly and wonderfully *augmented* in volume, as to subtend no less than thirty-nine degrees in apparent angular diameter! I was thunderstruck! No words can give any adequate idea of the extreme, the absolute horror and astonishment, with which I was seized, possessed, and altogether overwhelmed. My knees tottered beneath me— my teeth chattered—my hair started up on end. 'The balloon, then, had actually burst!' These were the first tumultuous ideas that hurried through my mind: 'The balloon had positively burst!—I was falling—falling with the most impetuous, the most unparalleled velocity! To judge by the immense distance already so quickly passed over, it could not be more than ten minutes, at the farthest, before I should reach the surface of the earth, and be hurled into annihilation!' But at length reflection came to my relief. I paused; I considered; and I began to doubt. The matter was impossible. I could not in any reason have so rapidly come down. Besides, although I was evidently approaching the surface below me, it was with a speed by no means commensurate with the velocity I had at first conceived. This consideration served to calm the perturbation of my mind, and I finally succeeded in regarding the phenomenon in its proper point of view. In fact, amazement must have fairly deprived me of my senses, when I could not see the vast difference, in appearance, between the surface below me, and the surface of my mother earth. The latter was indeed over my head, and completely hidden by the balloon, while the moon—the moon itself in all its glory—lay beneath me, and at my feet.

"The stupor and surprise produced in my mind by this extraordinary change in the posture of affairs, was, perhaps, after all, that part of the adventure least susceptible of explanation. For the *bouleversement* in itself was not only natural and inevitable, but had been long actually anticipated as a circumstance to be expected whenever I should arrive at that exact point of my voyage where the attraction of the planet should be superseded by the attraction of the satellite—or, more precisely, where the gravitation of the balloon toward the earth should be less powerful than its gravitation toward the moon. To be sure I arose from a sound slumber, with all my senses in confusion, to the contemplation of a very startling phenomenon, and one which, although expected, was not expected at the moment. The revolution itself must, of course, have taken place in an easy and gradual manner, and it is by no means clear that, had I even been awake at the time of the occurrence, I should have been made aware of it by any *internal* evidence of an inversion—that is to say, by any inconvenience or disarrangement, either about my person or about my apparatus.

"It is almost needless to say that, upon coming to a due sense of my situation, and emerging from the terror which had absorbed every faculty of my soul, my attention was, in the first place, wholly directed to the contemplation of the general physical appearance of the moon. It lay beneath me like a chart—and although I judged it to be still at no inconsiderable distance, the indentures of its surface were defined to my vision with a most striking and altogether unaccountable distinctness. The entire absence of ocean or sea, and indeed of any lake or river, or body of water whatsoever, struck me, at first glance, as the most extraordinary feature in its geological condition. Yet, strange to say, I beheld vast level regions of a character decidedly alluvial, although by far the greater portion of the hemisphere in sight was covered with innumerable volcanic mountains, conical in shape, and having more the appearance of artificial than of natural protuberances. The highest among them does not exceed three and three-quarter miles in perpendicular elevation; but a map of the volcanic districts of the Campi Phlegræi would afford to your Excellencies a better idea of their general surface than any unworthy description I might think proper to attempt. The greater part of them were in a state of evident eruption, and gave me fearfully to understand their fury and their power, by the repeated thunders of the miscalled meteoric stones, which now rushed upward by the balloon with a frequency more and more appalling.

"*April 18th.* Today I found an enormous increase in the moon's apparent bulk—and the evidently accelerated velocity of my descent began to fill me with alarm. It will be remembered, that, in the earliest stage of my speculations upon the possibility of a passage to the moon, the existence, in its vicinity, of an atmosphere, dense in proportion to the bulk of the planet, had entered largely into my calculations; this too in spite of many theories to the contrary, and, it may be added, in spite of a general disbelief in the existence of any lunar atmosphere at all. But, in addition to what I have already urged in regard to Encke's comet and the zodiacal light, I had been strengthened in my opinion by certain observations of Mr. Schroeter, of Lilienthal. He observed the moon when two days and a half old, in the evening soon after sunset, before the dark part was visible, and continued to watch it until it became visible. The two cusps appeared tapering in a very sharp faint prolongation, each exhibiting its farthest extremity faintly illuminated by the solar rays, before any part of the dark hemisphere was visible. Soon afterward, the whole dark limb became illuminated. This prolongation of the cusps beyond the semicircle, I thought, must have arisen from the refraction of the sun's rays by the moon's atmosphere. I computed, also, the height of the atmosphere (which could refract light enough into its dark hemisphere to produce a twilight more luminous than the light reflected from the earth when the moon is about 32° from the new) to be 1356 Paris feet; in this view, I supposed the greatest height capable of refracting the solar ray, to be 5376 feet. My ideas on this topic had also received confirmation by a passage in the eighty-second volume of the *Philosophical Transactions,* in which it is stated, that, an occultation of Jupiter's satellites, the third disappeared after having been about 1″ or 2″ of time indistinct, and the fourth became indiscernible near the limb.*

"Upon the resistance or, more properly, upon the support of an atmosphere, existing in the state of density imagined, I had, of course, entirely depended for the safety of my ultimate descent. Should I then, after all, prove to have been mistaken, I had in consequence nothing better to expect, as a *finale* to my adventure, than being dashed into atoms against the rugged surface of the satellite. And, indeed, I had now every reason to be terrified. My distance from the moon was comparatively trifling, while the labour required by the condenser was diminished not at all, and I could discover no indication whatever of a decreasing rarity in the air.

"*April 19th.* This morning, to my great joy, about nine

---

*Hevelius writes that he has several times found, in skies perfectly clear, when even stars of the sixth and seventh magnitude were conspicuous, that, at the same altitude of the moon, at the same elongation from the earth, and with one and the same excellent telescope, the moon and its maculæ did not appear equally lucid at all times. From the circumstances of the observation, it is evident that the cause of this phenomenon is not either in our air, in the tube, in the moon, or in the eye of the spectator, but must be looked for in something (an atmosphere?) existing about the moon.

Cassini frequently observed Saturn, Jupiter, and the fixed stars, when approaching the moon to occultation, to have their circular figure changed into an oval one; and, in other occultations, he found no alteration of figure at all. Hence it might be supposed, that *at some times,* and not at others, there is a dense matter encompassing the moon wherein the rays of the stars are refracted.

o'clock, the surface of the moon being frightfully near, and my apprehensions excited to the utmost, the pump of my condenser at length gave evident tokens of an alteration in the atmosphere. By ten, I had reason to believe its density considerably increased. By eleven, very little labour was neecessary at the apparatus; and at twelve o'clock, with some hesitation, I ventured to unscrew the *tourniquet,* when, finding no inconvenience from having done so, I finally threw open the gum-elastic chamber, and unrigged it from around the car. As might have been expected, spasms and violent headache were the immediate consequences of an experiment so precipitate and full of danger. But these and other difficulties attending respiration, as they were by no means so great as to put me in peril of my life, I determined to endure as I best could, in consideration of my leaving them behind me momently in my approach to the denser *strata* near the moon. This approach, however, was still impetuous in the extreme; and it soon became alarmingly certain that, although I had probably not been deceived in the expectation of an atmosphere dense in proportion to the mass of the satellite, still I had been wrong in supposing this density, even at the surface, at all adequate to the support of the great weight contained in the car of my balloon. Yet this *should* have been the case, and in an equal degree as at the surface of the earth, the actual gravity of bodies at either planet supposed in the ratio of the atmospheric condensation. That it *was not* the case, however, my precipitous downfall gave testimony enough; *why* it was not so, can only be explained by a reference to those possible geological disturbances to which I have formerly alluded. At all events I was now close upon the planet, and coming down with the most terrible impetuosity. I lost not a moment, accordingly, in throwing overboard first my ballast, then my water-kegs, then my condensing apparatus and gum-elastic chamber, and finally every article within the car. But it was all to no purpose. I still fell with horrible rapidity, and was now not more than half a mile from the surface. As a last resource, therefore, having got rid of my coat, hat, and boots, I cut loose from the balloon *the car itself,* which was of no inconsiderable weight, and thus, clinging with both hands to the net-work, I had barely time to observe that the whole country, as far as the eye could reach, was thickly interspersed with diminutive habitations, ere I tumbled headlong into the very heart of a fantastical-looking city, and into the middle of a vast crowd of ugly little people, who none of them uttered a single syllable, or gave themselves the least trouble to render me assistance, but stood, like a parcel of idiots, grinning in a ludicrous manner, and eyeing me and my balloon askant, with their arms set akimbo. I turned from them in contempt, and, gazing upward at the earth so lately left, and left perhaps for ever, beheld it like a huge, dull, copper shield, about two degrees in diameter, fixed immovably in the heavens over-head, and tipped on one of its edges with a crescent border of the most brilliant gold. No traces of land or water could be discovered, and the whole was clouded with variable spots, and belted with tropical and equatorial zones.

"Thus, may it please your Excellencies, after a series of great anxieties, unheard-of dangers, and unparalleled escapes, I had, at length, on the nineteenth day of my departure from Rotterdam, arrived in safety at the conclusion of a voyage undoubtedly the most extraordinary, and the most momentous, ever accomplished, undertaken, or conceived by any denizen of earth. But my adventures yet remain to be related. And indeed your Excellencies may well imagine that, after a residence of five years upon a planet not only deeply interesting in its own peculiar character, but rendered doubly so by its intimate connection, in capacity of satellite, with the world inhabited by man, I may have intelligence for the private ear of the States' College of Astronomers of far more importance than the details, however wonderful, of the mere *voyage* which so happily concluded. This is, in fact, the case. I have much—very much which it would give me the greatest pleasure to communicate. I have much to say of the climate of the planet; of its wonderful alternations of heat and cold; of unmitigated and burning sunshine for one fortnight, and more than polar frigidity for the next; of a constant transfer of moisture, by distillation like that *in vacuo,* from the point beneath the sun to the point the farthest from it; of a variable zone of running water; of the people themselves; of their manners, customs, and political institutions; of their peculiar physical construction; of their ugliness; of their want of ears, those useless appendages in an atmosphere so peculiarly modified; of their consequent ignorance of the use and properties of speech; of their substitute for speech in a singular method of inter-communication; of the incomprehensible connection between each particular individual in the moon with some particular individual on the earth—a connection analogous with, and depending upon, that of the orbs of the planet and the satellite, and by means of which the lives and destinies of the inhabitants of the one are interwoven with the lives and destinies of the inhabitants of the other; and above all, if it so please your Excellencies—above all, of those dark and hideous mysteries which lie in the outer regions of the moon—regions which, owing to the almost miraculous accordance of the satellite's rotation on its own axis with its sidereal revolution about the earth, have never yet been turned, and, by God's mercy, never shall be turned, to the scrutiny of the telescopes of man. All this, and more—much more—would I most willingly detail. But, to be brief, I must have my reward. I am pining for a return to my family and to my home; and as the price of any farther communication on my part—in consideration of the light which I have it in my power to throw upon many very important branches of physical and metaphysical science—I must solicit, through the influence of your honourable body, a pardon for the crime of which I have been guilty in the death of the creditors upon my departure from Rotterdam. This, then, is the object of the present paper. Its bearer, an inhabitant of the moon, whom I have prevailed upon, and properly instructed, to be my messenger to the earth, will await your Excellencies' pleasure, and return to me with the pardon in question, if it can, in any manner, be obtained.

"I have the honour to be, etc., your Excellencies' very humble servant,

HANS PFAALL."

Upon finishing the perusal of this very extraordinary document, Professor Rubadub, it is said, dropped his pipe upon the ground in the extremity of his surprise, and Mynheer

Superbus Von Underduk having taken off his spectacles, wiped them, and deposited them in his pocket, so far forgot both himself and his dignity, as to turn round three times upon his heel in the quintessence of astonishment and admiration. There was no doubt about the matter—the pardon should be obtained. So at least swore, with a round oath, Professor Rubadub, and so finally thought the illustrious Von Underduk, as he took the arm of his brother in science, and without saying a word, began to make the best of his way home to deliberate upon the measures to be adopted. Having reached the door, however, of the burgomaster's dwelling, the professor ventured to suggest that as the messenger had thought proper to disappear—no doubt frightened to death by the savage appearance of the burghers of Rotterdam—the pardon would be of little use, as no one but a man of the moon would undertake a voyage to so vast a distance. To the truth of this observation the burgomaster assented, and the matter was therefore at an end. Not so, however, rumours and speculations. The letter, having been published, gave rise to a variety of gossip and opinion. Some of the over-wise even made themselves ridiculous by decrying the whole business as nothing better than a hoax. But hoax, with these sort of people, is, I believe, a general term for all matters above their comprehension. For my part, I cannot conceive upon what data they have founded such an accusation. Let us see what they say:

Imprimis. That certain wags in Rotterdam have certain especial antipathies to certain burgomasters and astronomers.

Secondly. That an odd little dwarf and bottle conjurer, both of whose ears, for some misdemeanour, have been cut off close to his head, has been missing for several days from the neighbouring city of Bruges.

Thirdly. That the newspapers which were stuck all over the little balloon were newspapers of Holland, and therefore could not have been made in the moon. They were dirty papers—very dirty—and Gluck, the printer, would take his Bible oath to their having been printed in Rotterdam.

Fourthly. That Hans Pfaall himself, the drunken villain, and the three very idle gentlemen styled his creditors, were all seen, no longer than two or three days ago, in a tippling house in the suburbs, having just returned, with money in their pockets, from a trip beyond the sea.

Lastly. That it is an opinion very generally received, or which ought to be generally received, that the College of Astronomers in the city of Rotterdam, as well as all other colleges in all other parts of the world—not to mention colleges and astronomers in general—are, to say the least of the matter, not a whit better, nor greater, nor wiser than they ought to be.

The Horror
of the Heights

Sir Arthur Conan Doyle

The idea that the extraordinary narrative which has been called the Joyce-Armstrong Fragment is an elaborate practical joke evolved by some unknown person, cursed by a perverted and sinister sense of humour, has now been abandoned by all who have examined the matter. The most *macabre* and imaginative of plotters would hesitate before linking his morbid fancies with the unquestioned and tragic facts which reinforce the statement. Though the assertions contained in it are amazing and even monstrous, it is none the less forcing itself upon the general intelligence that they are true, and that we must readjust our ideas to the new situation. This world of ours appears to be separated by a slight and precarious margin of safety from a most singular and unexpected danger. I will endeavour in this narrative, which reproduces the original document in its necessarily somewhat fragmentary form, to lay before the reader the whole of the facts up to date, prefacing my statement by saying that, if there be any who doubt the narrative of Joyce-Armstrong, there can be no question at all as to the facts concerning Lieutenant Myrtle, RN, and Mr. Hay Connor, who undoubtedly met their end in the manner described.

The Joyce-Armstrong Fragment was found in the field

which is called Lower Haycock, lying one mile to the westward of the village of Withyham, upon the Kent and Sussex border. It was on the fifteenth of September last that an agricultural labourer, James Flynn, in the employment of Mathew Dodd, farmer, of the Chauntry Farm, Withyham, perceived a briar pipe in Lower Haycock. A few paces farther on he picked up a pair of broken binocular glasses. Finally, among some nettles in the ditch, he caught sight of a flat, canvas-backed book, which proved to be a note-book with detachable leaves, some of which had come loose and were fluttering along the base of the hedge. These he collected, but some, including the first, were never recovered, and leave a deplorable hiatus in this all-important statement. The note-book was taken by the labourer to his master, who in turn showed it to Dr. J.H. Atherton, of Hartfield. This gentleman at once recognized the need for an expert examination, and the manuscript was forwarded to the Aero Club in London, where it now lies.

The first two pages of the manuscript are missing. There is also one torn away at the end of the narrative, though none of these affect the general coherence of the story. It is conjectured that the missing opening is concerned with the record of Mr. Joyce-Armstrong's qualifications as an aeronaut, which can be gathered from other sources and are admitted to be unsurpassed among the air-pilots of England. For many years he has been looked upon as the most daring and the most intellectual of flying men, a combination which has enabled him to both invent and test several new devices, including the common gyroscopic attachment which is known by his name. The main body of the manuscript is written neatly in ink, but the last few lines are in pencil and are so ragged as to be hardly legible—exactly, in fact, as they might be expected to appear if they were scribbled off hurriedly from the seat of a moving aeroplane. There are, it may be added, several stains, both on the last page and on the outside cover which have been pronounced by the Home Office experts to be blood—probably human and certainly mammalian. The fact that something closely resembling the organism of malaria was discovered in this blood, and that Joyce-Armstrong is known to have suffered from intermittent fever, is a remarkable example of the new weapons which modern science has placed in the hands of our detectives.

And now a word as to the personality of the author of this epoch-making statement. Joyce-Armstrong, according to the few friends who really knew something of the man, was a poet and a dreamer, as well as a mechanic and an inventor. He was a man of considerable wealth, much of which he had spent in the pursuit of his aeronautical hobby. He had four private aeroplanes in his hangars near Devizes, and is said to have made no fewer than one hundred and seventy ascents in the course of last year. He was a retiring man with dark moods, in which he would avoid the society of his fellows. Captain Dangerfield, who knew him better than anyone, says that there were times when his eccentricity threatened to develop into something more serious. His habit of carrying a shot-gun with him in his aeroplane was one manifestation of it.

Another was the morbid effect which the fall of Lieutenant Myrtle had upon his mind. Myrtle, who was attempting the height record, fell from an altitude of something over thirty thousand feet. Horrible to narrate, his head was entirely obliterated, though his body and limbs preserved their configuration. At every gathering of airmen, Joyce-Armstrong, according to Dangerfield, would ask, with an enigmatic smile: "And where, pray, is Myrtle's head?"

On another occasion after dinner, at the mess of the Flying School on Salisbury Plain, he started a debate as to what will be the most permanent danger which airmen will have to encounter. Having listened to successive opinions as to air-pockets, faulty construction, and over-banking, he ended by shrugging his shoulders and refusing to put forward his own views, though he gave the impression that they differed from any advanced by his companions.

It is worth remarking that after his own complete disappearance it was found that his private affairs were arranged with a precision which may show that he had a strong premonition of disaster. With these essential explanations I will now give the narrative exactly as it stands, beginning at page three of the blood-soaked notebook:

"Nevertheless, when I dined at Rheims with Coselli and Gustav Raymond I found that neither of them was aware of any particular danger in the higher layers of the atmosphere. I did not actually say what was in my thoughts, but I got so near to it that if they had any corresponding idea they could not have failed to express it. But then they are two empty, vainglorious fellows with no thought beyond seeing their silly names in the newspaper. It is interesting to note that neither of them had ever been much beyond the twenty-thousand-foot level. Of course, men have been higher than this both in balloons and in the ascent of mountains. It must be well above that point that the aeroplane enters the danger zone—always presuming that my premonitions are correct.

"Aeroplaning has been with us now for more than twenty years, and one might well ask: Why should this peril be only revealing itself in our day? The answer is obvious. In the old days of weak engines, when a hundred horse-power Gnome or Green was considered ample for every need, the flights were very restricted. Now that three hundred horse-power is the rule rather than the exception, visits to the upper layers have become easier and more common. Some of us can remember how, in our youth, Garros made a worldwide reputation by attaining nineteen thousand feet, and it was considered a remarkable achievement to fly over the Alps. Our standard now has been immeasurably raised, and there are twenty high flights for one in former years. Many of them have been undertaken with impunity. The thirty-thousand-foot level has been reached time after time with no discomfort beyond cold and asthma. What does this prove? A visitor might descend upon this planet a thousand times and never see a tiger. Yet tigers exist, and if he chanced to come down into a jungle he might be devoured. There are jungles of the upper air and there are worse things than tigers which inhabit them. I believe in time they will map these jungles accurately out. Even at the present moment I could name two of them. One of them lies over the Pau-Biarritz district of France. Another is just over my head as I write here in my house in Wiltshire. I rather think there is a third in the Homburg-Wiesbaden district.

"It was the disappearance of the airmen that first set me

thinking. Of course, everyone said that they had fallen into the sea, but that did not satisfy me at all. First, there was Verrier in France; his machine was found near Bayonne, but they never got his body. There was the case of Baxter also, who vanished, though his engine and some of the iron fixings were found in a wood in Leicestershire. In that case, Dr. Middleton, of Amesbury, who was watching the flight with a telescope, declares that just before the clouds obscured the view he saw the machine, which was at an enormous height, suddenly rise perpendicularly upwards in a succession of jerks in a manner that he would have thought to be impossible. That was the last seen of Baxter. There was a correspondence in the papers, but it never led to anything. There were several other similar cases, and then there was the death of Hay Connor. What a cackle there was about an unsolved mystery of the air, and what columns in the halfpenny papers, and yet how little was ever done to get to the bottom of the business! He came down in a tremendous vol-plané from an unknown height. He never got off his machine and died in his pilot's seat. Died of what? 'Heart disease,' said the doctors. Rubbish! Hay Connor's heart was as sound as mine is. What did Venables say? Venables was the only man who was at his side when he died. He said that he was shivering and looked like a man who had been badly scared. 'Died of fright,' said Venables, but could not imagine what he was frightened about. Only said one word to Venables, which sounded like 'Monstrous.' They could make nothing of that at the inquest. But I could make something of it. Monsters! That was the last word of poor Harry Hay Connor. And he *did* die of fright, just as Venables thought.

"And then there was Myrtle's head. Do you really believe—does anybody really believe—that a man's head could be driven clean into his body by the force of a fall? Well, perhaps it may be possible, but I, for one, have never believed that it was so with Myrtle. And the grease upon his clothes—'all slimy with grease,' said somebody at the inquest. Queer that nobody got thinking after that! I did— but, then, I had been thinking for a good long time. I've made three ascents—how Dangerfield used to chaff me about my shot-gun—but I've never been high enough. Now, with this new, light Paul Veroner machine and its one hundred and seventy-five Robur, I should easily touch the thirty thousand tomorrow. I'll have a shot at the record. Maybe I shall have a shot at something else as well. Of course, it's dangerous. If a fellow wants to avoid danger he had best keep out of flying altogether and subside finally into flannel slippers and a dressing-gown. But I'll visit the air-jungle tomorrow—and if there's anything there I shall know it. If I return, I'll find myself a bit of a celebrity. If I don't, this note-book may explain what I am trying to do, and how I lost my life in doing it. But no drivel about accidents or mysteries, if *you* please.

"I chose my Paul Veroner monoplane for the job. There's nothing like a monoplane when real work is to be done. Beaumont found that out in very early days. For one thing it doesn't mind damp, and the weather looks as if we should be in the clouds all the time. It's a bonny little model and answers my hand like a tender-mouthed horse. The engine is a ten-cylinder rotary Robur working up to one hundred and seventy-five. It has all the modern improvements—enclosed fuselage, high-curved landing skids, brakes, gyroscopic steadiers, and three speeds, worked by an alteration of the angle of the planes upon the Venetian-blind principle. I took a shot-gun with me and a dozen cartridges filled with buck-shot. You should have seen the face of Perkins, my old mechanic, when I directed him to put them in. I was dressed like an Arctic explorer, with two jerseys under my overalls, thick socks inside my padded boots, a storm-cap with flaps, and my talc goggles. It was stifling outside the hangars, but I was going for the summit of the Himalayas, and had to dress for the part. Perkins knew there was something on and implored me to take him with me. Perhaps I should if I were using the biplane, but a monoplane is a one-man show—if you want to get the last foot of lift out of it. Of course, I took an oxygen bag; the man who goes for the altitude record without one will either be frozen or smothered—or both.

"I had a good look at the planes, the rudder-bar, and the elevating lever before I got in. Everything was in order so far as I could see. Then I switched on my engine and found that she was running sweetly. When they let her go she rose almost at once upon the lowest speed. I circled my home field once or twice just to warm her up, and then, with a wave to Perkins and the others, I flattened out my planes and put her on her highest. She skimmed like a swallow down wind for eight to ten miles until I turned her nose up a little and she began to climb in a great spiral for the cloud-bank above me. It's all-important to rise slowly and adapt yourself to the pressure as you go.

"It was a close, warm day for an English September, and there was the hush and heaviness of impending rain. Now and then there came sudden puffs of wind from the south-west—one of them so gusty and unexpected that it caught me napping and turned me half-round for an instant. I remember the time when gusts and whirls and air-pockets used to be things of danger—before we learned to put an overmastering power into our engines. Just as I reached the cloud-banks, with the altimeter marking three thousand, down came the rain. My word, how it poured! It drummed upon my wings and lashed against my face, blurring my glasses so that I could hardly see. I got down on to a low speed, for it was painful to travel against it. As I got higher it became hail, and I had to turn tail to it. One of my cylinders was out of action—a dirty plug, I should imagine, but still I was rising steadily with plenty of power. After a bit the trouble passed, whatever it was, and I heard the full, deep-throated purr—the ten singing as one. That's where the beauty of our modern silencers comes in. We can at last control our engines by ear. How they squeal and squeak and sob when they are in trouble! All those cries for help were wasted in the old days, when every sound was swallowed up by the monstrous racket of the machine. If only the early aviators could come back to see the beauty and perfection of the mechanism which have been bought at the cost of their lives!

"About nine-thirty I was nearing the clouds. Down below me, all blurred and shadowed with rain, lay the vast expanse of Salisbury Plain. Half a dozen flying-machines were doing hackwork at the thousand-foot level, looking like little black swallows against the green background. I dare say they were wondering what I was doing up in cloud-land. Suddenly a grey curtain drew across beneath me and the wet folds of vapours were swirling round my face. It was clammily cold and miserable. But I was above the hail-storm, and that was something gained. The cloud was as dark and thick as a London fog. In my anxiety to get clear, I cocked her nose up until the automatic alarm-bell rang, and I actually began to slide backwards. My sopped and dripping wings had made me heavier than I thought, but presently I was in lighter cloud, and soon had cleared the first layer. There was a second—opal-coloured and fleecy—at a great height above my head, a white unbroken ceiling above, and a dark unbroken floor below, with the monoplane labouring upwards upon a vast spiral between them. It is deadly lonely in these cloud-spaces. Once a great flight of some small waterbirds went past me, flying very fast to the westwards. The quick whirr of their wings and their musical cry were cheery to my ear. I fancy that they were teal, but I am a wretched zoologist. Now that we humans have become birds we must really learn to know our brethren by sight.

"The wind down beneath me whirled and swayed the broad cloud-plain. Once a great eddy formed in it, a whirlpool of vapour, and through it, as down a funnel, I caught sight of the distant world. A large white biplane was passing at a vast depth beneath me. I fancy it was the morning mail service betwixt Bristol and London. Then the drift swirled inwards again and the great solitude was unbroken.

"Just after ten I touched the lower edge of the upper cloud-stratum. It consisted of fine diaphanous vapour drifting swiftly from the westward. The wind had been steadily rising all this time and it was now blowing a sharp breeze—twenty-eight an hour by my gauge. Already it was very cold, though my altimeter only marked nine thousand. The engines were working beautifully, and we went droning steadily upwards. The cloud-bank was thicker than I had expected, but at last it thinned out into a golden mist before me, and then in an instant I had shot out from it, and there was an unclouded sky and a brilliant sun above my head—all blue and gold above, all shining silver below, one vast glimmering plain as far as my eyes could reach. It was a quarter past ten o'clock, and the barograph needle pointed to twelve thousand eight hundred. Up I went and up, my ears concentrated upon the deep purring of my motor, my eyes busy always with the watch, the revolution indicator, the petrol lever, and the oil pump. No wonder aviators are said to be a fearless race. With so many things to think of there is no time to trouble about oneself. About this time I noted how unreliable is the compass when above a certain height from earth. At fifteen thousand feet mine was pointing east and a point south. The sun and the wind gave me my true bearings.

"I had hoped to reach an eternal stillness in these high altitudes, but with every thousand feet of ascent the gale grew stronger. My machine groaned and trembled in every joint and rivet as she faced it, and swept away like a sheet of paper when I banked her on the turn, skimming down wind at a greater pace, perhaps than ever mortal man has moved. Yet I had always to turn again and tack up in the wind's eye, for it was not merely a height record that I was after. By all my calculations it was above little Wiltshire that my air-jungle lay, and all my labour might be lost if I struck the outer layers at some farther point.

"When I reached the nineteen-thousand-foot level, which was about midday, the wind was so severe that I looked with some anxiety to the stays of my wings, expecting momentarily to see them snap or slacken. I even cast loose the parachute behind me, and fastened its hook into the ring of my leathern belt, so as to be ready for the worst. Now was the time when a bit of scamped work by the mechanic is paid for by the life of the aeronaut. But she held together bravely. Every cord and strut was humming and vibrating like so many harp-strings, but it was glorious to see how, for all the beating and buffeting, she was still the conqueror of Nature and the mistress of the sky. There is surely something divine in man himself that he should rise so superior to the limitations which Creation seemed to impose—rise, too, by such unselfish, heroic devotion as this air-conquest has shown. Talk of human degeneration! When has such a story as this been written in the annals of our race?

"These were the thoughts in my head as I climbed that monstrous, inclined plane with the wind sometimes beating in my face and sometimes whistling behind my ears, while the cloud-land beneath me fell away to such a distance that the folds and hummocks of silver had all smoothed out into one flat, shining plain. But suddenly I had a horrible and unprecedented experience. I have known before what it is to be in what our neighbours have called a *tourbillon*, but never on such a scale as this. That huge, sweeping river of wind of which I have spoken had, as it appears, whirlpools within it which were as monstrous as itself. Without a moment's warning I was dragged suddenly into the heart of one. I spun round for a minute or two with such velocity that I almost lost my senses, and then fell suddenly, left wing foremost, down the vacuum funnel in the centre. I dropped like a stone, and lost nearly a thousand feet. It was only my belt that kept me in my seat, and the shock and breathlessness left me hanging half-insensible over the side of the fuselage. But I am always capable of a supreme effort—it is my one great merit as an aviator. I was conscious that the descent was slower. The whirlpool was a cone rather than a funnel, and I had come to the apex. With a terrific wrench, throwing my weight all to one side, I levelled my planes and brought her head away from the wind. In an instant I had shot out of the eddies and was skimming down the sky. Then, shaken but victorious, I turned her nose up and began once more my steady grind on the upward spiral. I took a large sweep to avoid the danger-spot of the whirlpool, and soon I was safely above it. Just after one o'clock I was twenty-one thousand feet above the sea-level. To my great joy I had topped the gale, and with every hundred feet of ascent the air grew stiller. On the other hand, it was very cold, and I was conscious of that peculiar nausea which goes with rarefaction of the air. For the first time I unscrewed the mouth of my oxygen bag and took an occasional whiff of the glorious gas. I could feel it running like a cordial through my veins, and I was exhilarated almost to the point of drunkenness. I shouted and sang as I soared upwards into the cold, still outer world.

"It is very clear to me that the insensibility which came upon Glaisher, and in a lesser degree upon Coxwell, when, in 1862, they ascended in a balloon to the height of thirty thousand feet, was due to the extreme speed with which a perpendicular ascent is made. Doing it at an easy gradient and accustoming oneself to the lessened barometric pressure by slow degrees, there are no such dreadful symptoms. At the same great height I found that even without my oxygen inhaler I could breathe without undue distress. It was bitterly cold, however, and my thermometer was at zero, Fahrenheit. At one-thirty I was nearly seven miles above the surface of the earth, and still ascending steadily. I found, however, that the rarefied air was giving markedly less support to my planes, and that my angle of ascent had to be considerably lowered in consequence. It was already clear that even with my light weight and strong engine-power there was a point in front of me where I should be held. To make matters worse, one of my sparking-plugs was in trouble again and there was intermittent misfiring in the engine. My heart was heavy with the fear of failure.

"It was about that time that I had a most extraordinary experience. Something whizzed past me in a trail of smoke and exploded with a loud, hissing sound, sending forth a cloud of steam. For the instant I could not imagine what had happened. Then I remembered that the earth is forever being bombarded by meteor stones, and would be hardly inhabitable were they not in nearly every case turned to vapour in the outer layers of the atmosphere. Here is a new danger for the high-altitude man, for two others passed me when I was nearing the forty-thousand-foot mark. I cannot doubt that at the edge of the earth's envelope the risk would be a very real one.

"My barograph needle marked forty-one thousand three hundred when I became aware that I could go no farther. Physically, the strain was not as yet greater than I could bear, but my machine had reached its limit. The attenuated air gave no firm support to the wings, and the least tilt developed into side-slip, while she seemed sluggish on her controls. Possibly, had the engine been at its best, another thousand feet might have been within our capacity, but it was still misfiring, and two out of the ten cylinders appeared to be out of action. If I had not already reached the zone for which I was searching then I should never see it upon this journey. But was it not possible that I had attained it? Soaring in circles like a monstrous hawk upon the forty-thousand-foot level I let the monoplane guide herself, and with my Mannheim glass I made a careful observation of my surroundings. The heavens were perfectly clear; there was no indication of those dangers which I had imagined.

"I have said that I was soaring in circles. It struck me suddenly that I would do well to take a wider sweep and open up a new air-tract. If the hunter entered an earth-jungle he would drive through it if he wished to find his game. My reasoning had led me to believe that the air-jungle which I had imagined lay somewhere over Wiltshire. This should be to the south and west of me. I took my bearings from the sun, for the compass was hopeless and no trace of earth was to be seen—nothing but the distant, silver cloud-plain. However, I got my direction as best I might and kept her head straight to the mark. I reckoned that my petrol supply would not last for more than another hour or so, but I could afford to use it to the last drop, since a single magnificent vol-plané could at any time take me to the earth.

"Suddenly I was aware of something new. The air in front of me had lost its crystal clearness. It was full of long, ragged wisps of something which I can only compare to very fine cigarette-smoke. It hung about in wreaths and coils, turning and twisting slowly in the sunlight. As the monoplane shot through it, I was aware of a faint taste of oil upon my lips, and there was a greasy scum upon the woodwork of the machine. Some infinitely fine organic matter appeared to be suspended in the atmosphere. There was no life there. It was inchoate and diffuse, extending for many square acres and then fringing off into the void. No, it was not life. But might it not be the remains of life? Above all, might it not be the food of life, of monstrous life, even as the humble grease of the ocean is the food for the mighty whale? The thought was in my mind when my eyes looked upwards and I saw the most wonderful vision that ever man has seen. Can I hope to convey it to you even as I saw it myself last Thursday?

"Conceive a jelly-fish such as sails in our summer seas, bell-shaped and of enormous size—far larger, I should judge, than the dome of St. Paul's. It was of a light pink colour veined with a delicate green, but the whole huge fabric so tenuous that it was but a fairy outline against the dark blue sky. It pulsated with a delicate and regular rhythm. From it there depended two long, drooping green tentacles, which swayed slowly backwards and forwards. This gorgeous vision passed gently with noiseless dignity over my head, as light and fragile as a soap-bubble, and drifted upon its stately way.

"I had half-turned my monoplane, that I might look after this beautiful creature, when, in a moment, I found myself amidst a perfect fleet of them, of all sizes, but none so large as the first. Some were quite small, but the majority about as big as an average balloon, and with much the same curvature at the top. There was in them a delicacy of texture and colouring which reminded me of the finest Venetian glass. Pale shades of pink and green were the prevailing tints, but all had a lovely iridescence where the sun shimmered through their dainty forms. Some hundreds of them drifted past me, a wonderful fairy squadron of strange, unknown argosies of the sky—creatures whose forms and substance were so attuned to these pure heights that one could not conceive anything so delicate within actual sight or sound of earth.

"But soon my attention was drawn to a new phenomenon—the serpents of the outer air. These were long, thin, fantastic coils of vapour-like material, which turned and twisted with great speed, flying round and round at such a pace that the eyes could hardly follow them. Some of these ghost-like creatures were twenty or thirty feet long, but it was difficult to tell their girth, for their outline was so hazy that it seemed to fade away into the air around them. These air-snakes were of a very light grey or smoke colour, with some darker lines within, which gave the impression of a definite organism. One of them whisked past my very face, and I was conscious of a cold, clammy contact, but their composition was so insubstantial that I could not connect them with any thought of physical danger, any more than the beautiful bell-like creatures which had preceded them. There was no more solidity in their frames than in the floating spume from a broken wave.

"But a more terrible experience was in store for me. Floating downwards from a great height there came a purplish patch of vapour, small as I saw it first, but rapidly enlarging as it approached me, until it appeared to be hundreds of square feet in size. Though fashioned of some transparent jelly-like substance, it was none the less of much more definite outline and solid consistency than anything which I had seen before. There were more traces, too, of a physical organization, especially two vast, shadowy, circular plates upon either side, which may have been eyes and a perfectly solid white projection between them which was as curved and cruel as the beak of a vulture.

"The whole aspect of this monster was formidable and threatening, and it kept changing its colour from a very light mauve to a dark, angry purple so thick that it cast a shadow as it drifted between my monoplane and the sun. On the upper curve of its huge body there were three great projections which I can only describe as enormous bubbles, and I was convinced as I looked at them that they were charged with some extremely light gas which served to buoy up the misshapen and semi-solid mass in the rarefied air. The creature moved swiftly along, keeping pace easily with the monoplane, and for twenty miles or more it formed my horrible escort, hovering over me like a bird of prey which is waiting to pounce. Its method of progression—done so swiftly that it was not easy to follow—was to throw out a long, glutinous streamer in front of it, which in turn seemed to draw forward the rest of the writhing body. So elastic and gelatinous was it that never for two successive minutes was it the same shape, and yet each change made it more threatening and loathsome than the last.

"I knew that it meant mischief. Every purple flush of its hideous body told me so. The vague, goggling eyes which were turned always upon me were cold and merciless in their viscid hatred. I dipped the nose of my monoplane downwards to escape it. As I did so, as quick as a flash there shot out a long tentacle from this mass of floating blubber, and it fell as light and sinuous as a whip-lash across the front of my machine. There was a loud hiss as it lay for a moment across the hot engine, and it whisked itself into the air again, while the huge, flat body drew itself together as if in sudden pain. I dipped to a vol-piqué, but again a tentacle fell over the monoplane and was shorn off by the propeller as easily as it might have cut through a smoke wreath. A long, gliding, sticky, serpent-like coil came from behind and caught me round the waist, dragging me out of the fuselage. I tore at it, my fingers sinking into the smooth, glue-like surface, and for an instant I disengaged myself, but only to be caught round the boot by another coil, which gave me a jerk that tilted me almost on to my back.

"As I fell over I blazed off both barrels of my gun, though, indeed, it was like attacking an elephant with a pea-shooter to imagine that any human weapon could cripple that mighty bulk. And yet I aimed better than I knew, for, with a loud report, one of the great blisters upon the creature's back exploded with the puncture of the buck-shot. It was very clear that my conjecture was right, and that these vast, clear bladders were distended with some lifting gas, for in an instant the huge, cloud-like body turned sideways, writhing desperately to find its balance, while the white beak snapped and gaped in horribly fury. But already I had shot away on the steepest glide that I dared to attempt, my engine still full on, the flying propeller and the force of gravity shooting me downwards like an aerolite. Far behind me I saw a dull, purplish smudge growing swiftly smaller and merging into the blue sky behind it. I was safe out of the deadly jungle of the outer air.

"Once out of danger I throttled my engine, for nothing tears a machine to pieces quicker than running on full power from a height. It was a glorious, spiral vol-plané from nearly eight miles of altitude—first, to the level of the silver cloud-bank, then to that of the storm-cloud beneath it, and finally, in beating rain, to the surface of the earth. I saw the Bristol Channel beneath me as I broke from the clouds, but, having still some petrol in my tank, I got twenty miles inland before I found myself stranded in a field half a mile from the village of Ashcombe. There I got three tins of petrol from a passing motor-car, and at ten minutes past six that evening I alighted gently in my own home meadow at Devizes, after such a journey as no mortal upon earth has ever yet taken and lived to tell the tale. I have seen the beauty and I have seen the horror of the heights—and greater beauty or greater horror than that is not within the ken of man.

"And now it is my plan to go once again before I give my

results to the world. My reason for this is that I must surely have something to show by way of proof before I lay such a tale before my fellow-men. It is true that others will soon follow and will confirm what I have said, and yet I should wish to carry conviction from the first. Those lovely iridescent bubbles of the air should not be hard to capture. They drift slowly upon their way, and the swift monoplane could intercept their leisurely course. It is likely enough that they would dissolve in the heavier layers of the atmosphere, and that some small heap of amorphous jelly might be all that I should bring to earth with me. And yet something there would surely be by which I could substantiate my story. Yes, I will go, even if I run a risk by doing so. These purple horrors would not seem to be numerous. It is probable that I shall not see one. If I do I shall dive at once. At the worst there is always the shot-gun and my knowledge of . . ."

Here a page of the manuscript is unfortunately missing. On the next page is written, in large, straggling writing:

"Forty-three thousand feet. I shall never see earth again. They are beneath me, three of them. God help me; it is a dreadful death to die!"

Such in its entirety is the Joyce-Armstrong fragment. Of the man nothing has since been seen. Pieces of his shattered monoplane have been picked up in the preserves of Mr. Budd-Lushington upon the borders of Kent and Sussex, within a few miles of the spot where the note-book was discovered. If the unfortunate aviator's theory is correct that this air-jungle, as he called it, existed only over the south-west of England, then it would seem that he had fled from it at the full speed of his monoplane, but had been overtaken and devoured by these horrible creatures at some spot in the outer atmosphere above the place where the grim relics were found. The picture of that monoplane skimming down the sky, with the nameless terrors flying as swiftly beneath it and cutting it off always from the earth while they gradually closed in upon their victim, is one upon which a man who valued his sanity would prefer not to dwell. There are many, as I am aware, who still jeer at the facts which I have here set down, but even they must admit that Joyce-Armstrong has disappeared, and I would commend to them his own words: "This note-book may explain what I am trying to do, and how I lost my life doing it. But no drivel about accidents or mysteries, if *you* please."

Spads and Spandaus

Capt. W. E. Johns

Biggles looked up from his self-appointed task of filling a machine-gun belt as the distant hum of an aero engine reached his ears; an S.E.5, flying low, was making for the aerodrome. The Flight-Commander watched it fixedly, a frown deepening between his eyes. He sprang to his feet, the loose rounds of ammunition falling in all directions.

"Stand by for a crash!" he snapped at the duty ambulance driver. "Grab a Pyrene, everybody," he called; "that fellow's hit; he's going to crash!"

He caught his breath as the S.E. made a sickening flat turn, but breathed a sigh of relief as it flattened out and landed clumsily. The visiting pilot taxied to the tarmac and pushed up his goggles to disclose the pale but smiling face of Wilkinson, of 287 Squadron.

"You hit, Wilks?" called Biggles anxiously.

"No."

Biggles grinned his relief and cast a quick, critical glance at the machine. The fabric of the wings was ripped in a dozen places; an interplane strut was shattered, and the tail-unit was as full of holes as the rose of a watering-can.

"Have you got a plague of rats or something over at your place?" he enquired, pointing at the holes. "You want to get some cats."

"The rats that did that have red noses, and it'll take more than cats to catch 'em," said Wilkinson meaningly, climbing stiffly out of the cockpit.

"Red noses, did you say?" said Biggles, the smile fading from his face. "You mean—"

"The Richthofen crowd have moved down, that's what I mean," replied Wilkinson soberly. "I've lost Browne and Chadwicke, although I believe Browne managed to get down just over our side of the line. There must have been over twenty Huns in the bunch we ran into."

"What were they flying?"

"Albatrosses. I counted sixteen crashes on the ground between Le Cateau and here, theirs and ours. There's an R.E.8 on its nose between the lines. There's a Camel and an Albatross piled up together in the Hun front-line trench. What are we going to do about it?"

"Pray for dud weather, and pray hard," said Biggles grimly. "See any Camels on your way?"

Wilkinson nodded. "I saw three near Mossyface Wood."

"That'd be Mac; he's got Batty and a new man with him."

"Well, they'll have discovered there's a war on by now," observed Wilkinson. "Do you feel like making Fokker fodder of yourself, or what about running down to Clarmes for a drink and talk things over?"

"Suits me," replied Biggles. "I've done two patrols today and I'm tired. Come on; I'll ask the C.O. if we have the tender."

Half an hour later they pulled up in front of the Hôtel de Ville, in Clarmes. In the courtyard stood a magnificent touring car which an American staff officer had just vacated. Lost in admiration, Biggles took a step towards it.

"Thinking of buying it?" said a voice at his elbow.

Turning, Biggles beheld a captain of the American Flying Corps. "Why, are you thinking of selling it?" he asked evenly.

As he turned and joined Wilkinson at a table, the American seated himself near them. "You boys just going to the line?" he asked. "Because if you are I'll give you a tip or two."

Biggles eyed the speaker coldly. "Are you just going up?" he enquired.

"Sure," replied the American. "I'm commanding the 299th Pursuit Squadron. We moved in today—we shall be going over tomorrow."

"I see," said Biggles slowly; "then I'll give *you* a tip. Don't cross the line under fifteen thousand."

The American flushed. "I wasn't asking you for advice," he snapped; "we can take care of ourselves."

Biggles finished his drink and left the room.

"That baby fancies himself a bit," observed the American to Wilkinson. "When he's heard a gun or two go off he won't be so anxious to hand out advice. Who is he?"

"His name's Bigglesworth," said Wilkinson civilly. "Officially, he's only shot down twelve Huns and five balloons, but to my certain knowledge he's got several more."

"That kid? Say, don't try that on me, brother. You've got a dozen Huns, too, I expect," jibed the American.

"Eighteen, to be precise," said Wilkinson, casually tapping a cigarette.

The American paused with his drink half-way to his lips. He set the glass back on the table. "Say, do you mean that?" he asked incredulously.

Wilkinson shrugged his shoulders, but did not reply.

"What did he mean when he said not to cross the line under fifteen thousand?" asked the American curiously.

"I think he was going to tell you that the Richthofen circus has just moved in opposite," explained Wilkinson.

"I've heard of that lot," admitted the American. "Who are they?"

Wilkinson looked at him in surprise. "They are a big bunch of star pilots each with a string of victories to his credit. They hunt together, and are led by Manfred Richthofen, whose score stands at about seventy. With him he's got his brother, Lothar—with about thirty victories. There's Gussmann and Wolff and Weiss, all old hands at the game. There's Karjust, who has only one arm, but shoots better than most men with two. Then there's Lowenhardt, Reinhard, Udet and—but what does it matter? A man who hasn't been over the line before meeting that bunch, has about as much chance as a rabbit in a wild-beast show," he concluded.

"You trying to put the wind up me?"

"No. I'm just telling you why Biggles said don't cross under 15,000 feet. You may have a chance to dive home, if you meet 'em. That's all. Well, cheerio; see you later perhaps."

"It's a thundering shame," raved Biggles, as they drove back to the aerodrome. "Some of these Americans are the best stuff in the world. One or two of 'em have been out here for months with our own squadrons and the French Lafayette and Cigognes Escadrilles. Now their brass-hats have pulled 'em out and rolled 'em into their own Pursuit Squadrons. Do they put them in charge because they know the game? Do they? No! They hand 'em over to some poor boob who had done ten hours' solo in Texas or somewhere, but has got a command because his sister's in the Follies; and they've got to follow where he leads 'em. Bah! It makes me sick. You heard that poor prune just now? He'll go beetling over at five thousand just to show he knows more about it than we do. Well, he'll be pushing up the Flanders poppies by this time tomorrow night unless a miracle happens. He'll take his boys with him, that's the curse of it. Not one of 'em'll ever get back—you watch it," he concluded, bitterly.

"We can't let 'em do that," protested Wilkinson.

"What can we do?"

"I was just thinking."

"I've got it," cried Biggles. "Let them be the bait to bring the Huns down. With your S.E.s and our Camels together we'll knock the spots off that Hun circus. How many S.E.s can you raise?"

"Eight or nine."

"Right. You ask your C.O. and let me know tonight. I'll ask Major Mullen for all the Camels we can get in the air. That should even things up a bit; we'll be strong enough to take on anything the Huns can send against us. I'll meet you over Mossyface at six. How's that?"

"Suits me. I hope it's a fine day," yawned Wilkinson.

The show turned out to be a bigger one than Biggles anticipated. Major Mullen had decided to lead the entire Squadron himself, not so much on account of the possibility of the American Squadron being massacred, as because he realized the necessity of massing his machines to meet the new menace.

Thus it came about that the morning following his conversation with Wilkinson found Biggles leading his Flight behind the C.O. On his right was "A" Flight, led by Mahoney, and on his left "B" Flight, with MacLaren at their head. Each Flight comprised three machines, and these, with Major Mullen's red-cowled Camel, made ten in all. Major Sharp, commanding the S.E.5 Squadron, had followed Major Mullen's example, and from time to time Biggles looked upwards and backwards to where a formation of nine tiny dots, 6000 feet above them, showed where the S.E.s were watching and waiting. A concerted plan of action had been decided upon, and Biggles impatiently awaited its consummation.

Where were the Americans? He asked himself the question for the tenth time; they were a long time showing up. Where was the Boche circus? Sooner or later there was bound to be a clash, and Biggles thrilled at the thought of the coming dog-fight.

It was a glorious day; not a cloud broke the serenity of the summer sky. Biggles kept his eyes downwards, knowing that the S.E.s would prevent molestation from above. Suddenly, a row of minute moving objects caught his eye, and he stared in amazement. Then he swore. A formation of nine Spads was crossing the line far below. "The fools; the unutterable lunatics!" he growled. "They can't be an inch higher than four thousand. They must think they own the sky, and they haven't even seen us yet. Oh, well, they'll wake up presently, or I'm no judge."

The Spad Squadron was heading out straight into enemy sky, and Biggles watched them with amused curiosity, uncertain as to whether to admire their nerve or curse their stupidity. "They must think it's easy," he commented grimly, as his lynx-eyed leader altered his course slightly to follow the Americans.

Where were the Huns? He held his hand, at arm's length, over the sun, and extending his fingers squinted through the slits between them. He could see nothing, but the glare was terrific and might have concealed a hundred machines.

"They're there, I'll bet my boots," muttered the Flight-

Commander; "they are just letting those poor boobs wade right into the custard. How they must be laughing!"

Suddenly he stiffened in his seat. The major was rocking his wings—pointing. Biggles followed the outstretched finger and caught his breath. Six brightly painted machines were going down in an almost vertical dive behind the Spads. Albatrosses! He lifted his hand high above his head, and then, in accordance with the plan, pushed the stick forward and, with Batson and Healy on either side, tore down diagonally to cut off the enemy planes. He knew that most of the Hun circus was still above, somewhere, waiting for the right moment to come down. How long would they wait before coming down, thus bringing the rest of the Camels and S.E.s down into the mix-up with them? Not long, he hoped, or he might find his hands full, for he could not count upon the inexperienced Spad pilots for help.

The Spad Squadron had not altered its course, and Biggles' lip curled as he realized that even now they had not seen the storm brewing above them. Ah, they knew now! The Albatrosses were shooting, and the Spads swerved violently, like a school of minnows at the sudden presence of a pike. In a moment formation was lost as they scattered in all directions. Biggles sucked in his breath quickly as a Spad burst into flames and dropped like a stone. He was among them now; a red-bellied machine appeared through his sights and he pressed his triggers viciously, cursing a Spad that nearly collided with him.

A green Albatross came at him head-on, and, as he charged it, another with a blue-and-white checked fuselage sent a stream of tracer through his top plane. The green machine swerved and he flung the Camel round behind it; but the checked machine had followed him and he had to pull up in a wild zoom to escape the hail of lead it spat at him.

"Strewth!" grunted Biggles, as his windscreen flew to pieces. "This is getting too hot. My gosh! what a mess!"

A Spad and an Albatross, locked together, careered earthwards in a flat spin. A Camel, spinning viciously, whirled past him, and another Albatross, wrapped in a sheet of flame, flashed past his nose, the doomed pilot leaping into space even as it passed.

Biggles snatched a swift glance upwards. A swarm of Albatrosses were dropping like vultures out of the sky into the fight; he had a fleeting glimpse of other machines far above and then he turned again to the work on hand. Where were the Spads? Ah, there was one, on the tail of an Albatross. He tore after it, but the Spad pilot saw him and waved him away. Biggles grinned. "Go to it, laddie," he yelled exultantly, but a frown swept the grin from his face as a jazzed machine darted in behind the Spad and poured in a murderous stream of lead. Biggles shot down on the tail of the Hun. The Spad pilot saw his danger and twisted sideways to escape, but an invisible cord seemed to hold the Albatross to the tail of the American machine. Biggles took the jazzed machine in his sights and raked it from end to end in a long deadly burst. There was no question of missing at that range; the enemy pilot slumped forward in his seat and the machine went to pieces in the air.

The Spad suddenly stood up on its tail and sent two white pencils of tracer across Biggles' nose at something he could not see. A Hun, upside down, went past him so closely that he instinctively flinched.

"Holy smoke!" muttered Biggles. "He saved *me* that time; that evens things up."

His lips closed in a straight line; a bunch of six Albatrosses were coming at him together. Biggles fired one shot, and went as cold as ice as his gun jammed. Bullets were smashing through his machine when a cloud of S.E.s appeared between him and the Hun, and he breathed again.

"Lord, what a dog-fight," he said again, as he looked around to see what was happening. Most of the enemy planes were in full retreat, pursued by the S.E.s. Two Camels and two Albatrosses were still circling some distance away and four more Camels were rallying above him. Biggles saw the lone Spad flying close to him. Seven or eight crashed machines were on the ground, two blazing furiously, but whether they were Spads or Camels he couldn't tell.

He pushed up his goggles and beckoned to the Spad pilot, whom he now recognized as his acquaintance of the previous day, to come closer.

The American waved gaily, and together they started

after the Camels, led by Major Mullen's red cowling, now heading for the line.

Biggles landed with the Spad still beside him; he mopped the burnt castor-oil off his face and walked across to meet the pilot. The American held out his hand. "I just dropped in to shake hands," he said. "Now I must be getting back to our field to see how many of the outfit got home. I'd like to know you better; maybe you'll give me a tip or two."

"I can't tell you much after what you've seen today," laughed Biggles, turning to wave to an S.E.5, which had swung low over them and then proceeded on its way.

"Who's that?" asked the American.

"That's Wilks, the big stiff you saw with me yesterday," replied Biggles. "He's a good scout. He'll be at the Hôtel de Ville tonight for certain; so shall I. Do you feel like coming along to tear a chop or two?"

"Sure," agreed the Spad pilot enthusiastically.

The Greatest People
in the World

"Flying Officer X" (H. E. Bates)

He was very young, and because he was also very fair, he sometimes looked too young to have any part in the war at all; and more than anything else, as always, he wanted to fly.

It was his fairness that made him look so very much like one of the aristocracy, or at least very upper middle class, and I was very surprised to find that his people were labourers from a village in Somerset. His father was a hedger and ditcher with a fancy for leaving little tufts of hawthorn unclipped above the line of hedge. These tufts would grow into little ornamental balls, and later were clipped, gradually, summer by summer, into the shapes of birds. His father hoped, Lawson would explain to me, that bullfinches would use them for nesting-places. I never met either his father or his mother, but I gathered that they must have been at least forty when he was born. I gathered too that his mother cleaned at the local rectory and that she worked in the fields, harvesting and haymaking and pea-picking and cabbage-planting, whenever she had the chance or the time.

It was not only that Lawson wanted to fly. He had never wanted to do anything else but fly. It was the only life he had had time to know. There must have been thousands of young men like him, all reading the technicalities of the job in flight magazines, all passionately studying new designs, all longing for a flip, all flying Spitfires in imagination. But there were certain circumstances which made the case of Lawson different.

The chief of these circumstances, and the one which was in fact never altered, was that his parents were poor. When Lawson heard other people with incomes of five or six hundred or more a year talking of having no money he thought of his parents. His father knocked up a regular wage of two pounds a week. In summer he managed to increase this by ten or twelve shillings by gardening in the evenings and his mother put in a weekly average of about sixteen hours at sixpence an hour at the rectory. As a boy, Lawson went harvesting and haymaking for about sixpence a day and doing odd jobs on Saturdays in the rectory kitchen. And somehow, out of this, they bought him an education.

I don't know who was at the back of this idea of education. It may have been the rector. Most likely it was the rector and the mother. Lawson's father, I gathered, was a solid, unimaginative man who was rather content to let things remain as they were. He worked hard for three hundred and sixty-two days of the year—he tended his own garden on Sundays—and then got roaring tight on Christmas Eve, Flower Show Saturday, and the local Easter Monday races. It obviously wasn't he who had the idea of education, yet once the idea had been conceived he was behind it wholly and with all the solidity of his nature. For two years he and the mother saved up every extra penny they earned; every pea picked, every potato picked up, every forkful of hay turned over was something extra to the account. The house where they lived was old and damp, with unplastered walls and a brick floor and cracks in the window-frames that were stuffed with paper. The only light they had was a little oil lamp which they carried from room to room if they wanted a light in another place. They bought half a hundredweight of coal each week and on Friday afternoons the mother wetted the last shovelful of coal and banked up the fire so that it would last till evening.

When Lawson was fourteen they were able to send him to the local grammar school. Or at least they were going to send him. Everything was arranged for him to start in

September when one of those little accidents happened that often greatly affect the course of people's lives. Lawson fell off a bridge and broke his left arm. By the time it was better the vacancies in the first school were filled and he was sent instead to a school about fifteen miles away. He travelled there every day by train.

It was at this school that he heard the remark that was to affect, and crystallize, his whole life. The third term he was there, within a week or so of his fifteenth birthday, he heard a lecture in the school hall on the work of the R.A.F. When the lecture began, he told me, he really wasn't very interested. When he came out he could not get out of his mind something the lecturer had said about those who fly. "I often think," the lecturer said, "that they are the greatest people in the world."

When I knew Lawson the war was two years old. He had graduated rather uneventfully in the usual way, up through Moths and Ansons and so to light bombers, until now he was captain of a Stirling. There was even then a kind of premature immobility about him, especially about his eyes, so that the pupils sometimes looked seared, cauterized, burnt out. His first trouble was to have been made a bomber pilot at all. He had been through the usual Spitfire complex; all roaring glory and victory rolls. The thought of long flights of endurance, at night, with nothing to be seen except the flak coming up at you in slow sinister curls, the earth in the light of a flare, and then the flare-path at base if you were lucky and the fog hadn't come down, shook him quite a lot. It may have been this that accounted for what happened afterwards.

He stayed at school until he was eighteen, and had virtually walked straight out of school into the Air Force. What struck me most was that there was no disruption, no disloyalty, between himself and his parents. There might well have been. Their life, simple, bound to earth, lighted by that cheap paraffin lamp which they carried from room to room, compressed into the simple measure of hard work, saving, and devotion, was like the life of another age compared with the life they had chosen for him. I don't know what education exactly meant to them; I don't know what ambitions they had for him. But neither could have been connected with his flying a bomber. Yet they never uttered the smallest reproach or protest to what must have been rather a terrifying prospect to them. They might have thought that it would be better for him to be ploughing his own good Somerset clay. They probably did. But if they did they didn't once say so. They simply knew he wanted to fly and they let him fly because it was the thing that was nearest his heart.

His own part was just as straightforward and steadfast. As I became acquainted with it. I didn't wonder at all that he had been made a bomber pilot. The qualities for it were all there in his behaviour towards these two simple, self-sacrificial people. They had sent him to a pretty expensive school—to them it must have been fabulous—and he might easily have turned his back on them. A touch of swollen head and he might easily have decided that he was too good for that shabby little cottage, with the unplastered walls, the windows stuffed with paper, and the one cheap paraffin lamp carried from room to room. But I don't suppose he ever dreamed of it. He not only remained loyal to them but loyal in a positive way. He sent home to them a third of his pay every month: which for a Pilot Officer meant practically the same sacrifice as they had made for him.

He couldn't in fact have been more steadfast and careful. Perhaps he was too steadfast and, if it's possible as the captain of a crew of seven in a very expensive piece of aircraft, too careful. Yet nothing went right for him. Before his first big trip with a Stirling he felt the same dry mental tension, and the same sour wet slackness of the stomach, that you feel before a race. It was a sort of cold excitement. He felt it get worse as he taxied the aircraft across the field. It was winter and there was a kind of smokiness in the falling twilight over the few distant trees, and the hangars, looming up with their red lights burning, looked enormous. The runway seemed foreshortened and it looked practically impossible not to prang something on take-off. He was certain it would be all right once he was up, but it was the idea of lugging thirty-two tons of aircraft off the wet runway, that was soft in places, and in half-light, which worried him.

He was worked up to a very high state of tension, with the

kite actually on the runway, when Control informed him that the whole show would be scrubbed. His crew swore and mouthed at everybody and everything all the way back to dispersal. He felt too empty to say anything. He felt as if his stomach had dropped out and that he might be going to pieces. The awful anti-climax of the thing was too much.

That night he didn't sleep very well. He fell asleep and then woke up. His blankets had slipped and he was very cold and he did not know what time it was. He could hear his watch ticking very loudly. Someone had left a light on in the passage outside and it shone through the fan-light of the bedroom door. He lay for hours watching it, sleepless, cold, his mind full of the impression of the wet runway, the hangars looming up in the twilight, the idea that he was about to prang something on take-off.

Then he fell asleep and dreamed that he really did prang something. He was taking off and his port wing hit the control tower, which had wide, deep, circular windows. Through these windows he could see Brand, the control officer, and a little Flying Officer named Danvers, and the two orderlies, one wearing earphones. The two officers were drinking tea and his wing knocked the cups out of their hands. The tea shot up in a brown wave that broke on Brand's tunic, and he saw vividly the look of helpless and terrified indignation on Brand's face a second before he was hit and died.

It was fantastic, but very real also, and he woke in a terrible sweat of fear, scared solely by the happenings of the dream. He was relieved to find it a waking dream; that it was already daylight beyond the drawn curtains. It was in fact already late and he got up hurriedly and went down to breakfast without shaving. After breakfast he went straight over to the hangars and hoped there would be flying that day. But the weather was worse: grey fenland distances, gathering ground mist, spits of cold rain. The Wing Commander usually got the crews running round the perimeter track for training, but that morning the weather was too bad, there was no running and by eleven o'clock the crews were fretting for an afternoon stand-down. Lawson went over to his aircraft, but everything was nicely fixed there and his stooges were sheltering under the wings, out of the rain, smoking. As he walked back in the rain to Control and went up to the concrete stairs to the room where, in his dream, he had crashed through the wide windows and had killed Brand and Danvers, he saw at once that Brand and Danvers were not on duty, and by this fact, the fact that Brand and Danvers had been on duty at the time of the dream, he felt the reality of the dream grow brighter instead of fade.

After he had had the orderly bring him a cup of tea he drank it quickly and then went out alone. The trouble was perhaps that he was at that time a stranger in the station. There was no one—and it would have been better if there had been someone—to whom he could say, joking: "Had a hell of a queer dream last night. Dreamt I pranged the control tower. Brand was stooging around as usual and got it in the neck. He looked pretty damned funny when I knocked the tea out of his hands." But he knew no one very well, and could say nothing about the dream. It was like a complex personal problem. Once you had explained it to someone else it was no longer personal; it ceased to be complex and finally it ceased to be a problem at all.

Unfortunately he could not do this, and unfortunately there was a recurrence of the dream that night. It was the same dream precisely, with one important exception. It was now not Brand or Danvers who were killed, but two men named Porter and Evans, the duty officers for that night. The painful brightness of the dream was identical; he could see the brown tea steaming as it splashed on Porter's jacket and he could see on his face, as on Brand's face, the indignant, ridiculous terror.

The next morning the weather was much better, and by noon it was certain there would be ops that night. At briefing he felt much as if he had a hangover. He concentrated hard on the met. talk, but his head ached and the green and pink and mauve contour lines of the map troubled his eyes. The target was Hamburg, a fairly long hard trip, and his own take-off was at 18:00 hours. By the time he reached his aircraft the light was no longer good, but there was no mist and only thin cloud in a wasting blue sky. For some reason he now felt better: clearer-headed, quite confident. His stomach was dry and tight and the period of distrust in himself was practically over.

Then something else happened. His outer port engine would not start. As he sat there in the aircraft, struggling to get things going, his crew on edge, his engineer bewildered and furious by this inexplicable behaviour of an engine that had been tested only that morning, he felt his confidence breaking down again. The light was dying rapidly on the fringes of the field and he knew what must happen any moment now. "It's just one of these bloody damn things," the engineer said over and over again. "Just one of these damn bloody aggravating bastard things." Some minutes later Lawson, not listening much now to the engineer, heard what he expected to hear from Control. The trip was off; the margin of time was past. "Is it understood?" said Control in the voice of an ironical automatic parrot. "Is it understood?"

After this second disappointment he went through the same nervous agony of not sleeping. Because the breaking of tension at a vital moment was the cause in both cases you might have said he was trying too hard. But the third occasion seemed to have nothing to do with this. He was again on operations, and again it was evening, with the fringes of the drome blue-grey with winter mist, the runway pooled with water, the red lights like beacons on the black mountains of the hangars. This time he actually got up off the runway. He had actually got over the sickening horror that for the third time running some damnable triviality would stop him from getting the kite airborne. But soon that was past, and he was following the others. The sun had already set, leaving huge cloud-broken lakes of pale green and yellow light for miles above the sunset point, and towards these immense spaces of rapidly fading light he watched the black wings of the Stirlings fading into the distance until at last it was too dark and the lakes of light and the planes were no longer there to see. Then for the first time for weeks he felt good: strained but calm, sure of himself, settled.

I suppose they had been flying about an hour when the icing began. They were over the sea when the kite began to make sickening and heavy plunges in the darkness: movements to which there was only one answer. Lawson felt suddenly up against all the old trouble again: the inexplicable bad luck, the frustration, the disastrous break of tension. He felt himself lose heart. His guts became wet and cold and sour and then seemed to drop out of him. His only piece of luck was that he had not flown far, and when he had safely jettisoned his bombs and turned the kite for home he bitterly told himself that it was the only piece of luck he had ever had as a pilot or was ever likely to have. But even that was not all. As he came in to land it was as if there were some evil and persistent Jonah in the kite with him: somebody for whom the simplest moments were inexplicably turned into pieces of hellish and ironical misfortune. Lawson landed perfectly in the darkness, but the runway was wet and greasy after rain. He put on the brakes, but nothing happened. The kite drove fast down the runway and then skidded into a ground loop that brought it to a standstill on the grass, the undercarriage smashed. To Lawson it was like the end of everything.

He expected to be grounded any moment after that. His despair was sour and keen and personal; he could tell no one about it. For about a week he did not sleep much. He did not dream either. He re-created the few moments of ill-luck until they were moments of positive and monstrous failure. And as if this were not enough he created new moments, sharp and terrible seconds of stalling, ground-looping, crash-landing, overshooting the drome. He imagined himself coming in too slow, another time too fast. It never mattered much. He was going to prang the control tower in any case, killing the occupants there as they drank their last over-sweetened steaming tea.

Then by accident he discovered it possible to get some sleep. He began to sleep with the light on. The station at that time was not very crowded; later two and even three people slept in a room. But now no one could see him giving way— not that he was ever the only one—to the fear of sleeping in the dark. In this way he slept quite well for about a week; it was fairly peaceful; he was not cold; he did not have the recurrent dream. And above all, they did not ground him.

I don't know if they were ever thinking of it; but it never

93

in fact became necessary. Another thing happened: this time not just ill-luck, frustration, a mistake, a private illusion about something, but a simple and terrible fact. It was a telegram from the rectory of his village in Somerset. His parents had been killed in a raid.

After that telegram he got compassionate leave and went home. The next morning he stood in the garden of the house, staring at the bony, burnt roof timbers, the red-grey dust and rubble, the bare scorched blue wallpaper, of the two rooms where the cheap little paraffin lamp had once been carried to and fro. It was winter time. Red dust lay on the frozen leaves of the brussels sprouts; the hawthorn twigs, fancifully clipped by his father above the line of hedge, were almost the only things about the place that remained untouched and as before. He did not stay very long; but while he stayed there he thought he saw his mother working in the fields, skirt pinned behind her, and his father with the hedge-hook in his hand and the black twigs flying in the air. He saw for a moment their lives with the simple clearness of grief, the lives remote from his own, so utterly simple and so utterly remote, yet bound to him elementally.

When he went back to the station three days later, he had forgotten about the dreams, the illusions, and all the rest of it; or at least it was as if he had forgotten. All the reality of the bad moments, if it had been reality, was now obscured by the simple reality of the dusty and fire-blackened little house.

All that he had to do now seemed also quite simple and clear; terribly simple and terribly clear. If he ever had been afraid, there was no longer any sign of it as he took off for a daylight raid over northern Germany two days later. It was a cold, clear winter afternoon; there was just enough power in the sunlight to reveal the colours of the fields. He used to say it was one of those trips where you felt the aircraft had been shot from a gun. You got away clean and smooth and easy; there was no hitch. Instinctively, from the first, you knew it was a piece of cake. You went over and did the job and no matter what came up at you you knew that, ultimately, it would be all right. That afternoon flak tore a strip off his flaps and for about half an hour his crew did nothing but yell gloriously through the intercom, that fighters were coming up from everywhere. Cannon fire hit his middle turret and put it out of action and sprayed the fuselage from end to end with raw ugly little holes. Inland over Germany he lost a lot of height chasing and finally shooting down an Me 109, and he discovered he could not regain his height as he came back over the coast and sea. But even that did not trouble him then. Everything was clear at last. His whole life was clear.

He came over the English coast and then the English fields, at about two or three hundred feet. The sun was still shining, but sometimes there were clouds and then it was light in patches on the fields below and dark in the upper air. He roared over fields and woods and roads and over the little dusty blue towns and over remote farms where he could even see the hens feeding and scuttling in the dark winter grass.

He came so low once that for a second or so he saw people in the fields. For an instant he saw a man and woman working. They raised flat, astonished faces to look at the great plane overhead. The woman perhaps was picking sticks and he thought he saw the man lean for a moment on a fork. They might have been old or young, he could not tell; they lifted their heads and in a second were cut off by the speed of the plane. But in this second, as he saw them transfixed on the earth below him and before the speed of the plane cut them off for ever, he remembered his own people. He remembered them as they lived, simple and sacrificing, living only for him, and he saw them alive again in the arrested figures of the two people in the field below: as if they were the same people, the same simple people, the same humble, faithful, eternal people, giving always and giving everything: the greatest people in the world.

They Shall
Not Grow Old

Roald Dahl

The two of us sat outside the hangar on wooden boxes.

It was noon. The sun was high and the heat of the sun was like a close fire. It was hotter than hell out there by the hangar. We could feel the hot air touching the inside of our lungs when we breathed and we found it better if we almost closed our lips and breathed in quickly; it was cooler that way. The sun was upon our shoulders and upon our backs, and all the time the sweat seeped out from our skin, trickled down our necks, over our chests and down our stomachs. It collected just where our belts were tight around the tops of our trousers and it filtered under the tightness of our belts where the wet was very uncomfortable and made prickly heat on the skin.

Our two Hurricanes were standing a few yards away, each with that patient, smug look which fighter planes have when the engine is not turning, and beyond them the thin black strip of the runway sloped down towards the beaches and towards the sea. The black surface of the runway and the white grassy sand on the sides of the runway shimmered and shimmered in the sun. The heat haze hung like a vapour over the aerodrome.

The Stag looked at his watch.

"He ought to be back," he said.

The two of us were on readiness, sitting there for orders to take off. The Stag moved his feet on the hot ground.

"He ought to be back," he said.

It was two and a half hours since Fin had gone and he certainly should have come back by now. I looked up into the sky and listened. There was the noise of airmen talking beside the petrol wagon and there was the faint pounding of the sea upon the beaches; but there was no sign of an aeroplane. We sat a little while longer without speaking.

"It looks as though he's had it," I said.

"Yep," said the Stag. "It looks like it."

The Stag got up and put his hands into the pockets of his khaki shorts. I got up too. We stood looking northwards into the clear sky, and we shifted our feet on the ground because of the softness of the tar and because of the heat.

"What was the name of that girl?" said the Stag without turning his head.

"Nikki," I answered.

The Stag sat down again on his wooden box, still with his hands in his pockets and he looked down at the ground between his feet. The Stag was the oldest pilot in the squadron; he was twenty-seven. He had a mass of coarse ginger hair which he never brushed. His face was pale, even after all this time in the sun, and covered with freckles. His mouth was wide and tight closed. He was not tall but his shoulders under his khaki shirt were broad and thick like those of a wrestler. He was a quiet person.

"He'll probably be all right," he said, looking up. "And anyway, I'd like to meet the Vichy Frenchman who can get Fin."

We were in Palestine fighting the Vichy French in Syria. We were at Haifa, and three hours before the Stag, Fin and I had gone on readiness. Fin had flown off in response to an urgent call from the Navy, who had phoned up and said that there were two French destroyers moving out of Beyrouth harbour. Please go at once and see where they are going, said the Navy. Just fly up the coast and have a look and come back quickly and tell us where they are going.

So Fin had flown off in his Hurricane. The time had gone by and he had not returned. We knew that there was no longer much hope. If he hadn't been shot down, he would have run out of petrol some time ago.

I looked down and I saw his blue RAF cap which was lying on the ground where he had thrown it as he ran to his aircraft, and I saw the oil stains on top of the cap and the shabby bent peak. It was difficult now to believe that he had gone. He had been in Egypt, in Libya and in Greece. On the aerodrome and in the mess we had had him with us all of the time. He was gay and tall and full of laughter, this Fin, with black hair and a long straight nose which he used to stroke up and down with the tip of his finger. He had a way of listening to you while you were telling a story, leaning back in his chair with his face to the ceiling but with his eyes looking down on the ground, and it was only last night at supper that he had suddenly said, "You know, I wouldn't mind marrying Nikki. I think she's a good girl."

The Stag was sitting opposite him at the time, eating baked beans.

"You mean just occasionally," he said.

Nikki was in a cabaret in Haifa.

"No," said Fin. "Cabaret girls make fine wives. They are never unfaithful. There is no novelty for them in being unfaithful; that would be like going back to the old job."

The Stag had looked up from his beans. "Don't be such a bloody fool," he said. "You wouldn't really marry Nikki."

"Nikki," said Fin with great seriousness, "comes of a fine family. She is a good girl. She never uses a pillow when she sleeps. Do you know why she never uses a pillow when she sleeps?"

"No."

The others at the table were listening now. Everyone was listening to Fin talking about Nikki.

"Well, when she was very young she was engaged to be married to an officer in the French Navy. She loved him greatly. Then one day when they were sunbathing together on the beach he happened to mention to her that he never used a pillow when he slept. It was just one of those little things which people say to each other for the sake of conversation. But Nikki never forgot it. From that time onwards she began to practise sleeping without a pillow. One day the French officer was run over by a truck and killed; but although to her it was very uncomfortable, she still went on sleeping without a pillow to preserve the memory of her lover."

Fin took a mouthful of beans and chewed them slowly. "It is a sad story," he said. "It shows that she is a good girl. I think I would like to marry her."

That was what Fin had said last night at supper. Now he was gone and I wondered what little thing Nikki would do in his memory.

The sun was hot on my back and I turned instinctively in order to take the heat upon the other side of my body. As I turned, I saw Carmel and the town of Haifa. I saw the steep pale green slope of the mountain as it dropped down towards the sea, and below it I saw the town and the bright colours of the houses shining in the sun. The houses with their whitewashed walls covered the sides of Carmel and the red roofs of the houses were like a rash on the face of the mountain.

Walking slowly towards us from the grey corrugated-iron hangar, came the three men who were the next crew on readiness. They had their yellow Mae Wests slung over their shoulders and they came walking slowly towards us, holding their helmets in their hands as they came.

When they were close, the Stag said, "Fin's had it," and they said, "Yes, we know." They sat down on the wooden boxes which we had been using, and immediately the sun was upon their shoulders and upon their backs and they began to sweat. The Stag and I walked away.

The next day was a Sunday and in the morning we flew up the Lebanon valley to ground-strafe an aerodrome called Rayak. We flew past Hermon who had a hat of snow upon his head, and we came down out of the sun on to Rayak and on to the French bombers on the aerodrome and began our strafing. I remember that as we flew past, skimming low over the ground, the doors of the French bombers opened. I remember seeing a whole lot of women in white dresses running out across the aerodrome; I remember particularly their white dresses.

You see, it was a Sunday and the French pilots had asked their ladies out from Beyrouth to look over the bombers. The Vichy pilots had said, come out on Sunday morning and we will show you our aeroplanes. It was a very Vichy French thing for them to do.

So when we started shooting, they all tumbled out and began to run across the aerodrome in their white Sunday dresses.

I remember hearing Monkey's voice over the radio, saying, "Give them a chance, give them a chance," and the whole squadron wheeled around and circled the aerodrome once while the women ran over the grass in every direction. One of them stumbled and fell twice and one of them was limping and being helped by a man, but we gave them time. I remember watching the small bright flashes of a machine-gun on the ground and thinking that they should at least have stopped their shooting while we were waiting for their white-dressed women to get out of the way.

That was the day after Fin had gone. The next day the Stag and I sat once more at readiness on the wooden boxes outside the hangar. Paddy, a big fair-haired boy, had taken Fin's place and was sitting with us.

It was noon. The sun was high and the heat of the sun was like a close fire. The sweat ran down our necks, down inside our shirts, over our chests and stomachs, and we sat there waiting for the time when we would be relieved. The Stag was sewing the strap on to his helmet with a needle and cotton and telling of how he had seen Nikki the night before in Haifa and of how he had told her about Fin.

Suddenly we heard the noise of an aeroplane. The Stag stopped his talking and we all looked up. The noise was coming from the north, and it grew louder and louder as the aeroplane flew closer, and then the Stag said suddenly, "It's a Hurricane."

The next moment it was circling the aerodrome, lowering its wheels to land.

"Who is it?" said the fair-haired Paddy. "No one's gone out this morning."

Then, as it glided past us on to the runway, we saw the number on the tail of the machine, H4427, and we knew that it was Fin.

We were standing up now, watching the machine as it taxied towards us, and when it came up close and swung round for parking we saw Fin in the cockpit. He waved his hand at us, grinned and got out. We ran up and shouted at him, "Where've you been?" "Where in the hell have you been?" "Did you force-land and get away again?" "Did you find a woman in Beyrouth?" "Fin, where in the hell have you been?"

Others were coming up and crowding around him now, fitters and riggers and the men who drove the fire tender, and they all waited to hear what Fin would say. He stood there pulling off his helmet, pushing back his black hair with his hand, and he was so astonished at our behaviour that at first he merely looked at us and did not speak. Then he laughed and he said, "What in the hell's the matter? What's the matter with all of you?"

"Where have you been?" we shouted. "Where have you been for two days?"

Upon the face of Fin there was a great and enormous astonishment. He looked quickly at his watch.

"Five past twelve," he said. "I left at eleven, one hour and five minutes ago. Don't be a lot of damn fools. I must go and report quickly. The Navy will want to know that those destroyers are still in the harbour at Beyrouth."

He started to walk away; I caught his arm.

"Fin," I said quietly, "you've been away since the day before yesterday. What's the matter with you?"

He looked at me and laughed.

"I've seen you organize much better jokes than this one," he said. "It isn't so funny. It isn't a bit funny." And he walked away.

We stood there, the Stag, Paddy and I, the fitters, the riggers and the men who drove the fire-engine, watching Fin as he walked away. We looked at each other, not knowing what to say or to think, understanding nothing, knowing nothing except that Fin had been serious when he spoke and that what he said he had believed to be true. We knew this because we knew Fin, and we knew it because when one has been together as we had been together, then there is never any doubting of anything that anyone says when he is talking about his flying; there can only be a doubting of one's self. These men were doubting themselves, standing there in the sun doubting themselves, and the Stag was standing by the wing of Fin's machine peeling off with his

101

fingers little flakes of paint which had dried up and cracked in the sun.

Someone said, "Well, I'll be buggered," and the men turned and started to walk quietly back to their jobs. The next three pilots on readiness came walking slowly towards us from the grey corrugated-iron hangar, walking slowly under the heat of the sun, and swinging their helmets in their hands as they came. The Stag, Paddy and I walked over to the pilots' mess to have a drink and lunch.

The mess was a small white wooden building with a veranda. Inside there were two rooms, one a sitting-room with armchairs and magazines and a hole in the wall through which you could buy drinks, and the other a dining-room with one long wooden table. In the sitting-room we found Fin talking to Monkey, our CO. The other pilots were sitting around listening and everybody was drinking beer. We knew that it was really a serious business in spite of the beer and the armchairs; that Monkey was doing what he had to do and doing it in the only way possible. Monkey was a rare man, tall with a handsome face, an Italian bullet wound in his leg and a casual friendly efficiency. He never laughed out loud, he just choked and grunted deep in his throat.

Fin was saying, "You must go easy, Monkey; you must help me to stop thinking that I've gone mad."

Fin was being serious and sensible, but he was worried as hell.

"I have told you all I know," he said. "That I took off at eleven o'clock, that I climbed up high, that I flew to Beyrouth, saw the two French destroyers and came back, landing at five past twelve. I swear to you that that is all I know."

He looked around at us, at the Stag and me, at Paddy and Johnny and the half-dozen other pilots in the room, and we smiled at him and nodded to show him that we were with him, not against him, and that we believed what he said.

Monkey said, "What in the hell am I going to say to Headquarters at Jerusalem? I reported you missing. Now I've got to report your return. They'll insist on knowing where you've been."

The whole thing was getting to be too much for Fin. He

was sitting upright, tapping with the fingers of his left hand on the leather arm of his chair, tapping with quick sharp taps, leaning forward, thinking, thinking, fighting to think, tapping on the arm of the chair and then he began tapping the floor with his foot as well. The Stag could stand it no longer.

"Monkey," he said, "Monkey, let's just leave it all for a bit. Let's leave it and perhaps Fin will remember something later on."

Paddy, who was sitting on the arm of the Stag's chair, said, "Yes, and meanwhile we could tell HQ that Fin had force-landed in a field in Syria, taken two days to repair his aircraft, then flown home."

Everybody was helping Fin. The pilots were all helping him. In the mind of each of us was the certain knowledge that here was something that concerned us greatly. Fin knew it, although that was all he knew, and the others knew it because one could see it upon their faces. There was a tension, a fine high-drawn tension in the room, because here for the first time was something which was neither bullets nor fire nor the coughing of an engine nor burst tyres nor blood in the cockpit nor yesterday nor today, nor even tomorrow. Monkey felt it too, and he said, "Yes, let's have another drink and leave it for a bit. I'll tell HQ that you force-landed in Syria and managed to get off again later."

We had some more beer and went in to lunch. Monkey ordered bottles of Palestine white wine with the meal to celebrate Fin's return.

After that no one mentioned the thing at all; we did not even talk about it when Fin wasn't there. But each one of us continued to think about it secretly, knowing for certain that it was something important and that it was not finished. The tension spread quickly through the squadron and it was with all the pilots.

Meanwhile the days went by and the sun shone upon the aerodrome and upon the aircraft and Fin took his place among us flying in the normal way.

Then one day, I think it was about a week later, we did another ground-strafe of Rayak aerodrome. There were six of us, with Monkey leading and Fin flying on his starboard side. We came in low over Rayak and there was plenty of light flak, and as we went in on the first run, Paddy's machine was hit. As we wheeled for the second run we saw his Hurricane wing gently over and dive straight to the ground at the edge of the aerodrome. There was a great billow of white smoke as it hit, then the flames, and as the flames spread the smoke turned from white to black and Paddy was with it. Immediately there was a crackle over the radio and I heard Fin's voice, very excited, shouting into his microphone, shouting, "I've remembered it. Hello, Monkey, I've remembered it all," and Monkey's calm, slow reply, "OK Fin, OK; don't forget it."

We did our second run and then Monkey led us quickly away, weaving in and out of the valleys, with the bare grey-brown hills far above us on either side, and all the way home, all through the half-hour's flight, Fin never stopped shouting over the RT. First he would call to Monkey and say, "Hello, Monkey, I've remembered it, all of it; every bit of it." Then he would say, "Hello, Stag, I've remembered it, all of it; I can't forget it now." He called me and he called Johnny and he called Wishful; he called us all separately over and over again, and he was so excited that sometimes he shouted too loudly into his mike and we could not hear what he was saying.

When we landed, we dispersed our aircraft and because Fin for some reason had to park his at the far side of the aerodrome, the rest of us were in the Operations room before him.

The Ops room was beside the hangar. It was a bare place with a large table in the middle of the floor on which there was a map of the area. There was another smaller table with a couple of telephones, a few wooden chairs and benches and at one end the floor was stacked with Mae Wests, parachutes and helmets. We were standing there taking off our flying clothing and throwing it on to the floor at the end of the room when Fin arrived. He came quickly into the doorway and stopped. His black hair was standing up straight and untidy because of the way in which he had pulled off his helmet; his face was shiny with sweat and his khaki shirt was dark and wet. His mouth was open and he was breathing quickly. He looked as though he had been running. He looked like a child who had rushed downstairs into a room full of grown-ups to say that the cat has had kittens in the nursery and who does not know how to begin.

We had all heard him coming because that was what we had been waiting for. Everyone stopped what they were doing and stood still, looking at Fin.

Monkey said, "Hello, Fin," and Fin said, "Monkey, you've got to believe this because it's what happened."

Monkey was standing over by the table with the telephones; the Stag was near him, square, short, ginger-haired Stag, standing up straight, holding a Mae West in his hand, looking at Fin. The others were at the far end of the room. When Fin spoke, they began to move up quietly until they were closer to him, until they reached the edge of the big map table which they touched with their hands. There they stood, looking at Fin, waiting for him to begin.

He started at once, talking quickly, then calming down and talking more slowly as he got into his story. He told everything, standing there by the door of the Ops room, with his yellow Mae West still on him and with his helmet and oxygen mask in his hand. The others stayed where they were and listened, and as I listened to him, I forgot that it was Fin speaking and that we were in the Ops room at Haifa; I forgot everything and went with him on his journey, and did not come back until he had finished.

"I was flying at about twenty thousand," he said. "I flew over Tyre and Sidon and over the Damour River and then I flew inland over the Lebanon hills, because I intended to approach Beyrouth from the east. Suddenly I flew into cloud, thick white cloud which was so thick and dense that I could see nothing except the inside of my cockpit. I couldn't understand it, because a moment before everything had been clear and blue and there had been no cloud anywhere.

"I started to lose height to get out of the cloud and I went down and down and still I was in it. I knew that I must not go too low because of the hills, but at six thousand the cloud was still around me. It was so thick that I could see nothing, not even the nose of my machine nor the wings, and the cloud condensed on the windshield and little rivers of water ran down the glass and got blown away by the slipstream. I have never seen cloud like that before. It was thick and white right up to the edges of the cockpit. I felt like a man on a magic carpet, sitting there alone in this little glass-topped cockpit, with no wings, no tail, no engine and no aeroplane.

"I knew that I must get out of this cloud, so I turned and flew west over the sea away from the mountains; then I came down low by my altimeter. I came down to five hundred feet, four hundred, three hundred, two hundred, one hundred, and the cloud was still around me. For a moment I paused. I knew that it was unsafe to go lower. Then, quite suddenly, like a gust of wind, came the feeling that there was nothing below me; no sea nor earth nor anything else and slowly, deliberately, I opened the throttle, pushed the stick hard forward and dived.

"I did not watch the altimeter; I looked straight ahead through the windshield at the whiteness of the cloud and I went on diving. I sat there pressing the stick forward, keeping her in the dive, watching the vast clinging whiteness of the cloud and I never once wondered where I was going. I just went.

"I do not know how long I sat there; it may have been minutes and it may have been hours; I know only that as I sat there and kept her diving, I was certain that what was below me was neither mountains nor rivers nor earth nor sea and I was not afraid.

"Then I was blinded. It was like being half asleep in bed when someone turns on the light.

"I came out of the cloud so suddenly and so quickly that I was blinded. There was no space of time between being in it and being out of it. One moment I was in it and the whiteness was thick around me and in that same moment I was out of it and the light was so bright that I was blinded. I screwed up my eyes and held them tight closed for several seconds.

"When I opened them everything was blue, more blue than anything that I had ever seen. It was not a dark blue, nor was it a bright blue; it was a blue blue, a pure shining colour which I had never seen before and which I cannot describe. I looked around. I looked up above me and behind me. I sat up and peered below me through the glass of the cockpit and everywhere it was blue. It was bright and clear, like pleasant sunlight, but there was no sun.

"Then I saw them.

"Far ahead and above I saw a long thin line of aircraft flying across the sky. They were moving forward in a single black line, all at the same speed, all in the same direction, all close up, following one behind the other, and the line stretched across the sky as far as the eye could see. It was the way they moved ahead, the urgent way in which they pressed forward like ships sailing before a great wind, it was from this that I knew everything. I do not know why or how I knew it, but I knew as I looked at them that these were the pilots and aircrews who had been killed in battle, who now, in their own aircraft were making their last flight, their last journey.

"As I flew higher and closer I could recognize the machines themselves. I saw in that long procession nearly every type there was. I saw Lancasters and Dorniers, Halifaxes and Hurricanes, Messerschmitts, Spitfires, Sterlings, Savoia 79s, Junkers 88s, Gladiators, Hampdens, Macchi 200s, Blenheims, Focke-Wulfs, Beaufighters, Swordfish and Heinkels. All these and many more I saw, and the moving line reached across the blue sky both to the one side and to the other until it faded from sight.

"I was close to them now and I began to sense that I was being sucked towards them regardless of what I wished to do. There was a wind which took hold of my machine, blew it over and tossed it about like a leaf and I was pulled and sucked as by a giant vortex towards the other aeroplanes. There was nothing I could do for I was in the vortex and in the arms of the wind. This all happened very quickly, but I remember it clearly. I felt the pull on my aircraft becoming stronger. I was whisked forward faster and faster, and then suddenly I was flying in the procession itself, moving forward with the others, at the same speed and on the same course. Ahead of me, close enough for me to see the colour of the paint on its wings, was a Swordfish, an old Fleet Air Arm Swordfish. I could see the heads and helmets of the observer and the pilot as they sat in their cockpits, the one behind the other. Ahead of the Swordfish there was a Dornier, a Flying Pencil, and beyond the Dornier there were others which I could not recognize from where I was.

"We flew on and on. I could not have turned and flown away even if I had wanted to. I do not know why, although it may have been something to do with the vortex and with the wind, but I knew that it was so. Moreover, I was not really flying my aircraft; it flew itself. There was no manoeuvring to reckon with, no speed, no height, no throttle, no stick, no nothing. Once I glanced down at my instruments and saw that they were all dead, just as they are when the machine is sitting on the ground.

"So we flew on. I had no idea how fast we went. There was no sensation of speed and, for all I know, it was a million miles an hour. Now I come to think of it, I never once during that time felt either hot or cold or hungry or thirsty; I felt none of those things. I felt no fear, because I knew nothing of which to be afraid. I felt no worry, because I could remember nothing or think of nothing about which to be worried. I felt no desire to do anything that I was not doing or to have anything that I did not have, because there was nothing that I wished to do and there was nothing that I wished to have. I felt only pleasure at being where I was, at seeing the wonderful light and the beautiful colour around me. Once I caught sight of my face in the cockpit mirror and I saw that I was smiling, smiling with my eyes and with my mouth, and when I looked away I knew that I was still smiling, simply because that was the way I felt. Once, the observer in the Swordfish ahead of me turned and waved his hand. I slid back the roof of my cockpit and waved back. I remember that even when I opened the cockpit, there was no rush of air and no rush of cold or heat, nor was there any pressure of the slipstream on my hand. Then I noticed that they were all waving at each other, like children on a roller-coaster and I turned and waved at the man in the Macchi behind me.

"But there was something happening along the line. Far up in front I could see that the aeroplanes had changed course, were wheeling around to the left and losing height. The whole procession, as it reached a certain point, was banking around and gliding downwards in a wide, sweeping circle. Instinctively I glanced down over the cockpit and there I saw spread out below me a vast green plain. It was green and smooth and beautiful; it reached to the far edges of the horizon where the blue of the sky came down and merged with the green of the plain.

"And there was the light. Over to the left, far away in the distance was a bright white light, shining bright and without any colour. It was as though the sun, but something far bigger than the sun, something without shape or form whose light was bright but not blinding, was lying on the far edge of the green plain. The light spread outwards from a centre of brilliance and it spread far up into the sky and far out over the plain. When I saw it, I could not at first look away from it. I had no desire to go towards it, into it, and almost at once the desire and the longing became so intense that several times I tried to pull my aircraft out of the line and fly straight towards it; but it was not possible and I had to fly with the rest.

"As they banked around and lost height I went with them, and we began to glide down towards the green plain below. Now that I was closer, I could see the great mass of aircraft upon the plain itself. They were everywhere, scattered over the ground like currants upon a green carpet. There were hundreds and hundreds of them, and each minute, each second almost, their numbers grew as those in front of me landed and taxied to a standstill.

"Quickly we lost height. Soon I saw that the ones just in front of me were lowering their wheels and preparing to land. The Dornier next but one to me levelled off and touched down. Then the old Swordfish. The pilot turned a little to the left out of the way of the Dornier and landed beside him. I turned to the left of the Swordfish and levelled off. I looked out of the cockpit at the ground, judging the height, and I saw the green of the ground blurred as it rushed past me and below me.

"I waited for my aircraft to sink and to touch down. It seemed to take a long time. 'Come on,' I said. 'Come on, come on.' I was only about six feet up, but she would not sink. 'Get down,' I shouted, 'please *get down*.' I began to panic. I became frightened. Suddenly I noticed that I was gaining speed. I cut all the switches, but it made no difference. The aircraft was gathering speed, going faster and faster, and I looked around and saw behind me the long procession of aircraft dropping down out of the sky and sweeping in to land. I saw the mass of machines upon the ground, scattered far across the plain and away on one side I saw the light, that shining white light which shone so brightly over the great plain and to which I longed to go. I know that had I been able to land, I would have started to run towards that light the moment I got out of my aircraft.

"And now I was flying away from it. My fear grew. As I flew faster and farther away, the fear took hold of me until soon I was fighting crazy mad, pulling at the stick, wrestling with the aeroplane, trying to turn it around, back towards the light. When I saw that it was impossible, I tried to kill myself. I really wanted to kill myself then. I tried to dive the aircraft into the ground, but it flew on straight. I tried to jump out of the cockpit, but there was a hand upon my shoulder which held me down. I tried to bang my head against the sides of the cockpit, but it made no difference and I sat there fighting with my machine and with everything until suddenly I noticed that I was in cloud. I was in the same thick white cloud as before; and I seemed to be climbing. I looked behind me, but the cloud had closed in all round. There was nothing now but this vast impenetrable whiteness. I began to feel sick and giddy. I did not care any longer what happened one way or the other, I just sat there limply, letting the machine fly on by itself.

"It seemed a long time and I am sure that I sat there for many hours. I must have gone to sleep. As I slept, I dreamed. I dreamed not of the things that I had just seen, but of the things of my ordinary life, of the squadron, of Nikki and of the aerodrome here at Haifa. I dreamed that I was sitting at readiness outside the hangar with two others, that a request came from the Navy for someone to do a quick recce over Beyrouth; and because I was first up, I jumped into my Hurricane and went off. I dreamed that I passed over Tyre and Sidon and over the Damour River, climbing up to twenty thousand as I went. Then I turned inland over the Lebanon hills, swung around and approached Beyrouth from the east. I was above the town, peering over the side of the cockpit, looking for the harbour and trying to find the two French destroyers. Soon I saw them, saw them clearly, tied up close alongside each other by the wharf, and I banked around and dived for home as fast as I could.

"The Navy's wrong, I thought to myself as I flew back. The destroyers are still in the harbour. I looked at my watch. An hour and a half. 'I've been quick,' I said. 'They'll be pleased.' I tried to call up on the radio to give the information, but I couldn't get through.

"Then I came back here. When I landed, you all crowded around me and asked me where I had been for two days, but I could remember nothing. I did not remember anything except the flight to Beyrouth until just now, when I saw Paddy being shot down. As his machine hit the ground, I found myself saying, 'You lucky bastard. You lucky, lucky bastard,' and as I said it, I knew why I was saying it and remembered everything. That was when I shouted to you over the radio. That was when I remembered."

Fin had finished. No one had moved or said anything all the time that he had been talking. Now it was only Monkey who spoke. He shuffled his feet on the floor, turned and looked out of the window and said quietly, almost in a whisper, "Well, I'll be damned," and the rest of us went slowly back to the business of taking off our flying clothing and stacking it in the corner of the room on the floor; all except the Stag, square short Stag, who stood there watching Fin as Fin walked slowly across the room to put away his clothing.

After Fin's story, the squadron returned to normal. The tension which had been with us for over a week, disappeared. The aerodrome was a happier place in which to be. But no one ever mentioned Fin's journey. We never once spoke about it together, not even when we got drunk in the evening at the Excelsior in Haifa.

The Syrian campaign was coming to an end. Everyone could see that it must finish soon, although the Vichy people were still fighting fiercely south of Beyrouth. We were still flying. We were flying a great deal over the fleet, which was bombarding the coast, for we had the job of protecting them from the Junkers 88s which came over from Rhodes. It was on the last one of these flights over the fleet that Fin was killed.

We were flying high above the ships when the Ju-88s came over in force and there was a battle. We had only six Hurricanes in the air; there were many of the Junkers and it was a good fight. I do not remember much about what went on at the time. One never does. But I remember that it was a hectic, chasing fight, with the Junkers diving for the ships, with the ships barking at them, throwing up everything into the air so that the sky was full of white flowers which blossomed quickly and grew and blew away with the wind. I remember the German who blew up in mid-air, quickly, with just a white flash, so that where the bomber had been, there was nothing left except tiny little pieces falling slowly downwards. I remember the one that had its rear turret shot away, which flew along with the gunner hanging out of the tail by his straps, struggling to get back into the machine. I remember one, a brave one who stayed up above to fight us while the others went down to dive-bomb. I remember that we shot him up and I remember seeing him turn slowly over on to his back, pale green belly upwards like a dead fish, before finally he spun down.

And I remember Fin.

I was close to him when his aircraft caught fire. I could see the flames coming out of the nose of his machine and dancing over the engine cowling. There was black smoke coming from the exhaust of his Hurricane.

I flew up close and I called to him over the RT. "Hello, Fin," I called, "you'd better jump."

His voice came back, calm and slow. "It's not so easy."

"Jump," I shouted, "jump quickly."

I could see him sitting there under the glass roof of the cockpit. He looked towards me and shook his head.

"It's not so easy," he answered. "I'm a bit shot up. My arms are shot up and I can't undo the straps."

"Get out," I shouted. "For God's sake, get out," but he did not answer. For a moment his aircraft flew on, straight and level, then gently, like a dying eagle, it dipped a wing and dived towards the sea. I watched it as it went; I watched the thin trail of black smoke which it made across the sky, and as I watched, Fin's voice came again over the radio, clear and slow. "I'm a lucky bastard," he was saying. "A lucky, lucky bastard."

Winter's Morning

Len Deighton

Major Richard Winter was a tall man with hard black eyes, a large nose and close-cropped hair. He hated getting out of bed, especially when assigned to dawn patrols on a cold morning. As he always said—and by now the whole Officers' Mess could chant it in unison—"If there must be dawn patrols in winter, let there be no Winter in the dawn patrols."

Winter believed that if they stopped flying them, the enemy would also stop. In 1914, the front-line soldiers of both armies had decided to live and let live for a few weeks. So now, during the coldest weather, some squadrons had allowed the dawn patrol to become a token couple of scouts hurrying over the frosty wire of no-man's-land after breakfast. The warm spirit of humanity that Christmas 1914 conjured had given way to the cold reality of self-preservation. Those wiser squadrons kept the major offensive patrol until last light, when the sun was mellow and the air less turbulent. At St. Antoine Farm airfield, however, dawn patrol was still a gruelling obligation that none could escape.

"Oatmeal, toast, eggs and sausage, sir." Like everyone else in the Mess tent—except Winter—the waiter spoke in a soft whisper that befitted the small hours. Winter preferred his normal booming voice. "Just coffee," he said. "But hot, really hot."

"Very good, Major Winter, sir."

The wind blew with enough force to make the canvas flap and roar, as though at any moment the whole tent would blow away. From outside they heard the sound of tent pegs being hammered more firmly into the hard chalky soil.

A young Lieutenant sitting opposite offered his cigarette case, but Winter waved it aside in favour of a dented tin from which he took cheap dark tobacco and a paper to fashion a misshapen cigarette. The young officer did not light one of his own in the hope that he would be invited to share in this ritual. But Winter lit up, blew the noxious smoke across the table, coughed twice and pushed the tin back into his pocket.

Each time someone entered through the flap there was a clatter of canvas and ropes and a gust of cold air, but Winter looked in vain for a triangle of grey sky. The only light came from six acetylene lamps that were placed along the breakfast table. The pump of one of them was faulty; its light was dull and it left a smell of mould on the air. The other lamps hissed loudly and their eerie greenish light shone upon the Mess silver, folded linen and empty plates. The table had been set the previous night for the regular squadron breakfast at 8 a.m., and the Mess servants were anxious that these three early-duty pilots shouldn't disarrange it too much.

Everyone stiffened as they heard the clang of the engine cylinder and con. rod that hung outside for use as a gas warning. Winter laughed when Ginger, the tallest pilot in the squadron, emerged from the darkness rubbing his head and scowling in pain. Ginger walked over to the ancient piano and pulled back the edge of the tarpaulin that protected it from damp. He played a silly melody with one finger.

"Hot coffee, sir." The waiter emphasized the word "hot," and the liquid spluttered as it poured over the metal spout. Winter clamped his cold hands round the pot like a drowning man clinging to flotsam. He twisted his head to see Ginger's watch. Six twenty-five. What a time to be having breakfast: it was still night.

Winter yawned and wrapped his ankle-length fur coat

round his legs. New pilots thought that his fur overcoat had earned him the nickname of "the Bear," but that had come months before the coat.

The others kept a few seats between themselves and Winter. They spoke only when he addressed them, and then answered only in brief formalities.

"You flying with me, Lieutenant?"

The young ex-cavalry officer looked around the table. Ginger was munching his bread and jam, and gave no sign of having heard.

"Yes, sir," said the young man.

"How many hours?"

Always the same question. Everyone here was graded solely by flying time, though few cared whether the hours had been spent stunting, fighting or just hiding in the clouds. "Twenty-eight and a half, solo, sir."

"Twenty-eight *and a half*," nodded Winter. "Twenty-eight *and a half!* Solo! Did you hear that, Lieutenant?" The question was addressed to Ginger, who was paying unusually close attention to the sugar bowl. Winter turned back to the new young pilot. "You'd better watch yourself."

Winter divided new pilots into assets and liabilities at either side of seventy hours. Assets sometimes became true friends and close comrades. Assets might even be told your misgivings. The demise of assets could spread grief through the whole Mess. This boy would be dead within a month, Winter decided. He looked at him: handsome, in the pallid, aristocratic manner of such youngsters. His tender skin was chapped by the rain and there were cold sores on his lip. His blond hair was too long for Winter's taste, and his eyebrows girlish. This boy's kit had never known a quartermaster's shelf. It had come from an expensive tailor: a cavalry tunic fashionably nipped in at the waist, tight trousers and boots as supple as velvet. The ensemble was supplemented by accessories from the big department stores. His cigarette case was the sort that, it was advertised, could stop a bullet.

The young man returned Richard Winter's close examination with interest. So this rude fellow, so proud of his chauffeur's fur coat, was the famous Bear Winter who had twenty-nine enemy aircraft to his credit. He was a blotchy-faced devil, with bloodshot eyes and a fierce twitching eyebrow that he sometimes rubbed self-consciously, as if he knew that it undid his carefully contrived aplomb. The youngster wondered whether he would end up looking like this: dirty shirt, long finger-nails, unshaven jaw and a cauliflower-knobbly head, shaved razor-close to avoid lice. Except for his quick eyes and occasional wry smile Winter looked like the archetypal Prussian *Schweinhund*.

Major Richard Winter had been flying in action for nearly two years without a leave. He was a natural pilot who'd flown every type of plane the makers could provide, and some enemy planes too. He could dismantle and assemble an engine as well as any squadron fitter, and as a precaution against jams he personally supervised the loading of every bullet he would use. Why must he be so rude to young pilots who hero-worshipped him, and would follow him to hell itself? And yet that too was part of the legend.

The young officer swallowed. "May I ask, sir, where you bought your magnificent fur coat?"

Winter gulped the rest of his coffee and got to his feet as he heard the first of the scout's engines start. "Came off a mug I shot down in September," he bellowed. "It's from a fashionable shop, I'm told. Never travelled much myself, except here to France." Winter poked his fingers through four holes in the front. Did the boy go a shade paler, or had he imagined it in the glare of the gas lights? "Don't let some smart bastard get your overcoat, sonny."

"No, sir," said the boy. Behind him Ginger grinned. The Bear was behaving true to form. Ginger dug his knife into a tin of butter he'd scrounged from the kitchen and then offered it to the cavalry officer. The boy sniffed the tin doubtfully. It smelled rancid but he scraped a little on to his bread and swamped it with jam to hide the taste.

"This your first patrol?" asked Ginger.

"No, sir. Yesterday one of the chaps took me as far as Cambrai to see the lie of the land. Before that I did a few hours around the aerodrome here. These scouts are new to me."

"Did you see anything at Cambrai yesterday?"

"Anti-aircraft gunfire."

Winter interrupted. "Let's see if we can't do better than that for you today, sonny." He leaned close to the boy and asked in his most winning voice, "Think you could down a couple before lunch?"

The boy didn't answer. Winter winked at Ginger and buttoned his fur coat. The other motors had started, so Winter shouted, "That's it, sonny. Don't try to be a hero. Don't try to be an ace in the first week you're out here. Just keep under my stinking armpit. Just keep close. Close, you understand? Bloody damn close." Winter flicked his cigarette end on to the canvas floor of the tent and put his heel on it. He coughed and growled, "Hurry up," although he could see that the others were waiting for him.

From the far side of the wind-swept tarmac, Major Winter's Sergeant fitter saw a flash of greenish light as the Mess tent flap opened and the duty pilots emerged. Winter came towards him out of the darkness, walking slowly because of his thick woollen underwear and thigh-length fleece boots. His hands were tucked into his sleeves for warmth, and his head was sunk into the high collar that stood up around his ears like a cowl. Exactly like a monk, thought the Sergeant, not for the first time. Perhaps Winter cultivated this resemblance. He'd outlived all the pilots who had been here when he arrived, to become as high in rank as scout pilots ever became. Yet his moody introspective manner and his off-hand attitude to high and low had prevented him from becoming the commanding officer. So Winter remained a taciturn misanthrope, without any close companions, except for Ginger who had the same skills of survival and responded equally coldly to overtures of friendship from younger pilots.

The Sergeant fitter—Pops—had been here even longer than the Bear. He'd always looked after his aeroplane, right from his first patrol when Winter was the same sort of noisy friendly fool as the kid doing his first patrol this morning. Aeroplanes, he should have said: the Bear had written off seven of them. Pops spat as the fumes from the engine collected in his lungs. It was a bad business, watching these kids vanish one by one. Last year it had been considered lucky to touch Pops's bald head before take-off. For twelve months the fitter had refused leave, knowing that the pilots were truly anxious about their joke. But Pops's bald head had proved as fallible as all the other talismans. One after another the faces had been replaced by similar faces until they were all the same pink-faced smiling boy.

Pops spat again, then cut the motor and climbed out of the cockpit. The other planes were also silent. From the main road came the noise of an army convoy hurrying to get to its destination before daylight made it vulnerable to attack. Any moment now artillery observers would be climbing into the balloons that enabled them to see far across no-man's-land.

"Good morning, Major."

"Morning, Pops."

"The old firm, eh, sir?"

"Yes, you, me and Ginger," said Winter, laughing in a way that he'd not done in the Mess tent. "Sometimes I think we are fighting this war all on our own, Pops."

"We are," chuckled Pops. This was the way the Bear used to laugh. "The rest of them are just part-timers, sir."

"I'm afraid they are, Pops," said Winter. He climbed stiffly into the cramped cockpit and pulled the fur coat round him. There was hardly enough room to move his elbows and the tiny seat creaked under his weight. The instruments were simple: compass, altimeter, speedometer and rev-counter. The workmanship was crude and the finish was hasty, like a toy car put together by a bungling father. "Switches off," said Pops. Winter looked at the brass switches and then pressed them as if not sure of his vision. "Switches off," he said.

"Fuel on," said Pops.

"Fuel on."

"Suck in."

"Suck in."

Pops cuddled the polished wooden prop blade to his ear. It was cold against his face. He walked it round to prime the cylinders. That was the thing Pops liked about Winter: when he said off, you knew it was off. Pops waited while Winter pulled on his close-fitting flying helmet; its fur trimmed a tonsure of leather that had faded to the colour of flesh.

"Contact."

"Contact." Pops stretched high into the dark night and brought the blade down with a graceful sweep of his hands.

Like brass and percussion responding to a conductor, the engine began its performance with a blinding sheet of yellow flame and a drum roll. Winter throttled back, slowing the drum and changing the shape and colour of the flame to a gaseous feather of blue that danced around the exhaust pipes and made his face swell and contract as the shadows exploded and died. Winter held a blue flickering hand above his head. He felt the wheels lurch forward as the chocks were removed and he dabbed at the rudder bar so that he could see around the aircraft's nose. There was no brake or pitch adjustment and Winter let her gather speed while keeping the tail skid tight down upon the ground.

They took off in a vic three, bumping across frozen ruts in the balding field with only the glare of the exhausts to light their going. It was easy for Winter; as formation leader he relied on the others to watch his engine and formate on him accordingly. At full screaming throttle they climbed over the trees at the south end of the airfield. A gusty crosswind hit them. Winter banked a wing-tip dangerously close to the tree tops rather than slew into the boy's line of flight. Ginger did the same to avoid his Major. The boy, unused to these heavy operational machines with high-compression engines, found his aircraft almost wrenched from his grasp. He yawed across the trees, a hundred yards from the others, before he put her nose up to regain his position in formation. Close, he must keep close. Winter spared him only a brief glance over the shoulder between searching the sombre sky for the minuscule dots of other aeroplanes. For by now the black lid of night had tilted and an orange wedge prised open the eastern horizon. Winter led the way to the front lines, the others tight against his tailplane.

The first light of the sun revealed a land covered by a grey eiderdown of mist, except where a loose thread of river matched the silver of the sky. Over the front line they turned south. Winter glanced eastwards, where the undersides of some low clouds were leaking dribbles of gold paint on to the earth. As the world awakened stoves were lit and villages were marked by dirty smoke that trailed southwards.

Major Winter noted the north wind and glanced back to

see Ginger's aeroplane catch the first light of the sun as it bent far enough over the horizon to reach them at fifteen thousand feet above the earth. The propeller blades made a perfect circle of yellow gauze, through which reflections from the polished-metal cowling winked and wavered as the aeroplanes rose and sank gently on the clear morning air.

Here, on the Arras section of the front, the German and French lines could be clearly seen as careless scrawls in the livid chalk. Near the River Scarpe at Feuchy, Winter saw a constant flicker of artillery shells exploding: "the morning hate." Pinheads of pink, only just visible through the mist. Counter-battery fire he guessed, from its concentration some way behind the lines.

He pulled his fur collar as high round his face as it could go, then raised his goggles. The icy wind made his eyes water, but not before he had scanned the entire horizon and banked enough to see below him. He pulled the goggles down again. It was more comfortable, but they acted like blinkers. Already ice had formed in the crevices of his eyes and he felt its pin-pricks like daggers. His nose was numb and he let go of the stick to massage it.

The cavalry officer—Willy, they called him—was staring anxiously at the other two aeroplanes. He probably thought that the banking search was a wing-rocking signal that the enemy was sighted. They read too many cheap magazines, these kids; but then so had Winter before his first posting out here: *Ace of the Black Cross, Flying Dare-Devils, True War Stories.*

Well, now Winter knew true war stories. When old men decided to barter young men for pride and profit, the transaction was called war. It was another Richard Winter who had come to war. An eighteen-year-old child with a scrapbook of cuttings about Blériot and the Wright brothers, a roomful of models which his mother wasn't permitted to dust and thirteen hours of dangerous experiments on contraptions that were bigger, but no more airworthy, than his dusty models. That Richard Winter was long-since dead. Gone was the gangling boy whose only regret about the war was leaving his mongrel dog. Winter smiled as he remembered remonstrating with some pilots who were using fluffy yellow chicks for target practice on the pistol range. That was before he'd seen men burned alive, or, worse, men half-burned alive.

He waved to frightened little Willy who was desperately trying to fly skilfully enough to hold formation on his bad-tempered flight commander. Poor little swine. Two dots almost ahead of them to the south-east. Far below. Ginger had seen them already but the boy wouldn't notice them until they were almost bumping into him. All the new kids were like that. It's not a matter of eyesight, it's a matter of knowledge. Just as a tracker on a safari knows that a wide golden blob in the shadow of a tree at midday is going to be a pride of lions resting after a meal, so in the morning an upright golden blob in the middle of a plain is a cheetah waiting to make a kill. So at five thousand feet, that near the lines, with shellfire visible, they were going to be enemy two-seaters on artillery observation duty. First he must be sure that there wasn't a flight of scouts in ambush above them. He looked at the cumulus and decided that it was too far from the two-seaters to be dangerous. Brownish-black smoke patches appeared around the planes as the anti-aircraft guns went into action.

Winter raised his goggles. Already they had begun to mist up because of the perspiration generated by his excitement. He waggled his wings and began to lose height. He headed east to come round behind them from out of the sun. Ginger loosed off a short burst of fire to be sure his guns were not frozen. Winter and the boy did the same. The altitude had rendered him too deaf to hear it as more than a ticking, as of an anxious pulse.

Winter took another careful look around. Flashes of artillery shells were bursting on the ground just ahead of the enemy planes' track. The ground was still awash with blue gloom, although here and there hillocks and trees were crisply golden in the harsh oblique light of morning. The hedges and buildings threw absurdly long shadows, and a church steeple was bright yellow. Winter now saw that there were four more two-seaters about a mile away. They were beginning to turn.

Winter put down his nose and glanced in his mirror to be sure the others were close behind. The airspeed indicator showed well over a hundred miles an hour and was still rising. The air stream sang across the taut wires with a contented musical note. He held the two aeroplanes steady on his nose, giving the stick and rudder only the lightest of touches as the speed increased their sensitivity.

Five hundred yards: these two still hadn't seen their attackers. The silly bastards were hanging over the side anxious not to get their map references wrong. Four hundred.

The boy saw them much later than Ginger and Winter. He stared in wonder at these foreign aeronauts. At a time when only a handful of madmen had ever tried this truly magical science, and when every flight was a pioneering experiment to discover more about this new world, he hated the idea of killing fellow enthusiasts. He would much rather have exchanged anecdotes and information with them.

Ginger and Winter had no such thoughts. Their minds were delivered to their subconscious. They were checking instruments, cocking guns and judging ever-changing altitudes, range and deflection.

If that stupid kid fires too early . . . damn him, damn him! Oh, well. Ginger and Winter opened fire too. Damn, a real ace gets in close, close, close. They'd both learned that, if nothing else. Stupid boy! The artobs leader pulled back on the stick and turned so steeply as almost to collide with the two-seater to his left. He knew what he was doing; he was determined to make himself a maximum-deflection shot. Winter kept his guns going all the way through the turn. The tracer bullets seemed unnaturally bright because his eyes had become accustomed to the morning's gloom. Like glow-worms they were eating the enemy's tailplane. This is what decided a dogfight: vertical turns, tighter and tighter still. Control stick held into the belly, with toes and eyes alert so that the aeroplane doesn't slide an inch out of a turn that glued him to the horizon. It was sheer flying skill. The sun—a watery blob of gold—seemed to drop through his mainplane and on to his engine. Winter could feel the rate of turn by the hardness of his seat. He pulled even harder on the stick to make the tracers crawl along the fuselage. The smell from his guns was acrid and the thin smoke and heat from the blurring breechblocks caused his target to wobble like a jelly. First the observer was hit, then the pilot, throwing up their hands like badly made marionettes. The two-seater stalled, falling suddenly like a dead leaf. Winter rolled. Two more aeroplanes slid across his sights. He pushed his stick forward to follow the damaged two-seater down. Hearing bullets close to his head, he saw the fabric of his upper plane prodded to tatters by invisible fingers which continued their destruction to the point of breaking a centre-section strut and throwing its splinters into his face. His reflexes took over and he went into a vertical turn tighter than any two-seater could manage. Aeroplanes were everywhere. Bright green and blue wings and black crosses passed across his sights, along with roundels and dark green fabric. One of them caught the light of the sun and its wings flashed with brilliant blue. All the time Winter kept an eye upon his rear-view mirror. A two-seater nosed down towards his tail, but Winter avoided him effortlessly. Ginger came under him, thumping his machine-guns with one of the hammers which they all kept in their cockpits. He was red-faced with exertion as he tried to clear the stoppage by force. At this height every movement was exhausting. Ginger wiped his face with the back of his gauntlet and his goggles came unclipped and blew away in the air stream.

Winter had glimpsed Ginger for only a fraction of a second but he'd seen enough to tell him the whole story. If it was a split round he'd never unjam it. Trees flashed under him. The combat had brought them lower and lower, as it always did.

The new boy was half a mile away and climbing. Winter knew it was his job to look after the kid but he'd not leave Ginger with a jammed gun. A plane rushed past before he had a chance to fire. Winter saw one of the two-seaters behind Ginger. My God, they were tough, these fellows. You'd think they'd be away, with their tails between their legs. Hold on, Ginger, here I come. Dive, climb, roll; a perfect Immelmann turn. The world upside down; above him the dark earth, below him the dawn sky like a rasher of streaky bacon. Hold that. He centred the stick, keeping the enemy's huge mainplane centred in his sight. Fire. The guns shook the whole airframe and made a foul stink. He kicked the rudder and slid down past the enemy's tail with no more than six feet to spare. A white-faced observer was frozen in fear. Up. Up. Up. Winter leaned out of his cockpit to see below him. The new boy is in trouble. One of the two-seaters is pasting him. The poor kid is trying for the cloud bank but that's half a mile away. Never throttle back in combat, you fool. White smoke? Radiator steam? No, worse: vaporizing petrol from a punctured tank of fractured lead. If it touches a hot pipe he'll go up like a torch. You should have kept close, sonny. What did I tell you. What do I always tell them. Winter flick-rolled and turned to cover Ginger's tail.

Woof: a flamer. The boy: will he jump or burn? The whole world was made up of jumpers or burners. There were no parachutes for pilots yet, so either way a man died. The machine was breaking up. Burning pieces of fuel-soaked wreckage fell away. It would be difficult to invent a more efficient bonfire. Take thin strips of timber, nail them into a framework, stretch fabric over it and paint it with highly inflammable dope. Into the middle of this build a metal tank for 30 gallons of high-grade fuel. Move air across it at 50 m.p.h. Winter couldn't decide whether the boy had jumped. A pity, the chaps in the Mess always wanted to know that, even though few could bear to ask.

The dogfight had scattered the aeroplanes in every direction, but Ginger was just below him and a two-seater was approaching from the south. Ginger waved. His gun was working. Winter side-slipped down behind a two-seater and gave it a burst of fire. The gunner was probably dead, for no return fire came and the gun rocked uselessly on its mounting. The pilot turned steeply on full throttle and kept going in an effort to come round in a vertical turn to Winter's rear. But Ginger was waiting for that. They'd been through this many times. Ginger fired as the two-seater was half-way through the turn, raking it from engine to tail. The whole aeroplane lurched drunkenly, and then the port mainplane snapped, its main spar eaten through by Ginger's bullets. As it fell, nose-down, the wings folded back along the fuselage like an umbrella being closed. The shapeless mess of broken struts and tangled steel wire fell vertically to earth, weighted by its heavy engine which was still roaring at full throttle. It was so low that it hit the ground within seconds.

Winter throttled back and came round in a gentle turn to see the wreckage: not a movement. It was just a heap of junk in a field. Ginger was circling it, too. From this height the sky was a vast bowl as smooth and shiny as Ming. They both looked round it but the other two-seaters had gone. There were no planes in sight. Winter increased his throttle and came alongside Ginger. He pushed his goggles up. Ginger was laughing. The artillery fire had stopped, or perhaps its explosions were lost in the mist. They turned for home, scampering across the trees and hedges like two schoolboys.

Winter and Ginger came over the airfield in echelon. Eight aeroplanes were lined up outside the canvas hangars that lacked only bunting to be a circus. A dozen officers fell over themselves scrambling out of the Mess tent. One of them waved. Winter's machine, painted bright green with wasp-like white bands, was easily recognized. Winter circled the field while Ginger landed. He'd literally lived in this French field for almost a year and knew each tree, ditch and bump. He'd seen it from every possible angle. He remembered praying for a sight of it with a dead motor and a bootful of blood. Also how he'd focused on blurred blades of its cold dewy grass, following a long night unconscious after a squadron booze-up. He'd vomited, excreted, crashed and fornicated on this field. He couldn't imagine being anywhere else.

For the first time in a month the sun shone, but it gave no warmth. As he switched off his engine the petrol fumes made the trees bend and dance on the heavy vapour. Pops hurried across to him but couldn't resist a quick inspection of the tail before saluting.

"Everything in order, Herr Major?"

Winter was still a little deaf but he guessed what the Sergeant was saying. He always said the same thing. "Yes, Sergeant. The strut is damaged but apart from that it probably just needs a few patches."

Winter unclipped his goggles, unwound his scarf and took off his leather helmet. The cordite deposits from his Spandaus had made a black band across his nose and cheeks.

"Another Englishman?" said Pops. He warmed his hands before the big Mercedes engine, which was groaning softly.

"Bristols: one forced down, one destroyed. We lost the

new young officer, though." Winter was ashamed that he
didn't know the boy's name, but there were so many of
them. He knew he was right to remain unfriendly to all of
them. Given half a chance new kids would treat him like
some sort of divinity, and that made him feel like hell when
they went west.

Winter wiped the protective grease from his face. He was
calm. Briefly he watched his own unshaking hand with a
nod of satisfaction. He knew himself to be a nerveless and
relentless killer, and like any professional assassin he took
pride in seeing a victim die. Only such men could become
aces.

My Dream of Flying
to Wake Island

J. G. Ballard

Melville's dream of flying to Wake Island—a hopeless ambition, given all his handicaps—came alive again when he found the crashed aircraft buried in the dunes above the beach-house. Until then, during these first three months at the abandoned resort built among the sand-hills, his obsession with Wake Island had rested on little more than a collection of fraying photographs of this Pacific atoll, a few vague memories of its immense concrete runways, and an unfulfilled vision of himself at the controls of a light aircraft, flying steadily westwards across the open sea.

With the discovery of the crashed bomber in the dunes, everything had changed. Instead of spending his time wandering aimlessly along the beach, or gazing from the balcony at the endless sand-flats that stretched towards the sea at low tide, Melville now devoted all his time to digging the aircraft out of the dunes. He cancelled his evening games of chess with Dr. Laing, his only neighbour at the empty resort, went to bed before the television programmes began, and was up by five, dragging his spades and land-lines across the sand to the excavation site.

The activity suited Melville, distracting him from the sharp frontal migraines that had begun to affect him again. These returning memories of the prolonged ECT treatment unsettled him more than he had expected, with their unequivocal warning that in the margins of his mind the elements of a less pleasant world were waiting to reconstitute themselves. The dream of escaping to Wake Island was a compass bearing of sorts, but the discovery of the crashed aircraft gave him a chance to engage all his energies and, with luck, hold these migraine attacks at bay.

A number of wartime aircraft were buried near this empty resort. Walking across the sand-flats on what Dr. Laing believed were marine-biology specimen hunts, Melville often found pieces of Allied and enemy fighters shot down over the Channel. Rusting engine blocks and sections of cannon breeches emerged from the sand, somehow brought to the surface by the transits of the sea, and then subsided again without trace. During the summer weekends a few souvenir hunters and World War II enthusiasts picked over the sand, now and then finding a complete engine or wing spar. Too heavy to move, these relics were left where they lay. However, one of the weekend groups, led by a former advertising executive named Tennant, had found an intact Messerschmitt 109 a few feet below the sand half a mile along the coast. The members of the party parked their sports-cars at the bottom of the road below Melville's beach-house, and set off with elaborate pumps and lifting tackle in a reconditioned DUKW.

Melville noticed that Tennant was usually suspicious and standoffish with any visitors who approached the Messerschmitt, but the advertising man was clearly intrigued by this solitary resident of the deserted resort who spent his time ambling through the debris on the beach. He offered Melville a chance of looking at the aircraft. They drove out across the wet sand to where the fighter lay like a winged saurian inside its galvanized-iron retaining wall a few feet below the surface of the flat. Tennant helped to lower Melville into the blackened cockpit, an experience which promptly brought on his first fugue.

Later, when Tennant and his co-workers had returned him to the beach-house, Melville sat for hours massaging his arms and hands, uneasily aware of certain complex digital skills that he wanted to forget but were beginning to reassert themselves in unexpected ways. Laing's solarium, with its dials and shutters, its capsulelike interior, unsettled him even more than the cockpit of the 109.

Impressive though the find was, the rusting hulk of the World War II fighter was insignificant beside Melville's discovery. He had been aware of the bomber, or at least of a large engineered structure, for some time. Wandering among the dunes above the beach-house during the warm afternoons, he had been too preoccupied at first with the task of settling in at the abandoned resort, and above all with doing nothing. Despite the endless hours he had spent in the hospital gymnasium, during his long recuperation after the aviation accident, he found that the effort of walking through the deep sand soon exhausted him.

At this stage, too, he had other matters to think about. After arriving at the resort he had contacted Dr. Laing, as instructed by the after-care officers at the hospital, expecting the physician to follow him everywhere. But whether deliberately or not Laing had not been particularly interested in Melville, this ex-pilot who had turned up here impulsively in his expensive car and was now prowling restlessly around the solarium as if hunting for a chromium rat. Laing worked at the Science Research Council laboratory five miles inland, and clearly valued the privacy of the prefabricated solarium he had erected on the sandbar at the southern end of the resort. He greeted Melville without comment, handed him the keys to the beach-house, and left him to it.

This lack of interest was a relief to Melville, but at the same time threw him onto himself. He had arrived with two suitcases, one filled with newly purchased and unfamiliar clothes, the other holding the hospital X-ray plates of his head and the photographs of Wake Island. The X-ray plates he passed to Dr. Laing, who raised them to the light, scrutinizing these negatives of Melville's skull as if about to point out some design error in its construction. The photographs of Wake Island he returned without comment.

These illustrations of the Pacific atoll, with its vast concrete runways, he had collected over the previous months. During his convalescence at the hospital he had

130

joined a wildlife conservation society, ostensibly in support of its campaign to save the Wake Island albatross from extinction—tens of thousands of the goony birds nested at the ends of the runways, and would rise in huge flocks into the flightpaths of airliners at takeoff. Melville's real interest had been in the island itself, a World War II airbase and now refuelling point for trans-Pacific passenger jets. The combination of scuffed sand and concrete, metal shacks rusting by the runways, the total psychological reduction of this man-made landscape, seized his mind in a powerful but ambiguous way. For all its arid, oceanic isolation, the Wake Island in Melville's mind soon became a zone of intense possibility. He daydreamed of flying there in a light aircraft, island-hopping across the Pacific. Once he touched down he knew that the migraines would go away forever. He had been discharged from the Air Force in confused circumstances, and during his convalescence after the accident the military psychiatrists had been only too glad to play their parts in what soon turned out to be an underrehearsed conspiracy of silence. When he told them that he had rented a house from a doctor in this abandoned resort, and intended to live there for a year on his back pay, they had been relieved to see him go, carrying away the X-ray plates of his head and the photographs of Wake Island.

"But why Wake Island?" Dr. Laing asked him on their third chess evening. He pointed to the illustrations that Melville had pinned to the mantelpiece, and the technical abstracts lavishly documenting its geology, rainfall, seismology, flora, and fauna. "Why not Guam? Or Midway? Or the Hawaiian chain?"

"Midway would do, but it's a naval base now—I doubt if they'll give me landing clearance. Anyway, the atmosphere is wrong." Discussing the rival merits of various Pacific islands always animated Melville, feeding this potent re-mythologizing of himself. "Guam is forty miles long, covered with mountains and dense jungle, New Guinea in miniature. The Hawaiian islands are an offshore suburb of the United States. Only Wake has real time."

"You were brought up in the Far East?"

"In Manila. My father ran a textile company there."

"So the Pacific area has a special appeal for you."

"To some extent. But Wake is a long way from the Philippines."

Laing never asked if Melville had actually been to Wake Island. Clearly Melville's vision of flying to this remote Pacific atoll was unlikely to take place outside his own head.

However, Melville then had the good luck to discover the aircraft buried in the dunes.

When the tide was in, covering the sand-flats, Melville was forced to walk among the dunes above his beach-house. Driven and shaped by the wind, the contours of the dunes varied from day to day, but one afternoon Melville noticed that a section below the ridge retained its rectilinear form, indicating that some man-made structure lay below the sand, possibly the detached room of a metal barn or boathouse.

Irritated by the familiar drone of a single-engined aircraft flying from the light airfield behind the resort, Melville clambered up to the ridge through the flowing sand and sat down on the horizontal ledge that ran among the clumps of wild grass. The aircraft, a privately owned Cessna, flew in from the sea directly towards him, banked steeply and circled overhead. Its pilot, a dentist and aviation enthusiast in her early thirties, had been curious about Melville for some time—the mushy drone of her flat six was forever dividing the sky over his head. Often, as he walked across the sand-flats four hundred yards from the shore, she would fly past him, wheels almost touching the streaming sand, throttling up her engine as if trying to din something into his head. She appeared to be testing various types of auxiliary fuel tank. Now and then he saw her driving her American sedan through the deserted streets of the resort towards the airfield. For some reason the noise of her light aircraft began to unsettle him, as if the furniture of his brain was being shifted around behind some dark curtain.

The Cessna circled above him like a dull, unwearying bird. Trying to look as though he was engaged in his study of beach ecology, Melville cleared away the sand between his feet. Without realizing it, he had exposed a section of grey, riveted metal, the skin of an all-too-familiar aerodynamic structure. He stood up and worked away with both hands, soon revealing the unmistakable profile of an aerofoil curvature.

The Cessna had gone, taking the lady dentist back to the airstrip. Melville had forgotten about her as he pushed the heavy sand away, steering it down the saddle between the dunes. Although nearly exhausted, he continued to clear the starboard wing-tip now emerging from the dune. He took off his jacket and beat away the coarse white grains, at last revealing the combat insignia, star and bars of a USAAF roundel.

As he knew within a few minutes, he had discovered an intact wartime B-17. Two days later, by a sustained effort, he had dug away several tons of sand and exposed to view almost the entire starboard wing, the tail and rear turret. The bomber was virtually undamaged—Melville assumed that the pilot had run out of fuel while crossing the Channel and tried to land on the sand-flats at low tide, overshot the wet surface and ploughed straight through the dunes above the beach. A write-off, the Fortress had been abandoned where it lay, soon to be covered by the shifting sandhills. The small resort had been built, flourished briefly, and declined without anyone's realizing that this relic of World War II lay in the ridge a hundred yards behind the town.

Systematically, Melville organized himself in the task of digging out, and then renovating, this antique bomber. Working by himself, he estimated that it would take three months to expose the aircraft, and a further two years to strip it down and rebuild it from scratch. The precise details of how he would straighten the warped propeller blades and replace the Wright Cyclone engines remained hazy in his mind, but already he visualized the shingle-reinforced earth-and-sand ramp which he would construct with a rented bulldozer from the crest of the dunes down to the beach. When the sea was out, after a long late-summer day, the sand along the tide-line was smooth and hard . . .

Few people came to watch him. Tennant, the former advertising man leading the group digging out the Messerschmitt, came across the sand-flats and gazed philosophically at the emerging wings and fuselage of the Fortress. Neither of the men spoke to each other—both, as Melville knew, had something more important on their minds.

In the evening, when Melville was still working on the aircraft, Dr. Laing walked along the beach from his solarium. He climbed the shadow-filled dunes, watching Melville clear away the sand from the chin turret.

"What about the bomb-load?" he asked. "I'd hate to see the whole town levelled."

"It's an officially abandoned wreck." Melville pointed to the stripped-down gun turret. "Everything has been removed, including the machine-guns and bomb-sight. I think you're safe from me, Doctor."

"A hundred years ago you'd have been digging a diplodocus out of a chalk cliff," Laing remarked. The Cessna was circling the sandbar at the southern end of the resort, returning after a navigation exercise. "If you're keen to fly, perhaps Helen Winthrop will take you on as a copilot. She was asking me something about you the other day. She's planning to break the single-engine record to Cape Town."

This item of news intrigued Melville. The next day, as he worked at his excavation site, he listened for the sound of the Cessna's engine. The image of this determined woman preparing for her solo flight across Africa, testing her aircraft at this abandoned airfield beside the dunes, coincided powerfully with his own dream of flying to Wake Island. He knew full well now that the elderly Fortress he was laboriously digging from the sand-dunes would never leave its perch on the ridge, let alone take off from the beach. But the woman's aircraft offered a feasible alternative. Already he mapped out a route in his mind, calculating the capacity of her auxiliary tanks and the refuelling points in the Azores and Newfoundland.

Afraid that she might leave without him. Melville decided to approach her directly. He drove his car through the deserted streets of the resort, turned onto the unmade road that led to the airfield, and parked beside her American sedan. The Cessna, its engine cowlings removed, stood at the end of the runway.

She was working at an engineering bench in the hangar, welding together the sections of a fuel tank. As Melville approached she switched off the blowtorch and removed her mask, her intelligent face shielded by her hands.

"I see we're involved in a race to get away first," she called out reassuringly to him when he paused in the entrance to the hangar. "Dr. Laing told me that you'd know how to strengthen these fuel tanks."

For Melville, her nervous smile cloaked a complex sexual metaphor.

From the start Melville took it for granted that she would abandon her plan to fly to Cape Town, and instead embark on a round-the-world flight with himself as her copilot. He outlined his plans for their westward flight, calculating the reduced fuel load they would carry to compensate for his weight. He showed her his designs for the wing spars and braces that would support the auxiliary tanks.

"Melville, I'm flying to Cape Town," she told him wearily. "It's taken me years to arrange this—there's no question of setting out anywhere else. You're obsessed with this absurd island."

"You'll understand when we get there," Melville assured her. "Don't worry about the aircraft. After Wake you'll be on your own. I'll strip off the tanks and cut all these braces away."

"You intend to stay on Wake Island?" Helen Winthrop seemed unsure of Melville's seriousness, as if listening to an overenthusiastic patient in her surgery chair outlining the elaborate dental treatment he had set his heart on.

"Stay there? Of course . . ." Melville prowled along the mantelpiece of the beach-house, slapping the line of photographs. "Look at those runways, everything is there. A big airport like the Wake field is a zone of tremendous possibility—a place of beginnings, by the way, not ends."

Helen Winthrop made no comment on this, watching Melville quietly. She no longer slept in the hangar at the airstrip, and during her weekend visits moved into Melville's beach-house. Needing his help to increase the Cessna's range, and so reduce the number of refuelling stops with their built-in delays, she put up with his restlessness and childlike excitement, only concerned by his growing dependence on her. As he worked on the Cessna, she listened for hours to him describing the runways of the island. However, she was careful never to leave him alone with the ignition keys.

While she was away, working at her dental practice, Melville returned to the dunes, continuing to dig out the crashed bomber. The port and starboard wings were now free of the sand, soon followed by the upper section of the fuselage. The weekends he devoted to preparing the Cessna for its long westward flight. For all his excitability, the state of controlled euphoria which his soon-to-be-realized dream of flying to Wake Island had brought about, his navigation plans and structural modification to the Cessna's airframe were carefully and professionally carried through.

Even the intense migraines that began to disturb Melville's sleep did little to dent his good humour. He assumed that these fragments of the past had been brought to the surface of his mind by the strains of his involvement with this overserious aviatrix, but later he knew that these elements of an unforgotten nightmare had been cued in by the aircraft emerging around him on all sides—Helen Winthrop's Cessna, the Fortress he was exposing to light, the blackened Messerschmitt which the advertising man was lifting from the seabed.

After a storm had disturbed the sand-flats, he stood on the balcony of the beach-house inhaling the carbonated air, trying to free himself from the uneasy dreams that had filled the night, a system of demented metaphors. In front of him the surface of the sand-flats was covered with dozens of pieces of rusting metal, aircraft parts shaken loose by the storm. As Helen Winthrop watched from the bedroom window, he stepped onto the beach and walked across the ruffled sand, counting the fragments of carburettor and exhaust manifold, trim-tab and tail-wheel, that lay around him as if left here by the receding tide of his dreams.

Already other memories were massing around him, fragments that he was certain belonged to another man's life, details from the case-history of an imaginary patient whose role he had been tricked into playing. As he worked on the Fortress high among the dunes, brushing the sand away from the cylinder vanes of the radial engines, he remembered other aircraft he had been involved with, vehicles without wings.

The bomber was completely exposed now. Knowing that his work was almost over, Melville opened the ventral crew hatch behind the chin turret. Ever since he had first revealed the cockpit of the plane he had been tempted to climb through the broken starboard windshield and take his seat at the controls, but the experience of the Messerschmitt cautioned him. With Helen Winthrop, however, he would be safe.

Throwing down his spade, he clambered across the sand to the beach-house.

"Helen! Come up here!" He pointed with pride to the exposed aircraft on the ridge, poised on its belly as if at the end of a takeoff ramp. While Helen Winthrop tried to calm him, he steered her up the shifting slopes, hand over hand along the rope-line.

As they climbed through the crew hatch, he looked back for the last time across the sand-flats, littered with their rusting aircraft parts. Inside the fuselage they searched their way around the barbette of the roof turret, stepping through the debris of old R/T gear, life-jackets, and ammunition boxes. After all his efforts, the interior of the fuselage seemed to Melville like a magical arbour, the grottolike cavern within some archaic machine.

Sitting beside Helen in the cockpit, happy that she was with him as she would be on their flight across the Pacific, he took her through the controls, moving the throttles and trim wheels.

"Right, now. Mixture rich, carb heat cold, pitch full fine, flaps down for takeoff . . ."

As she held his shoulders, trying to pull him away from the controls, Melville could hear the engines of the Fortress starting up within his head. As if watching a film, he remembered his years as a military test-pilot, and his single abortive mission as an astronaut. By some grotesque turn of fate, he had become the first astronaut to suffer a mental breakdown in space. His nightmare ramblings had disturbed millions of television viewers around the world, as if the terrifying image of a man going mad in space had triggered off some long-buried innate releasing mechanism.

Later that evening, Melville lay by the window in his bedroom, watching the calm sea that covered the sand-flats. He remembered Helen Winthrop leaving him in the cockpit, and running away along the beach to find Dr. Laing. Careful though he was, the physician was no more successful at dealing with Melville than the doctors at the institute of aviation medicine, who had tried to free him from his obsession that he had seen a fourth figure on board the three-man craft. This mysterious figure, either man or bird, he was convinced he had killed. Had he, also, committed the first murder in space? After his release he resolved to make his worldwide journey, externally to Wake Island, and internally across the planets of his mind.

As the summer ended and the time of their departure drew nearer, Melville was forced to renew his efforts at digging out the crashed Fortress. In the cooler weather the night winds moved the sand across the ridge, once again covering the fuselage of the aircraft.

Dr. Laing visited him more frequently. Worried by Melville's deteriorating condition, he watched him struggle with the tons of sliding sand.

"Melville, you're exhausting yourself." Laing took the spade from him and began to shovel away. Melville sat down on the wing. He was careful now never to enter the cockpit. Across the sand-flats Tennant and his team were leaving for the winter, the broken-backed Me 109 carried away on two trucks. Conserving his strength, he waited for the day when he and Helen Winthrop would leave this abandoned resort and take off into the western sky.

"All the radio aids are ready," he told her on the weekend before they were due to leave. "All you need to do now is file your flight plan."

Helen Winthrop watched him sympathetically as he stood by the mantelpiece. Unable to stand his nervous vomiting, she had moved back to the hangar. Despite, or perhaps because of, their brief sexual involvement, their relationship now was almost matter-of-factly neutral, but she tried to reassure him.

"How much luggage have you got? You've packed nothing."

"I'm taking nothing—only the photographs."

"You won't need them once you get to Wake Island."

"Perhaps—they're more real for me now than the island could ever be."

When Helen Winthrop left without him, Melville was surprised, but not disappointed. He was working up on the dunes as the heavily laden Cessna, fitted with the wing tanks he had installed, took off from the airstrip. He knew immediately from the pitch of the engine that this was not a trial flight. Sitting on the roof turret of the Fortress, he watched her climb away across the sand-flats, make a steady right-hand turn towards the sea and set off downwind across the Channel.

Long before she was out of sight, Melville had forgotten her. He would make his own way to the Pacific. During the following weeks he spent much of his time sheltering under the aircraft, watching the wind blow the sand back across the fuselage. With the departure of Helen Winthrop and the advertising executive with his Messerschmitt he found that his dreams grew calmer, shutting away his memories of the spaceflights. At times he was certain that his entire memory of having trained as an astronaut was a fantasy, part of some complex delusional system, an extreme metaphor of his real ambition. This conviction brought about a marked improvement in his health and self-confidence.

Even when Dr. Laing climbed the dunes and told him that Helen Winthrop had died two weeks after crashing her Cessna at Nairobi airport, Melville had recovered sufficiently to feel several days of true grief. He drove to the airfield and wandered around the empty hangar. Traces of her overhurried departure, a suitcase of clothes and a spare set of rescue flares, lay among the empty oil-drums.

Returning to the dunes, he continued to dig the crashed bomber from the sand, careful not to expose too much of it to the air. Although often exhausted in the damp winter air, he felt increasingly calm, sustained by the huge bulk of the Fortress, whose cockpit he never entered, and by his dream of flying to Wake Island.

Cat

Richard Bach

It was a cat, a grey Persian cat. It had no name and it sat very carefully in the tall grass at the end of the runway, studying the fighter planes as they touched down in France for the first time.

The cat did not flinch as the ten-ton jet fighters whistled airily by, nosewheels still in the air and drag chutes waiting to spring from their little houses beneath the tailpipes. Its yellow eyes watched calmly, appraising the quality of the touchdowns, angled ears listening for the faint pouf! of the late-blossoming drag chutes, head turning serenely after one landing to watch the final approach and touchdown of the next. Now and then a touchdown was hard, and the eyes narrowed ever so slightly for an instant as the soft paw-pads felt the jar of airplane and soil for an instant as an airplane did not correct for crosswind, and great gouts of blue rubber-smoke angled from tortured wheels.

The cat watched the landings for three hours in the cold of an October afternoon, until twenty-seven airplanes had landed and the sky was empty and the last whine of dying engines had faded from the parking revetments across the field. Then the Persian stood suddenly, and without even a feline stretch of its graceful body, trotted away to disappear in the tall grass. The 167th Tactical Fighter Squadron had arrived in Europe.

When a fighter squadron is reactivated after fifteen years of nonexistence, there are a few problems. With the barest nucleus of experienced pilots in a squadron of thirty, the 167th's problems centered around pilot proficiency. Twenty-four of its air crews had been graduated from gunnery training schools within the year before reactivation.

"We can do it, Bob, and do a good job of it," said Major Carl Langley to his squadron commander. "This isn't the first time I've been an operations officer, and I tell you I've never seen a bunch of pilots who are more eager to learn this business than the ones we have right here."

Major Robert Rider pounded his fist lightly against the rough wooden wall of his office-to-be. "That point I will grant you," he said. "But you and I have a job cut out for us. This is Europe, and you know European weather in the winter. Aside from our flight commanders, young Henderson has more weather time than any other pilot in the squadron, and he only has eleven hours of it. Eleven hours! Carl, are you looking forward to leading a four-ship flight of these pilots, in old F-84s, through twenty thousand feet of weather? Or to a GCA touchdown on a wet runway in a crosswind?" He glanced out the dirt-streaked window. High overcast, good visibility beneath, he noted unconsciously. "I'm going to run this squadron, and I'm going to run it well; but I'll tell you that I can't help but think that before the new 167th is a real combat-ready outfit, a couple of our boys are going to be scattered across the sides of mountains. I'm not looking forward to that."

Carl Langley's ice-blue eyes sparkled with the challenge. He was at his best doing the job that anyone else would have called impossible. "They've got the knowledge. They probably know instrument flying better than you and I, they're so fresh out of school. All they need is experience. We've got a Link. We can run that thing ten hours a day and fill our pilots with every instrument approach for every base in France. They volunteered to join the 167th, and they want to work for the squadron. It's up to you and me to work 'em.''

The squadron commander smiled suddenly. "When you talk like that, I can almost accuse you of being eager yourself." He paused, and then spoke slowly. "I remember the old 167th, in England in 1944. We had the new Thunderbolt then, and we painted our little Persian battle-cat on its side. We weren't afraid of anything the Luftwaffe could get into the air. Eager in peace is brave in war, I guess." He nodded to his operations officer. "Can't say that I think we won't have our share of in-flight emergencies with this old airplane or that we won't need a lot of good luck before the boys start giving a meaning back to this squadron," he said. "But draw up your Link and flying schedules starting tomorrow and we'll begin to see just how good our youngsters really are."

In a moment Major Robert Rider stood alone in his darkening office, and he thought of the old 167th. Sadly. Of Lieutenant John Buckner, trapped in a burning Thunder-bolt, who still attacked a pair of unwary Focke-Wulfs and took one of them with him into the hard ground of France. Of Lieutenant Jack Bennett, with six kills and glory assured, who deliberately rammed an Me 109 that was closing to destroy a crippled B-17 over Strasburg. Of Lieutenant Alan Spencer, who brought back a Thunderbolt so badly dam-aged by cannonfire that he had to be freed from the wreckage of his crash landing by a crew with cutting torches. Rider had seen him after the crash. "It was the same '190 that got Jim Park," he had said from the whiteness of the hospital bed. "Black snakes down the side of the fuselage. And I said, 'Today, Al, it's going to be you or him, but one of us isn't going to make it home.' I was the lucky one." Alan Spencer volunteered to go back into combat when he was released from the hospital, and he did not return from his next mission over France. No one heard him call, no one saw his airplane hit. He simply didn't come back. Despite their battle-cat insignia, the 167th pilots did not have nine lives. Or even two.

Eager in peace is brave in war, Rider thought, looking absently at the scar along the back of his left hand, his throttle hand. It was wide and white, the kind of scar left only after an encounter with a Messerschmitt's thirty-calibre machine-gun bullet. But eagerness is not enough. If we're going to make it through the winter without losing a pilot, we'll need more than eagerness. We've got to have skill and we've got to have experience. So thinking, he walked outside into the overcast night.

The days whipped quickly by for Second Lieutenant Jonathan Heinz. All this talk of weather and look out for Europe in the winter was nonsense, sheer nonsense. November was bright and spilling with sun. December was ready to spring onto the calendar and the base had had only four days of low ceilings, which the pilots spent working on the ops officer's latest instrument quiz. Major Langley's instrument quizzes had become a standard of the squadron; a new one every third day, twenty questions, one wrong answer allowed. Fail a test and you stay another three hours at the flight line with the instrument manuals, until you pass the alternate test, one wrong answer allowed.

Heinz pressed the starter switch of his ageing Thunderstreak, winced in the concussion of a good start, and taxied to the runway behind Bob Henderson's airplane. But that's the way to get to know instruments, he thought. At first everyone was staying the three hours and cursing the day that they volunteered for the 167th Tactical Fighter Squadron. Tactical Instrument Squadron, they called it. Then you got the knack of it, and it seemed somehow that you knew more and more of the answers. It was pretty rare now to have to stay the three hours.

There was a little thud in the engine's roar when Heinz retracted his engine screens before takeoff, but all the engine instruments showed normal, and strange noises and little thuds are not unusual in the F-84. Oddly enough, though, at a time when he usually noticed little but the instruments and the leader's airplane rocking firmly against full throttle and locked brakes, Jonathan Heinz noticed a grey Persian cat sitting calmly at the edge of the runway a few hundred feet ahead of his airplane. Cat must be completely deaf, he thought. His engine, linked to the thick black throttle under his left glove, crackled and roared and spun blue fire through stainless-steel turbine blades to unchain seventy-eight hundred pounds of thrust within his airplane.

He was ready to roll, and he nodded to Henderson. Then, for no reason, he pressed the microphone button under his left thumb on the throttle. "There's a cat out on the edge of the runway," he said into the microphone set into his green-rubber oxygen mask. There was a short silence.

"Roj on the cat," Henderson said seriously, and Heinz felt foolish. He saw the mobile control officer in his minia-ture control tower at the right side of the runway reach for his binoculars. Why did I say a dumb stupid thing like that, he thought. I will not say one more word this flight. Radio discipline, Heinz, radio discipline! He released his brakes at the nod of Henderson's white helmet, and the two airplanes gathered a great reserve of speed and lifted into the air.

Eight minutes later Heinz was talking again. "Sahara Leader, I got an aft overheat light and the rpm's surging about five per cent. Power's back, light's still on. Check me for smoke, will you?" What a calm voice you have, he thought. You talk too much, but at least you're calm. Sixty hours in the '84 and you should be calm. Take it easy now and try not to sound like a little kid on the radio. I'll turn around and drop the external tanks, fly a simulated flame-out pattern, and land. I couldn't be on fire.

"No sign of smoke, Sahara Two. How's it doing now?"

Calm voice, Heinz. "Still surging, Leader. Fuel flow and tailpipe temp are going back and forth with it. I'm going to drop the tanks and land."

"OK, Two, I'll keep an eye for smoke and handle the radio calls if you'd like. But be ready to jump out of the bird if she starts to burn."

"Roj." I'm ready to jump out, Heinz thought. Just raise the ejection-seat armrest and squeeze the trigger. But I think I can get the airplane back down all right. He listened to Henderson declare an emergency, and as he descended slowly into the flameout pattern he saw the square red fire trucks burst from their garages and race to their alert slots at the taxiways. He could feel the engine surge in the throttle. It will be sort of touch-and-go here. I'll drop the tanks on final approach before I get down to five hundred feet, I'll pull the nose up and eject. Below five hundred feet, I'll have to take it on in, no matter what. He brought the throttle back to give an engine speed of fifty-eight per cent rpm, and the heavy airplane dropped more quickly through the pattern. Flaps down. I have the field made, for sure . . . Gear down. The wheels locked in place. He passed through four hundred feet. Thud. Thudthud. A big surge.

"There's a lot of smoke from your tailpipe, Sahara."

Wouldn't you know it! This thing's going to explode on me, and I'm too low to bail out. What do I do now? He pressed the drop tank jettison button and the airplane bounced a little as four thousand pounds of fuel fell away. A harsh grinding from the engine, behind him. He noticed, suddenly, that the oil pressure was at zero.

A frozen engine, Heinz! You got no flight control with a frozen engine. What now, what now? The control stick went solid and immovable in his gloves.

The officer in mobile control did not know about the frozen engine. He did not know that Sahara Two would make a gentle roll to the right and strike the ground inverted, or that Jonathan Heinz was helpless and committed to die. "You have a cat by the runway," the mobile officer said, with the mild relaxed humour of one who knows that danger has passed.

And it came to Heinz suddenly. In a burst of light. Emergency hydraulic pump, the electric pump! His airplane was beginning to roll, a hundred feet in the air. His glove smashed the pump switch to EMERG, and the stick came alive again, quickly. Wings level, nose up, nose up, and a beautiful touchdown in front of mobile. At least it felt beautiful. Throttle off, drag chute out, fuel off, battery off, canopy open and be ready to jump out of the thing. The giant square fire trucks, scarlet lights blazing atop their cabs, roared along next to him as he slowed through thirty knots on the landing roll. His airplane was completely quiet, and Heinz could hear the truck engines, sounding like great inboard cruiser engines, labouring in high gear. In a moment he had rolled to a stop, unstrapped from the cockpit, and jumped down to stand behind a fire truck that hosed thick white foam on a broad patch of discoloured aluminum aft of the wing root.

The airplane looked forlorn, unwilling to be the centre of such concentrated attention. But it was down, and it was in one piece. Jonathan Heinz was very much alive, and not a little bit famous. "Nice going, ace," the pilots would say, and they'd ask him about how it felt and what he thought and what he did and when, and there would be the routine accident investigation and there could be no other conclusion than well done, Lieutenant Heinz. No one would guess that he came within a few seconds of dying because he had completely forgotten, like a brand-new pilot, about the emergency hydraulic pump. Completely forgotten . . . and what had reminded him? What had snapped his thought to the red-covered switch at the last instant that it could save him? Nothing. It had just come to him.

Heinz thought some more. It had not just come. Mobile control told me about the cat by the runway, and I remembered the pump. There's an odd one for you. I'd like to meet that cat.

He looked down the long white runway. He could see no cat. Even the mobile control officer, with his binoculars, could not then have seen any cat. The squadron was later to ride him unmercifully about his lucky cat, but at that moment, by the runway or across the whole of the base, there was no such thing as a grey Persian cat.

It happened again, less than a week later, to another second lieutenant. Jack Willis had almost finished his first simulated combat mission after completing his checkout in the F-84. It had been a good mission, but now, in the landing pattern, he was worried. Twenty-knot crosswind, where did that come from? It was ten knots down the runway when we took off, and now it's twenty knots across. He rolled his airplane level on the downwind leg of the pattern. "Say again the wind, please, tower," he called.

"Roj," the tower's last explanation was entirely unnecessary. The wind was as cross as it could possibly be.

"OK, Two, let's watch the crosswind," said Major Langley, and called, "Eagle Lead is turning base, gear down, pressure up, brakes checked."

"Cleared to land," the tower operator replied.

Willis reached forward with his left glove and slammed the landing-gear lever to DOWN. OK, OK, he thought, this will be no problem. I'll just keep the right wing way down through the roundabout, touch on the right wheel, and follow through with plenty of rudder. Plenty of rudder.

He turned toward the runway, and pressed the microphone button. Haven't run off a runway yet, and I don't intend to do it today. "Eagle Two is turning base . . ." The right main gear indicator, the green light that should have been shining, was out. Left main was locked down, nosegear was locked down. But the right main gear was still retracted. The red warning light in the transparent plastic landing-gear handle was shining, and the squeal of the "gear unsafe" warning horn filled the cockpit. He heard the horn in his own earphones as he held the microphone button down. On their radios, the tower operators would hear the horn. He lifted his thumb, then pressed it down again. "Eagle Two is going to make a low approach; requests a gear check by mobile control."

An odd feeling, to have something wrong with the airplane. The landing gear usually works so well. He levelled at one hundred feet over the runway and flew past the miniature glass tower. The mobile control officer stood outside, in the blowing waves of autumn grass. Willis watched him for a second as he passed. The mobile control officer was not using binoculars. Then he was gone, and the solitary F-84 whipped over the far end of the runway, above Eagle Lead, safely on the ground.

"Your right main gear is up and locked," the voice came flatly from mobile control.

"Roj. I'll cycle the gear." Willis was pleased with his voice. He climbed slowly to one thousand feet, raised the landing gear, and lowered it again. The right main "safe" light remained stubbornly out, and the warning light in the plastic handle persisted redly. Another fifteen minutes of fuel. Four times Willis recycled the landing gear, and four times the right main gear indicated unsafe. He pulled the handle out a half inch and pressed it to EMERG DOWN. There was a faint click from the right, but the condition was the same. He was concerned. There was no time for the fire trucks to lay a strip of foam down the runway, if he was forced to land with the right gear still locked up. To land with it up on a hard dry runway, crosswind, would be inviting an end-over-end cartwheeling crash as soon as the unwheeled wing touched the concrete. The only alternative was bale-out. Here's a decision for you, he thought. And irrationally: one more flyby, maybe the gear is down now.

"It's still up," the mobile control officer said, before Willis had even flown by the miniature tower. The grass was waving greenly, briskly, and he noticed suddenly at the edge of the runway a small grey dot. With a shock of surprise, he realized that it was a cat. Heinz's lucky cat, he thought, and for no reason he smiled under his oxygen mask. He felt better. And a thought came from nowhere.

"Tower, Eagle Two is declaring an emergency. I'm going to make one more pass around; try to bounce on the left gear to knock the right one down."

"Understand you are declaring an emergency," the tower replied. The tower was primarily concerned with meeting its responsibility, which was to ring the bell that sent crash crews scrambling for the red trucks. Responsibility met, the tower became only an interested observer, and very little help.

Jack Willis, oddly, felt like a new person, enormously confident. The bounce on a left wheel in a strong right crosswind was a trick of coordination reserved for thousand-hour pilots, and Willis had just over four hundred hours in the air, sixty-eight in the F-84.

Those who watched the next approach called it the work of an old-time professional pilot. With left wing down, with hard right rudder, with controls only moderately responsive at landing airspeed, Second Lieutenant Jack Willis bounced his twenty-thousand-pound airplane six times on its left main landing gear. On the sixth bounce, the right gear swung suddenly down and locked into place. The third green light came on.

The crosswind landing that followed was simple by comparison, and his airplane touched smoothly down on its right wheel, then its left, and last of all, the nosewheel. Full left rudder in the landing roll and a touch of left brake as the airplane slowed and tried to weathervane into the wind, and the emergency was over. The crash crews in their bulky white suits of asbestos were unnecessary and out of their element in the normalcy that followed. "Nice job, Eagle Two," mobile said simply. And the grey Persian cat, that had watched the landing with uncatlike, one might almost say, professional interest, was gone. The 167th Tactical Fighter Squadron was gradually pulling itself into fighting shape.

The winter came. Low clouds moved in from the sea to become a permanent companion of the hilltops that surrounded the airbase. It rained much, and as the winter wore on, the rain became freezing rain and then snow. The runway was icy and drag chutes and very careful braking were necessary to keep the heavy airplanes on the concrete. The tall emerald grass turned pallid and lifeless. But a fighter squadron does not cancel its mission each winter, there is always flying and training to be done. There were incidents as the new pilots were faced with unusual aircraft problems and low ceilings, but they had been trained well on instruments and somehow the grey Persian cat sat carefully at the edge of the runway as each of the afflicted airplanes landed. The Persian became known to the pilots simply as "Cat."

One freezing afternoon, just as Wally Jacobs touched down uneventfully after a hydraulic-system failure and a no-flap, no-speed-brake approach through a five-hundred-foot ceiling, Captain Hendrick, on duty as mobile control officer, ventured to capture the cat. It sat quietly, looking down the runway, absorbed in watching Jacobs' airplane after it whistled past. Hendrick approached from behind and gently lifted the cat from the ground. At his first touch it became a ball of grey lightning. There was an instant slash of claw along Hendrick's cheek, and the Persian streaked to the ground and away, disappearing at once in the tall dry grass.

Five seconds later the brakes on Wally Jacobs' airplane failed completely, and he swerved off the runway at seventy knots into the not-quite-frozen dirt. The nosewheel strut sheared immediately. The airplane disappeared in a great sheet of flying mud, slewed to collapse the right main landing gear and split the droptank, and slid around, backward, for another two hundred feet. Jacobs left the cockpit at once, forgetting even to close the throttle. In a second, as Hendrick watched, the airplane burst into brilliant flame. It burned fiercely, and with the airplane was destroyed a record for flying safety unmatched by any other fighter squadron in Europe.

The findings of the investigation were that Lieutenant Jacobs was at fault for allowing the airplane to leave the runway and for neglecting to close the throttle, allowing the still-turning engine to ignite the fire. If he had not forgotten, like a grossly inexperienced pilot, to stopcock the throttle, the airplane would have been able to fly again.

The board's decision was not a popular one with the 167th Tactical Fighter Squadron, but the cause of the destruction of the airplane was laid to pilot error. Hendrick mentioned the cat, and an order, unwritten but official, was sent through the squadron: the Persian was never to be approached. From that moment, Cat was rarely mentioned.

But once in a while, as a young lieutenant brought an ailing airplane down through the weather, he would ask of mobile control, "Cat there?" And the mobile control officer would scan the runway edge for the sculptured grey Persian, and he would pick up his microphone and say, "He's there." And the airplane would land.

Winter wore on. The young pilots became older, absorbed experience. And as the weeks went by, Cat was seen less and less frequently at the edge of the runway. Norm Thompson brought in an airplane with the windscreen and canopy completely iced over. Cat was not waiting by the runway, but Thompson's GCA was a professional one, born of training and experience. He made a blind touchdown, jettisoned the canopy to be able to see, and rolled to an uneventful stop. Jack Willis, now with one hundred and thirty hours flying experience in the F-84, came back with an airplane heavily damaged by ricochets picked up after a firing run at a new strafing range laid over a base of solid rock. He landed smoothly, although Cat was nowhere to be seen.

The last time Cat appeared by the runway was in March. It was Jacobs again. He called that his oil pressure was falling, and that he was trying to make it back to the field. The ceiling was high, three thousand feet, when he broke into the clear after a radar vector and called the runway in sight.

Major Robert Rider had raced his staff car to mobile control as the notice of emergency in progress reached him. This is it, he thought. I'm going to see Jacobs die. He closed the glass door behind him as the pilot asked, "Cat happen to be down there?"

Rider reached for the binoculars and scanned the edge of the runway. The Persian sat quietly waiting. "Cat's here," the squadron commander told the mobile control officer seriously, and seriously the information was relayed to Jacobs.

"Oil pressure zero," the pilot said matter-of-factly. Then, "Engine's frozen, the stick is locking. I'll try to make it on the emergency hydraulic pump." A moment later he said, suddenly, "No I won't. I'm getting out." He turned his airplane toward the heavy forest to the west and ejected. Two minutes later he was sprawling in the frozen mud of a ploughed French field, his parachute settling like a tired white butterfly about him. It was over that quickly.

The investigation board was to find later that the airplane struck the ground with both hydraulic systems completely locked. The emergency hydraulic pump failed before impact, they discovered, and the airplane hit with controls frozen and immovable. Jacobs was later to be commended for his judgement in not attempting to land the stricken airplane.

But that was to be later. As Jacobs' parachute drifted down behind a low hill, Rider levelled the binoculars at the grey Persian, who stood suddenly and stretched luxuriously, claws digging into the frozen earth. Cat, he noticed, was not a perfect sculpture. Along his left side, from ribs to shoulder, ran a wide white scar that the battle-grey fur could not cover as he stretched. The graceful head turned as Rider watched, and the amber eyes gazed squarely at the commander of the 167th Tactical Fighter Squadron.

The cat blinked once, slowly, one might almost say amusedly, and walked to disappear for the last time in the tall grass.

The Argonauts
of the Air

H. G. Wells

One saw Monson's Flying Machine from the windows of the trains passing either along the South-Western main line or along the line between Wimbledon and Worcester Park—to be more exact, one saw the huge scaffoldings which limited the flight of the apparatus. They rose over the treetops, a massive alley of interlacing iron and timber, and an enormous web of ropes and tackle, extending the best part of two miles. From the Leatherhead branch this alley was foreshortened and in part hidden by a hill with villas; but from the main line one had it in profile, a complex tangle of girders and curving bars, very impressive to the excursionists from Portsmouth and Southampton and the West. Monson had taken up the work where Maxim had left it, had gone on at first with an utter contempt for the journalistic wit and ignorance that had irritated and hampered his predecessor, and had spent (it was said) rather more than half his immense fortune upon his experiments. The results, to an impatient generation, seemed inconsiderable. When some five years had passed after the growth of the colossal iron groves at Worcester Park, and Monson still failed to put in a fluttering appearance over Trafalgar Square, even the Isle of Wight trippers felt their liberty to smile. And such intelligent people as did not consider

Monson a fool stricken with the mania for invention, denounced him as being (for no particular reason) a self-advertising quack.

Yet now and again a morning trainload of season-ticket holders would see a white monster rush headlong through the airy tracery of guides and bars, and hear the further stays, nettings, and buffers snap, creak, and groan with the impact of the blow. Then there would be an efflorescence of black-set white-rimmed faces along the sides of the train, and the morning papers would be neglected for a vigorous discussion of the possibility of flying (in which nothing new was ever said by any chance), until the train reached Waterloo, and its cargo of season-ticket holders dispersed themselves over London. Or the fathers and mothers in some multitudinous train of weary excursionists returning exhausted from a day of rest by the sea, would find the dark fabric, standing out against the evening sky, useful in diverting some bilious child from its introspection, and be suddenly startled by the swift transit of a huge black flapping shape that strained upward against the guides. It was a great and forcible thing beyond dispute, and excellent for conversation; yet, all the same, it was but flying in leading-strings, and most of those who witnessed it scarcely counted its flight as flying. More of a switchback it seemed to the run of the folk.

Monson, I say, did not trouble himself very keenly about the opinions of the Press at first. But possibly he, even, had formed but a poor idea of the time it would take before the tactics of flying were mastered, the swift assured adjustment of the big soaring shape to every gust and chance movement of the air; nor had he clearly reckoned the money this prolonged struggle against gravitation would cost him. And he was not so pachydermatous as he seemed. Secretly he had his periodical bundles of cuttings sent him by Romeike, he had his periodical reminders from his banker; and if he did not mind the initial ridicule and scepticism, he felt the growing neglect as the months went by and the money dribbled away. Time was when Monson had sent the enterprising journalist, keen after readable matter, empty from his gates. But when the enterprising journalist ceased from troubling, Monson was anything but satisfied in his heart of hearts. Still day by day the work went on, and the multitudinous subtle difficulties of the steering diminished in number. Day by day, too, the money trickled away, until his balance was no longer a matter of hundreds of thousands, but of tens. And at last came an anniversary.

Monson, sitting in the little drawing-shed, suddenly noticed the date on Woodhouse's calendar.

"It was five years ago today that we began," he said to Woodhouse suddenly.

"Is it?" said Woodhouse.

"It's the alterations play the devil with us," said Monson, biting a paper-fastener.

The drawings for the new vanes to the hinder screw lay on the table before him as he spoke. He pitched the mutilated brass paper-fastener into the waste-paper basket and drummed with his fingers. "These alterations! Will the mathematicians ever be clever enough to save us all this patching and experimenting? Five years—learning by rule of thumb, when one might think that it was possible to calculate the whole thing out beforehand. The cost of it! I might have hired three senior wranglers for life. But they'd only have developed some beautifully useless theorems in pneumatics. What a time it has been, Woodhouse!"

"These mouldings will take three weeks," said Woodhouse. "At special prices."

"Three weeks!" said Monson, and sat drumming.

"Three weeks certain," said Woodhouse, an excellent engineer, but no good as a comforter. He drew the sheets towards him and began shading a bar.

Monson stopped drumming, and began to bite his fingernails, staring the while at Woodhouse's head.

"How long have they been calling this Monson's Folly?" he said suddenly.

"*Oh!* Year or so," said Woodhouse carelessly, without looking up.

Monson sucked the air in between his teeth, and went to the window. The stout iron columns carrying the elevated rails upon which the start of the machine was made rose up close by, and the machine was hidden by the upper edge of the window. Through the grove of iron pillars, red painted and ornate with rows of bolts, one had a glimpse of the pretty scenery towards Esher. A train went gliding noise-lessly across the middle distance, its rattle drowned by the hammering of the workmen overhead. Monson could imagine the grinning faces at the windows of the carriages. He swore savagely under his breath, and dabbed viciously at a blowfly that suddenly became noisy on the windowpane.

"What's up?" said Woodhouse, staring in surprise at his employer.

"I'm about sick of this."

Woodhouse scratched his cheek. "Oh!" he said, after an assimilating pause. He pushed the drawing away from him.

"Here these fools . . . I'm trying to conquer a new element—trying to do a thing that will revolutionize life. And instead of taking an intelligent interest, they grin and make their stupid jokes, and call me and my appliances names."

"Asses!" said Woodhouse, letting his eye fall again on the drawing.

The epithet, curiously enough, made Monson wince. "I'm about sick of it, Woodhouse, anyhow," he said, after a pause.

Woodhouse shrugged his shoulders.

"There's nothing for it but patience, I suppose," said Monson, sticking his hands in his pockets. "I've started. I've made my bed, and I've got to lie on it. I can't go back. I'll see it through, and spend every penny I have and every penny I can borrow. But I tell you, Woodhouse, I'm infernally sick of it, all the same. If I'd paid a tenth part of the money towards some political greaser's expenses—I'd have been a baronet before this."

Monson paused. Woodhouse stared in front of him with a blank expression he always employed to indicate sympathy, and tapped his pencil-case on the table. Monson stared at him for a minute.

"Oh, *damn!*" said Monson suddenly, and abruptly rushed out of the room.

Woodhouse continued his sympathetic rigour for perhaps half a minute. Then he sighed and resumed the shading of the drawings. Something had evidently upset Monson. Nice chap, and generous, but difficult to get on with. It was the way with every amateur who had anything to do with engineering—wanted everything finished at once. But Monson had usually the patience of the expert. Odd he was so irritable. Nice and round that aluminium rod did look now! Woodhouse threw back his head, and put it first this side then that, to appreciate his bit of shading better.

"Mr. Woodhouse," said Hooper, the foreman of the labourers, putting his head in at the door.

"Hullo!" said Woodhouse, without turning round.

"Nothing happened, sir?" said Hooper.

"Happened?" said Woodhouse.

"The governor just been up the rails swearing like a tornader."

"Oh!" said Woodhouse.

"It ain't like him, sir."

"No?"

"And I was thinking perhaps—"

"Don't think," said Woodhouse, still admiring the drawings.

Hooper knew Woodhouse, and he shut the door suddenly with a vicious slam. Woodhouse stared stonily before him for some further minutes, and then made an ineffectual effort to pick his teeth with a pencil. Abruptly he desisted, pitched that old, tried, and stumpy servitor across the room, got up, stretched himself, and followed Hooper.

He looked ruffled—it was visible to every workman he met. When a millionaire who has been spending thousands on experiments that employ quite a little army of people suddenly indicates that he is sick of the undertaking, there is almost invariably a certain amount of mental friction in the ranks of the little army he employs. And even before he indicates his intentions there are speculations and murmurs, a watching of faces and a study of straws. Hundreds of people knew before the day was out that Monson was ruffled, Woodhouse ruffled, Hooper ruffled. A workman's wife, for instance (whom Monson had never seen), decided to keep her money in the savings bank instead of buying a velveteen dress. So far-reaching are even the casual curses of a millionaire.

Monson found a certain satisfaction in going into the works and behaving disagreeably to as many people as possible. After a time even that palled upon him, and he rode off the grounds, to everyone's relief there, and through the lanes south-eastward, to the infinite tribulation of his house steward at Cheam.

And the immediate cause of it all, the little grain of annoyance that had suddenly precipitated all this discontent with his life-work was—these trivial things that direct all our great decisions!—half a dozen ill-considered remarks made by a pretty girl, prettily dressed; with a beautiful voice and something more than prettiness in her soft grey eyes. And of these half-dozen remarks, two words especially—"Monson's Folly." She had felt she was behaving charmingly to Monson; she reflected the next day how exceptionally effective she had been, and no one would have been more amazed than she, had she learned the effect she had left on Monson's mind. I hope, considering everything, that she never knew.

"How are you getting on with your flying-machine?" she asked. ("I wonder if I shall ever meet anyone with the sense not to ask that," thought Monson.) "It will be very dangerous at first, will it not?" ("Thinks I'm afraid.") "Jorgon is going to play presently; have you heard him before?" ("My mania being attended to, we turn to rational conversation.") Gush about Jorgon; gradual decline of conversation, ending with—"You must let me know when your flying-machine is finished, Mr. Monson, and then I will consider the advisability of taking a ticket." ("One would think I was still playing inventions in the nursery.") But the bitterest thing she said was not meant for Monson's ears. To Phlox, the novelist, she was always conscientiously brilliant. "I have been talking to Mr. Monson, and he can think of nothing, positively nothing, but that flying-machine of his. Do you know, all his workmen call that place of his 'Monson's Folly'? He is quite impossible. It is really very, very sad. I always regard him myself in the light of sunken treasure—the Lost Millionaire, you know."

She was pretty and well educated—indeed, she had written an epigrammatic novelette; but the bitterness was that she was typical. She summarized what the world thought of the man who was working sanely, steadily, and surely towards a more tremendous revolution in the appliances of civilization, a more far-reaching alteration in the ways of humanity than has ever been effected since history began. They did not even take him seriously. In a little while he would be proverbial. "I *must* fly now," he said on his way home, smarting with a sense of absolute social failure. "I must fly soon. If it doesn't come off soon, by God! I shall run amuck."

He said that before he had gone through his pass-book and his litter of papers. Inadequate as the cause seems, it was that girl's voice and the expression of her eyes that precipitated his discontent. But certainly the discovery that he had no longer even one hundred thousand pounds' worth of realizable property behind him was the poison that made the wound deadly.

It was on the next day after this that he exploded upon Woodhouse and his workmen, and thereafter his bearing was consistently grim for three weeks, and anxiety dwelt in Cheam and Ewell, Malden, Morden, and Worcester Park, places that had thriven mightily on his experiments.

Four weeks after that first swearing of his, he stood with Woodhouse by the reconstructed machine as it lay across the elevated railway, by means of which it gained its initial impetus. The new propeller glittered a brighter white than the rest of the machine, and a gilder, obedient to a whim of Monson's, was picking out the aluminium bars with gold. And looking down the long avenue between the ropes (gilded now with the sunset), one saw red signals, and two miles away an ant-hill of workmen busy altering the last falls of the run into a rising slope.

"I'll *come*," said Woodhouse. "I'll come right enough. But I tell you it's infernally foolhardy. If only you would give another year—"

"I tell you I won't. I tell you the thing works. I've given years enough—"

"It's not that," said Woodhouse. "We're all right with the machine. But it's the steering—"

"Haven't I been rushing, night and morning, backwards and forwards, through the squirrel's cage? If the thing steers true here, it will steer true all across England. It's just funk, I tell you, Woodhouse. We could have gone a year ago. And besides—"

"Well?" said Woodhouse.

"The money!" snapped Monson over his shoulder.

"Hang it! I never thought of the money," said Woodhouse, and then, speaking now in a very different tone to that with which he had said the words before, he repeated, "I'll come. Trust me."

Monson turned suddenly, and saw all that Woodhouse had not the dexterity to say, shining on his sunset-lit face. He looked for a moment, then impulsively extended his hand. "Thanks," he said.

"All right," said Woodhouse, gripping the hand, and with a queer softening of his features. "Trust me."

Then both men turned to the big apparatus that lay with its flat wings extended upon the carrier, and stared at it meditatively. Monson, guided perhaps by a photographic study of the flight of birds, and by Lilienthal's methods, had gradually drifted from Maxim's shapes towards the bird form again. The thing, however, was driven by a huge screw behind in the place of the tail; and so hovering, which needs an almost vertical adjustment of a flat tail, was rendered impossible. The body of the machine was small, almost cylindrical, and pointed. Forward and aft on the pointed ends were two small petroleum engines for the screw, and the navigators sat deep in a canoe-like recess, the foremost one steering, and being protected by a low screen, with two plate-glass windows, from the blinding rush of air. On either side a monstrous flat framework with a curved front border could be adjusted so as either to lie horizontally, or to be tilted upward or down. These wings worked rigidly together, or, by releasing a pin, one could be tilted through a small angle independently of its fellow. The front edge of either wing could also be shifted back so as to diminish the wing-area about one-sixth. The machine was not only not designed to hover, but it was also incapable of fluttering. Monson's idea was to get into the air with the initial rush of the apparatus, and then to skim, much as a playing-card may be skimmed, keeping up the rush by means of the screw at the stern. Rooks and gulls fly enormous distances in that way with scarcely a perceptible movement of the wings. The bird really drives along on an aerial switchback. It glides slanting downward for a space, until it has gained considerable momentum, and then, altering the inclination of its wings, glides up again almost to its original altitude. Even a Londoner who has watched the birds in the aviary in Regent's Park knows that.

But the bird is practising this art from the moment it leaves its nest. It has not only the perfect apparatus, but the perfect instinct to use it. A man off his feet has the poorest skill in balancing. Even the simple trick of the bicycle costs him some hours of labour. The instantaneous adjustments of the wings, the quick response to a passing breeze, the swift recovery of equilibrium, the giddy, eddying movements that require such absolute precision—all that he must learn, learn with infinite labour and infinite danger, if ever he is to conquer flying. The flying-machine that will start off some fine day, driven by neat "little levers," with a nice open deck like a liner, and all loaded up with bombshells and guns, is the easy dreaming of a literary man. In lives and in treasure the cost of the conquest of the empire of the air may even exceed all that has been spent in man's great conquest of the sea. Certainly it will be costlier than the greatest war that has ever devastated the world.

No one knew these things better than these two practical men. And they knew they were in the front rank of the coming army. Yet there is hope even in a forlorn hope. Men are killed outright in the reserves sometimes, while others who have been left for dead in the thickest corner crawl out and survive.

"If we miss these meadows—" said Woodhouse presently in his slow way.

"My dear chap," said Monson, whose spirits had been rising fitfully during the last few days, "we mustn't miss these meadows. There's a quarter of a square mile for us to hit, fences removed, ditches levelled. We shall come down all right—rest assured. And if we don't—"

"Ah!" said Woodhouse. "If we don't."

Before the day of the start, the newspaper people got wind of the alterations at the northward end of the framework, and Monson was cheered by a decided change in the comments Romeike forwarded him. "He will be off some day," said the papers. "He will be off some day," said the South-Western season-ticket holders one to another; the seaside excursionists, the Saturday-to-Monday trippers from Sussex and Hampshire and Dorset and Devon, the eminent literary people from Haslemere, all remarked eagerly one to another, "He will be off some day," as the familiar scaffolding came in sight. And actually, one bright morning, in full view of the ten-past-ten train from Basingstoke, Monson's flying-machine started on its journey.

They saw the carrier running swiftly along its rail, and the white and gold screw spinning in the air. They heard the rapid rumble of the wheels, and the thud as the carrier reached the buffers at the end of its run. Then a whirr as the flying-machine was shot forward into the networks. All that the majority of them had seen and heard before. The thing went with a drooping flight through the framework and rose again, and then every beholder shouted, or screamed, or yelled, or shrieked after his kind. For instead of the customary concussion and stoppage, the flying-machine flew out of its five years' cage like a bolt from a crossbow, and drove slantingly upward into the air, curved round a little, so as to cross the line, and soared in the direction of Wimbledon Common.

It seemed to hang momentarily in the air and grow smaller, then it ducked and vanished over the clustering blue tree-tops to the east of Coombe Hill, and no one stopped staring and gasping until long after it had disappeared.

That was what the people in the train from Basingstoke saw. If you had drawn a line down the middle of that train, from engine to guard's van, you would not have found a living soul on the opposite side to the flying-machine. It was a mad rush from window to window as the thing crossed the line. And the engine-driver and stoker never took their eyes off the low hills about Wimbledon, and never noticed that they had run clean through Coombe and Malden and Raynes Park, until, with returning animation, they found themselves pelting, at the most indecent pace, into Wimbledon station.

From the moment when Monson had started the carrier with a *"Now!"* neither he nor Woodhouse said a word. Both men sat with clenched teeth. Monson had crossed the line with a curve that was too sharp, and Woodhouse had opened and shut his white lips; but neither spoke. Woodhouse simply gripped his seat, and breathed sharply through his teeth, watching the blue country to the west rushing past, and down, and away from him. Monson knelt at his post forward, and his hands trembled on the spoked wheel that moved the wings. He could see nothing before him but a mass of white clouds in the sky.

The machine went slanting upward, travelling with an enormous speed still, but losing momentum every moment. The land ran away underneath with diminishing speed.

"Now!" said Woodhouse at last, and with a violent effort Monson wrenched over the wheel and altered the angle of the wings. The machine seemed to hang for half a minute motionless in mid-air, and then he saw the hazy blue house-covered hills of Kilburn and Hampstead jump up before his eyes and rise steadily, until the little sunlit dome of the Albert Hall appeared through his windows. For a moment he scarcely understood the meaning of this upward rush of the horizon, but as the nearer and nearer houses came into view, he realized what he had done. He had turned the wings over too far, and they were swooping steeply downward towards the Thames.

The thought, the question, the realization were all the business of a second of time. "Too much!" gasped Woodhouse. Monson brought the wheel half-way back with a jerk, and forthwith the Kilburn and Hampstead ridge dropped again to the lower edge of his windows. They had been a thousand feet above Coombe and Malden station; fifty seconds after they whizzed, at a frightful pace, not eighty feet above the East Putney station, on the Metropolitan District line, to the screaming astonishment of a platformful of people. Monson flung up the vanes against the air, and over Fulham they rushed up their atmospheric switchback again, steeply—too steeply. The buses went floundering across the Fulham Road, the people yelled.

Then down again, too steeply still, and the distant trees and houses about Primrose Hill leapt up across Monson's window, and then suddenly he saw straight before him the greenery of Kensington Gardens and the towers of the Imperial Institute. They were driving straight down upon South Kensington. The pinnacles of the Natural History Museum rushed up into view. There came one fatal second of swift thought, a moment of hesitation. Should he try and clear the towers, or swerve eastward?

He made a hesitating attempt to release the right wing, left the catch half released, and gave a frantic clutch at the wheel.

The nose of the machine seemed to leap up before him. The wheel pressed his hand with irresistible force, and jerked itself out of his control.

Woodhouse, sitting crouched together, gave a hoarse cry, and sprang up towards Monson. "Too far!" he cried, and then he was clinging to the gunwale for dear life, and Monson had been jerked clean overhead, and was falling backwards upon him.

So swiftly had the thing happened that barely a quarter of the people going to and fro in Hyde Park, and Brompton Road, and the Exhibition Road saw anything of the aerial catastrophe. A distant winged shape had appeared above the clustering houses to the south, had fallen and risen, growing larger as it did so; had swooped swiftly down towards the Imperial Institute, a broad spread of flying wings, had swept round in a quarter circle, dashed eastward and then suddenly sprang vertically into the air. A black object shot out of it, and came spinning downward. A man! Two men clutching each other! They came whirling down, separated as they struck the roof of the Students' Club, and bounded off into the green bushes on its southward side.

For perhaps half a minute, the pointed stem of the big machine still pierced vertically upward, the screw spinning desperately. For one brief instant, that yet seemed an age to all who watched, it had hung motionless in mid-air. Then a spout of yellow flame licked up its length from the stern engine, and swift, swifter, swifter, and flaring like a rocket, it rushed down upon the solid mass of masonry which was formerly the Royal College of Science. The big screw of white and gold touched the parapet, and crumpled up like wet linen. Then the blazing spindle-shaped body smashed and splintered, smashing and splintering in its fall, upon the north-westward angle of the building.

But the crash, the flame of blazing paraffin that shot heavenward from the shattered engines of the machine, the crushed horrors that were found in the garden beyond the

Students' Club, the masses of yellow parapet and red brick that fell headlong into the roadway, the running to and fro of people like ants in a broken ant-hill, the galloping of fire-engines, the gathering of crowds—all these things do not belong to this story, which was written only to tell how the first of all successful flying-machines was launched and flew. Though he failed, and failed disastrously, the record of Monson's work remains—a sufficient monument—to guide the next of that band of gallant experimentalists who will sooner or later master this great problem of flying. And between Worcester Park and Malden there still stands that portentous avenue of iron-work, rusting now, and dangerous here and there, to witness to the first desperate struggle for man's right of way through the air.

How Sleep the Brave

"Flying Officer X"
(H. E. Bates)

I

The sea moved away below us like a stream of feathers smoothed down by a level wind. It was grey and without light as far as we could see. Only against the coast of Holland, in a thin line of trimming that soon lost itself in the grey coasts of the North, did it break into white waves that seemed to remain frozen between sea and land. Down towards the Channel the sun, even from six thousand feet, had gone down at last below long layers of cloud. They had been orange and blue at first, then yellow and pale green, and then, as they were now, entirely the colour of slate. Above them there was nothing but a colourless sky that would soon be dark altogether.

There had been snow all over England that week. For two nights it had drifted against the huge wheels of the Stirlings in scrolls ten feet high. The wind had partially swept it from the smooth fabric of fuselages as it fell and then frost had frozen what remained of it into uneven drifts of papery dust. In the mornings gangs of soldiers worked at the runways, clearing them to black-white roads edged with low walls of snow, and lorries drove backwards and forwards along them, taking away like huge blocks of salt the carved-out drifts. In two more days the thaw came and yellow pools of snow-water lay in the worn places of the runways. It froze a little again late at night, leaving a muddy skin of ice on pools that looked dangerous with the sunlight level and cold on them in the early morning. It wasn't dangerous really and the wheels of the Stirlings smashed easily through the ice, splintering it like the silver glass toys on a Christmas tree. Then in the daytime the pools thawed again and if you watched the take-off from the control tower through a pair of glasses you saw the snow-water sparkle up from the wheels like brushes of silver feathers.

And now, beyond the hazy coast of Holland, with its thin white trimming that grew less white in the twilight as we flew towards it, we could see what reports had already told us. There was snow all over Europe. The day was too advanced to see it clearly. All you could see was a great hazy field of cotton-wool that had fewer marks on it than a layer of cloud. Far ahead of us, south and south-west and east, it ceased even to be white. It became the misty, colourless distances of all Europe, and suddenly as I looked at it, for almost the last time before darkness hit it altogether, I thought of what it would be like to fly on, southward, to the places I had never seen, the places without flak, the places in sunshine, the places beyond the war and the snow. It was one of those detached ideas that you get when flying, or rather that get you: a light-headed idea that seems to belong to the upper air and is gone as soon as its futility has played with you.

For a few more minutes the trimming of coast lay dead below us and then, in a moment, was gone past us altogether. For just a few minutes longer the misty cotton-wool of the snow over Europe meant something, and then I looked and could see it no longer. Darkness seemed to have floated suddenly between the snow and the Stirling. What was below us was just negative. It was not snow, or land, or Europe. It was just the negative darkness that would flare any moment into hostility.

This darkness was to be ours for five hours or more. I was already cold and the aircraft was bumping like a goods train. The most violent bumps seemed to jerk a little more blood out of my feet. I remembered this sensation from other trips and now tried moving my toes in my boots. But the boots were too thick and my toes were already partially dead. This was my fifteenth trip as flight engineer but even now I could not get rid of two sensations that had recurred on all those trips since the very first: the feeling that I had no feet and the feeling, even more awful than that, that I had swallowed something horribly sour, like vinegar, which had now congealed between my chest and throat. I never thought of it as fear. I was always slightly scared, in a numb way, before the trips began, and before Christmas, before the snow fell, I had been more scared than hell on the Brest daylights. But now I only thought of this sourness as discomfort. It always did something to my power of speech. I always kept the inter-comm. mouthpiece ready, but I rarely used it. I could hear other voices over the inter-comm. but I rarely spoke, unless it was very necessary, in reply. It wasn't that I didn't want to speak, and it had little to do with the fact that Ellis, Captain of K42, did not encourage talking. I think I was scared that by speaking I might give the impression that I was scared. So I kept my mouth shut and let the sourness bump in my throat and pretended, as perhaps the other six of us pretended, that I was tough and taciturn and did not care.

"A lot of light muck on the port side, Skipper."

"O.K."

The voice of Osborne, from the rear turret, came over the inter-comm., the Northern accent sharp and cold and almost an order in itself. Ossy, from Newcastle, five feet six, with the lean Newcastle face and grey monkey-wrinkled eyes, was the youngest of us. In battle-dress the wads of pictures in his breast pockets gave him a sort of oblong bust. In his Mae West this bust became quite big and handsome, so that he looked out of proportion, like a pouter pigeon. We always kidded Ossy about giving suck. But in his Mae West there was no room for his photographs; so always, before a trip, Ossy took them out and put them in his flying boots, one in each leg. In one leg of his boots he also carried a revolver, and in the other an American machine spanner. No one knew quite what this spanner was for, except perhaps that it was just one of those things that air-crews begin to carry about with them as foolish incidentals and that in the end become as essential as your right arm. So

Ossy never came on trips except he had with him, in the legs of his boots, the things that mattered: the revolver, the spanner, and the pictures of a young girl, light-haired, print-frocked, pretty in a pale Northern way, taken in the usual back-garden attitudes on Tyneside. "She's a wizard kid," he said.

As for the spanner, if it was a talisman, I knew that Ed Walker, the second dickey, carried two rabbits' feet. You might have expected the devotion to a good-luck charm from Ossy, who anyway had the good sense to carry a spanner. But it surprised you that Winchester hadn't taught Ed Walker anything better than a belief in rabbits' feet. They were very ordinary rabbits' feet. The tendons had been neatly severed and the hair was quite neat and tidy and smooth. Ed kept them hidden under his shirts in a drawer in his bedroom and he didn't know that anyone knew they were there. I shared the room with him and one day when I opened the wrong drawer by mistake there were the rabbits' feet under the shirts, hidden as a boy might have hidden a packet of cigarettes from his father. Ed was very tall and slow-eyed and limp. He took a long time to dress himself and did not talk much. Between Winchester at eighteen and a Stirling at nineteen there wasn't much life to be filled in. He was so big that sometimes he looked lost; as if he had suddenly found himself grown up too quickly. And sometimes I used to think he didn't talk much solely for the reason that he hadn't much to say. But just because of that, and because of the rabbits' feet and the big lazy helplessness that went with them and because we could lie in bed and not talk much and yet say the right things when we did talk, we were fairly devoted.

Between the coast of Holland and the first really heavy German flak I always felt in a half-daze. I always felt my mind foreshorten its view. It was like travelling on a very long journey in a railway train. You didn't look forward to the ultimate destination, but only to the next station. In this way it did not seem so long. If it were night you could never tell exactly where you were, and sometimes you were suddenly surprised by the lights of a station.

We had no station lights: that was the only difference. We bumped on against the darkness. I don't know why I always

felt it was against the darkness, and not in it or through it.
Darkness on these long winter trips seemed to solidify. The
power we generated seemed to cut it. We had to cut it to get
through.

If we got through—but we did not say that except as a
joke. At prayer-meeting, in the intelligence room, before the
trips, the Wing Commander always liked that joke. "When
you come back—*if* you come back." But he was the only
one, I think, who did like it, and most of us had given up
laughing now. It might have been rather funnier if, for
instance, he had said he hoped we had taken cases of light
ale on board, or that we might get drunk on Horlicks tablets
and black coffee. Not that this would have been very funny.
And the funniest joke in the world, coming from him,
wouldn't have given us any more faith than we had.

Faith is a curious thing to talk about. You can't put your
hand on it, but there it is. And I think what we and that crew
had faith in was not jokes or beam-approach or navigation
or the kite itself, but Ellis.

"It's like a duck's arse back here," Ossy suddenly said.
"One minute I'm in bloody Switzerland and the next I'm up
in the North Sea."

We laughed over the inter-comm.

"It's your ten-ton spanner," Ellis said.

"What spanner, Skipper, what spanner?"

"Drop it overboard!"

"What spanner, what—"

"Go on, drop it. I can feel the weight of the bloody thing
from here. You're holding us back."

"There's flak coming up like Blackpool illuminations,
Skip. Honest, Skip. Take plenty of evasive action—"

"Just drop the bloody spanner, Ossy, and shut up."

We all laughed again over the inter-comm. There was a
long silence, and then Ossy's voice again, now very slow:

"Spanner gone."

We laughed again, but it was broken by the voice of Ellis.
"What about this Blackpool stuff?"

"It's all Blackpool stuff. Just like the Tower Ball-room on
a carnival night."

They were pumping it up all round us, heavy and light,

and for a few minutes it was fairly violent. We were slapped about inside the kite like a collection of loose tools in a case.

Then from the navigation seat came the voice of Mac, the big Canadian from Winnipeg, slow and sardonic:

"Keep the milk warm, Ossy dear. It's baby's feed time." And we laughed again.

After that, for a long time, none of us spoke again. I always noticed that we did not speak much until Ellis started the talk. The voice of Ellis was rather abrupt. The words were shot out and cut off like sections of metal ejected by a machine. I sometimes wondered what I was doing on these trips, in that kite, with Ellis, as flight engineer. He knew more about aero-engines generally, and about these aero-engines particularly, than I should ever know. If ever a man had a ground-crew devoted by the terror of knowledge it was Ellis.

We too were devoted by something of the same feeling. He was a small man of about thirty, a little younger than myself, with those large raw hands that mechanics sometimes have: the large, angular, metallic hands that seem to get their shape and power from the constant handling of tools. These hands, his voice, and finally his eyes were the most remarkable things about him. They were dark eyes that looked at you as impersonally as the lens of a camera. Before them you knew you had better display yourself as you were and not as you hoped you might be.

If Ed Walker had not begun to live, Ellis had lived enough for both of them. For so small a man it was extraordinary how far you had to look up to him, and I think perhaps we looked up at him because of the fullness of that life. A man like Ed would always be insular, clinging to the two neat rabbits' feet of English ideals. The sea, on which Ellis had served for five or six years before the war, had beaten the insularity out of him. It had given him the international quality of a piece of chromium. He was small but he gave out a feeling of compression. You had faith in him because time had tested the pressure his resistances could hold. He did not drink much: hardly at all. Most of us got pretty puce after bad trips, or good trips too if it comes to that, and sometimes people like Ossy got tearful in the bar of the

Grenadier and looked wearily into the eyes of strangers and said, "We bloody near got wrapped up. Lost as hell. Would have been if it hadn't been for the Skipper," and probably in the morning did not remember what they said.

But all of us knew that, and did remember. We knew too why Ellis did not drink. It was because of us. The sea, I think, had taught him something about the cold results of sobriety.

The flak was all the time fairly violent and now and then we dropped into pockets of muck that lifted the sourness acidly into my throat and dragged it down again through my stomach. It was always bad here. We were a good way over now and I remembered the met. reports at prayer-meeting: about seven-tenths over Germany and then clearing over the target. We had many bombers out that night and I hoped it would be clear.

Thinking of the weather, I went for a moment into one of those odd mesmeric dazes that you get on long trips, and thought of myself. I was the eldest of the crew: thirty, with a wife I did not live with now. I had been a successful under-manager in Birmingham and we had at one time a very nice villa on the outskirts. For some reason, I don't know why, we quarrelled a lot about little things like my not cleaning the bath after I'd used it, and the fact that my wife liked vinegar with salmon. We were both selfish in the same ways. We were like two beans that want to grow up the same pole and then strangle each other trying to do so. I had been glad of the war because it gave me the chance to break from her, and now flying had beaten some of the selfishness out of me. My self was no longer assertive. It had lost part of its identity, and I hoped the worst parts of its identity, through being part of the crew. It had done me good to become afraid of losing my skin, and my only trouble really was that I suffered badly from cold. I now could not feel my feet at all.

Suddenly I could not feel anything. Something hit us with a crack that seemed to lift us straight up as if we had been shot through a funnel. The shock tore me sideways. It flung me violently down and up and down again as if I had been a loose nut in a revolving cylinder.

173

II

"O.K., everybody?"

We had been shaken like that before, on other trips, but never with quite that violent upward force. I lay on the floor of the aircraft and said something in answer to Ellis's voice. I hadn't any idea what it was. I wasn't thinking of myself, but only, at that moment, of the aircraft. I felt the blow had belted us miles upward, like a rocket.

I staggered about a bit and felt a little dazed. It seemed after a few moments that everybody was O.K. I looked at Mac, huge face immobile over the navigator's table, pinning down his charts and papers even harder with a violent thumb. I looked at his table and it was almost level. It did not tilt much with the motion of the aircraft and I knew then we were flying in a straight line. I looked at Allison, the radio operator, and his eyes, framed in a white circle between the earphones, looked back at me. He did not look any paler than usual. He did not look more fixed, more vacant, or more eaten up by trouble than usual. That was just the way he always looked. There had been a kind of cancerous emptiness on his face ever since a blitz had killed his child.

I grinned at him and then the next moment was not thinking of what had happened. The kite was flying well and I heard Ellis's voice again.

"Must be getting near, Mac?"

"About ten minutes' flying time."

"O.K."

She bumped violently once or twice as they spoke and seemed to slide into troughs of muck. The sick lump of tension bumped about in my throat and down into my bowels and up again.

"If I see so much as a flea's eyelash I'll feel bloody lucky," Mac said.

He got up and began to grope his way towards the forward hatch. In those days the navigator did the bomb-aiming. Huge and ponderous and blown out, he looked in the dim light like the man in the adverts for Michelin tyres. I sat down at his table. I felt sick and my head ached. Once as a boy, I had had scarlet fever and my head, as the fever came on, seemed to grow enormous and heavy, many times too large for my body. Now it was the same. It seemed like a colossal lump of helpless pulp on my shoulders. The light above the table seemed to flicker and splinter against my eyes.

I knew suddenly what it was. I wasn't getting my oxygen. It scared me for a moment and then I knew it must have been the fall. I don't quite know what I did. I must have fumbled about with the connections for a time and succeeded in finding what was wrong at last.

I felt as if I began to filter slowly back into the aircraft. I came back with that awful mental unhappiness, split finally apart by relief, that you get as you struggle out of anaesthesia. I came back to hear the voices of Ellis and Mac, exchanging what I knew must be the instructions over the target. They seemed like disembodied voices. I tried to shake my brain into clarity. It seemed muddy and weak.

At last I got some sense into myself, but it was like exchanging one trouble for another. By the voices over the inter-comm., I knew that we had trouble. The weather was violent and sticky and Mac could not see. Something very dirty and unexpected had come up to change that serene met. forecast at prayer-meeting: clearing over the target. It was not clearing. We were in the middle of something violent, caught up by one of those sinister weather changes that make you hate wind and rain and ice with impotent stupidity.

"Try again, Skip? I can't see a bloody thing."

"O.K. Again."

Whether it cleared or not I never knew. Ellis took her in hand and it was something like driving a springless car down a mountain pass half blocked by the blast of rocks. We went in as steadily as that. The flak beat under the body of the aircraft and once or twice seemed to suck it aside. I held myself tense, throttling my whole body back. If all you needed was good insides and no capacity for thought I was only half equipped. I was not thinking, but my emotions had dissolved into my guts like water.

"Bombs gone!"

"O.K.," Ellis said. "Thank Christ for that."

A second later I felt the aircraft pull upwards, as if, bombless, she were suddenly more powerful than the weather. The force of that upward surge seemed to pull me together. It seemed to clean the heaving taste of oil and sickness out of my throat. I was glad too of the voice of Ellis, ejecting smoothly the repeated "O.K., everybody?" We rocked violently, but I did not mind it. Whatever came now must be, I thought, an anti-climax to that moment. We had been in twice and out again. It was all that mattered now.

III

After two days' digging the rescue squad found the body of Allison's child, untouched but dead, pinned down into a cavity by a fallen door; and then Allison himself, his clothes plastered white as a limeworker's from the dust of debris washed by rain, crawled into the ruins and carried out the child in his own arms. She was still in her nightdress and she must have died as she was, the door falling but not striking her, making the little protective cavity, like a triangular coffin, in which she lay until they found her. Allison walked out of the bombed house and then, not knowing what he was doing, began to walk up the street, still carrying the child. He must have walked quite a long way, and quite fast, before anyone could stop him. He did not know what he was doing. He vaguely remembered a policeman and he remembered another man who took the child out of his arms. His idea was to take the child to his wife, who lay in hospital with a crushed shoulder and who had been crying out for the baby constantly for two days. He had an idea that it might help her if she saw the face of the child again.

It was my job among other things to watch the dials of the various engine pressures on the panel before me and to switch over the fuel tanks as and when it became necessary. On me depended, to a large extent, the balance of the aircraft. Sometimes you got a tank hit and the business of transferring the weight of fuel from one wing to another needed skill. There had been records of flight engineers who, in situations of this kind, and by their skill, had really brought an aircraft home.

I had never done anything as important as that and as I sat watching the dials on the panel I was thinking of Allison. You could never tell by his calm, white face what Allison was thinking. After the bomb had destroyed his house and child he had been away from the station for a couple of weeks. His wife got slowly better. He went back to see her quite often, for some days at a time, during the next six months. During this time he had fits of mutinous depression in which he wrote long letters to the boys, myself among them. They were always the same letters: the story of the child. He had nothing else to say because, obviously, there was nothing else in his life. He would always go back, for ever, to that moment; the moment when he carried the child from the house and up the street, himself like a dead person walking, until someone stopped him and took the child away. When he came back to operations with us he never once spoke of this; and none of us ever spoke of it either. I tried to understand for a time what Allison felt. Then I gave it up. I should have been surprised if he had felt anything at all. All that could be felt, whether it was fear or terror or anger or the mutilation of everything normal in you to utter despair, must have already been felt by Allison. He was inoculated for ever against terror and despair.

"Hell, it's the bloodiest night you ever saw," Mac said.

"I could have told you that," Thompson said. The voice of the sergeant in the mid-upper turret came over the intercomm. "And, Skip, they'll have us in a bloody cone any minute."

"God, it's dirty," Mac said.

"They're heading for the straight," Ossy said. "Arse-end Charlie two lengths behind. Sergeant Thompson well up—"

"Stop nattering!" Ellis said.

We were hit a moment later. It was not so violent as the hit which had forced us upward, earlier, as in a funnel. It seemed like a colossal hand-clap. Terrific and shattering, it beat at us from both port and starboard sides. There was a moment as if you were in a vacuum. Then you were blown out of it. It was like the impact of an enormous and violent wave at sea.

I don't know what happened, but the next moment we were on fire. The flames made a noise like the hiss of a rocket before it leaves the ground. They shot with a slight explosive sound all along the port side of the fuselage, forward from where I sat. I yelled something through the inter-comm. and I heard Mac yelling too. I got hold of the fire extinguisher and began to work it madly. I remember the aircraft bumping so violently that it knocked my hands upward and I shot the extinguisher liquid on the roof. I fell down and got up again, still playing the extinguisher. Then I got the jet straight on to the flames and for a moment it transformed them into smoke, which began to fill the fuselage, so that we could not see. Then the flames shot up again. They blew outward suddenly and violently like the blow-back from a furnace. I felt them slap my face, scorching my eyeballs. Then I saw them shoot back and they ran fiercely up the window curtains. At that moment the extinguisher ran dry and I began to tear down the curtains with my bare hands, which were already numb with cold so that I could not feel the flames. I don't know quite what I did with those curtains. I must have beaten the flames out of them by banging them against my boots because I remember once looking down and seeing the sheepskin smouldering, and I remember how the idea of being on fire myself terrified me more than the idea of the plane itself being on fire.

Sometime before this the inter-comm. had gone and suddenly I saw Ellis, who until that moment could not have known much of what we were doing back there, open the door behind the pilot's seat. His face ejected itself and remained for a second transfixed, yellow beyond the smoke. I shall never forget it. I saw the mouth open and move, and I must have yelled something in reply before the door closed again. I had an awful feeling suddenly that Ellis had gone for ever. We were shut off, alone, with the fire, Mac and Allison and myself, and there was nothing Ellis could do.

All this time Allison sat there as if nothing was happening. You hear of wireless operators at sea, when the ship is sinking, having a kind of supernatural power of concentration. Allison had that concentration. Mac and I must have behaved like madmen. We hit the flames with the screwed-up curtains and with our bare hands and once I saw Mac press his huge Michelin body against the fuselage and kill the flames by pressure as he might have killed an insect on his back. The flames had a sort of maddening elasticity. It was like putting back the inner tube of a bicycle tyre. You pushed it back in one place and it leapt out again in another. Several times the aircraft rocked violently and we fell on the floor. When we got up again we fell against each other. All the time Allison sat there. And I knew that although it was amazing it was also right. He had to sit there. Somehow, if it killed us, we had to keep the flames from him. There was no room for three of us in the confined space of the fuselage, and it was the best thing that Allison should sit there, as if nothing had happened, clamped down by his earphones, as if in a world of his own. Allison was our salvation.

It was very hot by this time and suddenly I was very tired. I could not see very clearly. It was as if the blow-back of the flames had scorched the pupils of my eyes. They were terribly raw and painful, and the smoke seemed to soak into them like acid. I had no idea where we were. There were no voices in the inter-comm., but after a time the pilot's door opened and Ed Walker crawled back to Allison, with a written message. Allison read it and nodded. I tried to shout something at Ed, but I began to cough badly and it was useless. Then the flames broke out in two new places; on the port side, aft of where I had been sitting, and in the roof above my head. When I went to lift my hands to beat the flames they would not rise. It was like trying to lift the whole aircraft. I felt sick and the sickness ran weakly and coldly down the arteries of my arms and out of the fingers.

Then suddenly I made a great effort. I had been standing there helplessly for what seemed a long time. It could not have been more than a few seconds but it was like a gap of agony in a dream. I wanted to move but I could not move and so at last because I could not throw my hands against the flames I threw my whole body. I let it fall with outstretched arms against the fuselage and I felt the slight bounce of my Mae West as it hit the metal. I lay there for about a second, very tired. My head was limp against the hot metal of the fuselage and my eyes were crying from the acid of the smoke. Then I raised my head. I had come to the moment of not caring. The flames were burning my legs and I was too tired to beat them out again. I was going to burn and die and it did not matter.

Then I lifted my eyes. Shrapnel had torn a hole in the fuselage and I could just see at an angle through the gap. It was like looking out of a window and seeing out in the darkness the reflection of the fire in the room. It was only that this fire was magnified. It was like a huge level dish of flame. It was horizontal and the edges of it were torn to violent shreds in the night.

"Oh! Christ," I said. "Oh! Christ, Christ Jesus!"

I expected at any moment to see that burning wing tear past my face. It was fantastic to see it riding with us. It did not seem part of us. It was like an enormous orange and crimson torch sailing wildly through the darkness.

All the time I knew that it must split and break, that in a moment now we were at the end. And in some curious way the idea gave me strength. For the first time since the fire began I could think clearly. My hands and my mind were not tired. I thought of my helmet and took it off. The fire must have burnt a hole in the fuselage somewhere forward, for air was now blowing violently in, clearing a gulley through the smoke. I held my helmet and then swung it. The moment was very clear. The flames crawled like big yellow insects up the slope of the fuselage and I began to hit them, with a sort of delirious and final calm, with the helmet. At the same time I saw the faces of Mac and Allison. Mac too must have known about the fire on the wing. His eyes were big and protuberant with desperation. But Allison still sat there as if nothing had happened; thin, pale, his head manacled by the earphones.

Then something happened. It was Ed Walker, coming in through the pilot's door with a message. I saw him go to Allison and again I saw Allison nod his head. Then he beckoned us and we went to Allison's seat. Leaning over, we read the message. "Over the sea. Take up ditching stations. Stand by for landing." We were coming down.

I must have put my helmet back on my head. I must have strapped it quite carefully in the few seconds' interval between reading the message and beginning to haul out the dinghy. Then Ed Walker came back with Ossy, the rear-gunner, and then the mid-upper gunner climbed down. The five of us stood there, braced for about a minute. The fuselage was still burning and through the window the flat plate of flame along the wing had thickened and broadened and looked more fantastic than ever.

I stood braced and ready with the axe. I no longer felt tired and I knew that I might have to hit the door, if it jammed, with all the strength I had. As we came down, throttled back, but the speed violent still, I drew in my insides and held them so taut that they seemed to tie themselves in a single knot of pain.

Next moment we hit the water. And in that moment, as the violence of the impact lifted all of us upward, I looked at Ossy. It was one of those silly moments that remained with me, clear and alive, long after the more confused moments of terror.

Ossy too was clenching something tightly in his hand. It was the spanner.

IV

K42 went down almost immediately, and except for a second or two when she was caught up in the light of her own fire, we never saw her again. I heard the port wing split with a crack before she went down, and I heard the explosive hiss of the sea beating over the flames. I could smell too the smell of fire and steam, dirty and hot and acid, blown at us on the wind. It remained in my mouth, sharp with the sourness of the sea-water, for a long time.

The next thing I knew was that we were in the dinghy. It was floating; it was right side up; and we were all there. I never knew at all how it happened. It was like a moment when, in a London raid, I had dived under a seat on a railway station. One moment I was standing waiting for the train; the next I was lying under the seat, my head under my arms, with a soldier and a girl. When I finally got up and looked under the seat it did not seem that there was room under it for a dog.

"Everybody O.K.?" Ellis said. "I can't see you. Better answer your names."

"I got a torch," Mac said.

"O.K. Let's have a look at you."

He shone the torch in our faces. The light burnt my eyes when I looked up.

"O.K. Everybody feel all right?"

"No, sir," Ossy said. "I'm bloody wet."

We all laughed with extra heartiness at that.

"What was the last contact with base?"

"Half an hour before we hit the drink," Allison said.

"You think they got you?"

"They were getting me then," Allison said. "But afterwards we were off course. The transmitter was u.s. after the fix."

"All right," Ellis said. "And listen to me." He shone the torch on his wrist. "It's now eleven ten. I'm going to call out the time every half-hour."

The torch went out. It seemed darker than ever. The dinghy rocked on the sea.

"Remember what the wind was, Mac?"

"She was north north-east," Mac said. "About thirty on the ground."

"Any idea where we should be?"

"We were on course until that bloody fire started. But Jesus, you did some evasive action after that. Christ knows where we went."

"We ought to be in the North Sea somewhere, just north-west of Holland."

"I guess so," said Mac.

"North north-east—that might blow us down-Channel."

"In time it might blow us to Canada," Mac said.

"As soon as it gets light we can get the direction of the wind," Ellis said. "We'll use the compass and then you'll all paddle like hell."

I sat there and did not say anything. I knew now that my hands were burnt, but I did not know how badly. I tried putting them in my pockets, but with the rocking of the dinghy I could not balance myself. The pain of my hands all that night was my chief concern. The pain of my eyes, which were scorched too, did not seem so bad. I could shut them against the wind, and for long intervals I did so, riding on the dinghy blindly, the swell of the waves magnified because I could not see. It was better to close my eyes. If I did so the wind, cold and steady but not really strong, could not reach the raw eyeballs. The sea-spray could not hit them and pain them any more.

But I could not shut my hands. Fire seemed to have destroyed the reflex action of the muscles. The fingers stood straight out. It was not so much the pain of burning as the pain of a paralysis in which the nerves had been stripped raw. I had to hold them in one position. In whatever way my body moved my hands remained outstretched and stiff. When the sea broke over the dinghy, as it did at the most unexpected moments, the spray splashed my hands and the salt was like acid on the burns and I could not dry it off. I had to sit there until the wind dried it for me. And then it was as if the wind was freezing every spit of spray into a flake of ice and that the flakes were burning my hands all over again.

I sat there all night, facing the wind. Every half-hour Ellis gave out the time. He said nothing about rations or about the rum. From this I gathered that he was not hopeful about our position. It seemed to mean that he expected us to be a long time in the dinghy and that we must apportion rations for two, three, or perhaps four days. I had noticed too that all through the period of snow, for the last week, the wind rose steadily with the sun. By mid-afternoon, on land, it blew at forty or fifty miles an hour, raising white frozen dust in savage little clouds on the runways. Then it dropped with the sun. So if in the morning the wind strengthened we should, I thought, have a hard job to paddle crossways against it; which was our way to England. We should drift towards the Channel, into the Straits, and then down Channel. Nothing could stop us. The wind would be strongest when we could paddle best, and weakest when we could not steer well. I saw that we might drift for days and end up, even if we were lucky, far down the French coast, certainly not east of Cherbourg. I did not see how we could reach England.

Perhaps it did me good to think like this. I know that afterwards Ellis thought much like it; except that he had a worse fear—that we might be so near the coast of Europe that, the night before we could realize our position, we might be blown into the shore of Germany or Holland. It was at least better than thinking like Ossy, who seemed so sure he would be in England in the morning and in Newcastle, on crash leave, in the afternoon.

And to think of this kept me from thinking of my hands. My mind, thinking of the possibility of future difficulties, went ahead of my pain. All night, too, there was little danger from the sea. It was very cold but the dinghy rode easily, if rather sluggishly, in the water. Our clothes were very wet and I could feel the water slapping about my boots in the well of the dinghy. We simply rode blindly in the darkness, without direction, under a sky completely without stars and on a sea completely without noise except for the flat slapping of waves on the rubber curve of the dinghy.

After a time I managed to bandage my hands very roughly with my handkerchief. The handkerchief was in my left trousers-pocket. I could not stand up or, in the confined space of the well that was full of feet, move my leg more than a few inches. But at last I straightened my thigh downward a little, and then my left hand downward against my thigh. The pain of touching the fabric filled my mouth with sickness. It was like pushing your hand into fire. When I pushed my hand still further down the sickness dried in my mouth and the roof of it and my tongue were dry and contracted, as if with alum. Then I pushed my hand further down. I could just feel the handkerchief between the tips of my fingers. I drew it out very slowly. The opening of the pocket, chafing against my hand, seemed to take off the flesh. The raw pain seemed to split my hand and long afterwards, when my hands were covered by the handkerchief and warm and almost painless, my head was cold with the awful sweat of pain.

I sat like that for the rest of the night, my hands roughly bound together.

V

We were all quite cheerful in the morning. The sky in the east was split into flat yellow bars of wintry light. As they fell on the yellow fabric of the dinghy it looked big and safe

and friendly. The wind was not strong and the air no colder.
The sea was everywhere the colour of dirty ice.

Ellis then told us what our position was.

"I am dividing the rations for three days," he said. I knew
afterwards that this was not true. He was reckoning on their
lasting for six days. "We eat in the morning. You get a tot of
rum at midday. Then a biscuit at night. That's all you'll
get."

We did not say anything.

"Now we paddle in turns, two at a time, fifteen minutes
each. If the wind is still north north-east it means steering at
right angles across it. We can soon check the wind when the
sun comes up. It ought to come almost behind the sun. It
means paddling almost north. The risk is that we'll bloody
well go down-Channel and never get back."

None of us said anything again.

"I'll dish the rations out and then we'll start. We'll start
with a drop of rum now, because it's the first time. Then
Ossy and Ed start paddling; then Mac and Ally; then
Thompson and—what's the matter with your hands?" he
said to me.

"Burnt a bit," I said.

"Can you hold anything?"

"They won't reflex or anything," I said. "But my wrists
are all right. I could hold the paddle with my wrists."

"Don't talk cock!" he said.

"I can't sit here doing nothing," I said.

"O.K.," he said, "you can call out the time. Every hour
now. And anyway it'll take us an hour to bandage those
hands."

Ossy and Ed started paddling. They were fresh and
paddled rather raggedly at first, over-eager, one long-armed
and one short so that the dinghy rocked.

"Take it steady," Ellis said. "Keep the sun on your right
cheek. Take long strokes. You've got all day."

"Not if I know it," Ossy said. "I got crash-leave coming,
so I'll catch the midnight to Newcastle."

"You've got damn all coming if you don't keep your
mouth shut. Do you want your guts full of cold air?"

Ellis got out his first-aid pack and peeled off the adhesive tape. He had changed places with Thompson and was sitting next to me.

"What did you do?" he said. "Try to fry yourself?"

"I dropped my gloves," I said.

"Take it easy," he said. "I'll take the handkerchief off."

He took off the handkerchief and for some moments I could not move my hands. The air seemed to burn again the shining swollen blisters. I sat in a vacuum of pain. Oh! Christ, I thought. Oh, Jesus, Jesus! I fixed my eyes on the horizon and held them there, blind to everything except the rising and falling line below the faint yellow bars of sun. I held my hands raw in the cold air and the wind savagely drove white-hot needles of agony down my fingers. Jesus, I thought, please, Jesus. I knew I could not bear it any more and then I did bear it. The pain came in waves that rose and fell with the motion of the dinghy. The waves swung me sickeningly up and down, my hands part of me for one second and then no longer part of me, the pain stretching away and then driving back like hot needles into my naked flesh.

I became aware after a time of a change of colour in the sea. This colour travelled slowly before my eyes and spewed violently into the dinghy. It was bright violet. I realized that it seemed one moment part of the sea and one moment part of the dinghy because it was, in reality, all over my hands. The motion of the dinghy raised it to the line of sea and spewed it down into the yellow wall of fabric.

I was not fully aware of what was happening now. I knew that the violet colour was the colour of the gentian ointment Ellis was squeezing on my hands; I knew that the pure whiteness that covered it was the white of bandage. For brief moments my mind was awake and fixed. Then violet and white and yellow and the grey of the sea were confused together. They suddenly became black and the blackness covered me.

When I could look at the sea again and not see those violent changes of colour the sun was well above the horizon and Mac and Allison were paddling. I did not then know they were paddling for the second time. I held my hands straight out, the wrists on my knees, and stared at the sea. It was roughened with tiny waves like frosted glass. I did not speak for a long time and the men in the dinghy did not speak to me. There was no pain in my hands now. And in my mind the only pain was the level negative pain of relief, the pain after pain, that had no violence or change.

I must have sat there all morning, not speaking. We might have drifted into the coast and I shouldn't have known it. I watched the sun clear itself of the low cloud lying above the sea, and then the sky itself clear slowly about the sun. It became a pale wintry blue and as the sun rose the sea was smoothed down, until it was like clean rough ice as far as you could see.

It must have been about midday that I was troubled with the idea that I ought to paddle. From watching the sea I found myself watching the faces of the others. They looked tired in the sun. I realized that I had been sitting there all morning, doing nothing. I did not know till afterwards that I had called out the time, from the watch on my wrist, every hour.

But now I wanted to paddle. I had to paddle. I had to pull my weight. It seemed agonizing and stupid to sit there, not moving or speaking, but only watching with sore and half-dazed eyes that enormous empty expanse of sea and sky. I had to do something to break the level pain of that monotony.

Thinking this, I must have tried to stand up.

"Sit down, you bloody fool! Sit down!" Ellis yelled. "Sit down!"

The words did not hurt me. I must have obeyed automatically, not knowing it. But in the second that Ellis shouted I was myself again. The stupefaction of pain was broken. For the first time since daybreak I looked at the men about me. They ceased being anonymous. I really saw their faces. They were no longer brown-yellow shapes, vague parts of the greater yellow shape of the dinghy. They were the men I knew, and I was consciously and fully with them, alive again.

"You feel better?" Ellis said.

"I'm all right."

"I gave you a shot," he said.

187

"I'm all right. I could paddle."

"You could bloody hell," he said.

"I could do something," I said. "I want to do something."

"O.K. Keep a look-out. Bawl as soon as you see anything that looks like a kite or a sail."

From that moment I felt better. I could not use my hands, but I had something on which to use my eyes. The situation in the morning had seemed bad. Now I turned it round. There was nothing so bad that it couldn't be worse. Supposing my eyes had been burnt out, and not my hands? I felt relieved and grateful and really quite hopeful now.

At one o'clock exactly we had a small tot of rum. The wind had risen, as I thought it would with the sun. But there was no cloud and no danger, that afternoon, of snow. Visibility was down to two or three miles and in the far distance there was a slight colourless haze on the face of the sea. But it was, as far as you could tell, good flying weather.

"So," as Ellis said, "there is a chance of a patrol. The vis. isn't improving, but it ought to be good enough. It all depends anyway on the next two hours."

No one paddled as we drank the rum. We rested for ten minutes. Then Ossy and Ed began paddling again. Helped by the rest, the rum, and the fact that the sun was so clear and bright on the water, we all felt much more hopeful. Occasionally a little water swilled over into the dinghy, but the next moment Allison, calm and methodical, bailed it out again with his hands.

I kept watching the sea and the sky. At two o'clock I called out the time. The hour seemed to have gone very quickly. I realized that we had one more hour in which we could hope to be seen by an aircraft; only two in which we could hope, even remotely, to be picked up. But I was not depressed. I do not think any of us were depressed. It was good that we were together, dependent, as we always had been, on each other. And we were so far only looking forward, not backward. We had no disappointment to feed on, but only the full hope of the afternoon. None of us knew that Ellis had already prepared himself, as early as one o'clock, for another night in the dinghy.

It must have been about half-past two when Allison shouted. He began waving his hands, too. It was the most excitable Allison I had ever seen, his hands waving, and his head thrown backward in the sun.

"You see it?" he shouted. "You see it?"

I saw the kite coming from north-westwards, about right angles to the sun. It was black and small, and flying at about six thousand.

"It's a single-engine job," Ossy said.

"A Spit," Thompson said.

She came towards us level and straight, no deviating at all. I felt the excitement pump into my throat. She seemed to be about a mile or two away and was coming fast. It was not like the approach of a ship. In a few seconds she would pass over us; she would go straight on or turn. It would be all over in a few seconds. "Come on, baby," Mac said. "For Pete's sake don't you know you got too much altitude? Come on, baby," he whispered, "blast and damn you, come on."

We had ceased paddling. The dinghy rocked slowly up and down. As the Spitfire came dead over us our seven faces must have looked to its pilot, if he had seen us at all, like seven empty white plates on the rim of a yellow table. They must have looked for one second like this before they tilted slowly down, and then finally upside down as we stared at our feet in the well of the dinghy.

"He'll be back," Ossy said. "He's bound to come back."

None of us spoke in answer, and it was some time after I heard the last sound of the plane that Mac and Allison began paddling again.

VI

The plane did not come back and the face of the sea began to darken about four o'clock. From the colour of slate on the western horizon the sunset rose through dirty orange to cold pale green above. The wind had almost dropped with the sun and except for the slap of the paddles hitting the water there was no sound.

Soon Ellis ordered the paddling to cease altogether. Then we sat for about half an hour between light and darkness, the dinghy rocking sluggishly up and down, and ate our evening meal.

"Flying Officer X" (H. E. Bates)

To each of us Ellis rationed out one biscuit and one piece, about two inches square, of plain chocolate. I could not hold either the biscuit or the chocolate in my hands, which Ellis had covered with long white muffs of bandage. Ellis therefore held them for me, giving me first a bite of chocolate, then a bite of the biscuit. I ate these very slowly, and in between the mouthfuls Ellis did something to my hands. "If she comes rough in the night you may get them wet," he said.

In the morning Ellis had saved the fabric of the first-aid pack and the adhesive tape that bound the biscuit tin. Now he undid another pack and put the bandages and the ointments and the lint inside his Mae West. Then with the two pieces of fabric he made bags for my hands. I put my hands into these bags and Ellis bound them about my wrists with the adhesive tape. It was a very neat job and I felt like a boxer.

"Now we'll work the night like we did the paddling," he said. "We'll split it into one-hour watches with two on a watch."

He gave me the last of the chocolate before he went on speaking. It clung to the roof of my mouth and I felt very thirsty. Below the taste of the chocolate there was still a faint taste, dry and acrid, of the burning plane.

"Ed and Ossy begin from five o'clock. Then Ally and Mac. Then Thompson and myself."

"What about me?" I said. "I'm all right."

"You've got your work cut out with your hands," he said.

"I'm O.K.," I said.

"Look after your hands," he said. "And don't go to sleep. You're liable to get bounced off this thing before the night's gone."

You did not argue with Ellis when the tone of his voice was final. Now it was very final and without answering I sat watching the western sky. It was colourless and clear now, with the first small stars, quite white, beginning to shine in the darker space about the sunset. I don't know how the others felt about these stars or if they noticed them at all, but they gave me a sense of comfort. I was determined not to be downcast. I was even determined not to be hopeful.

My hands did not seem very bad now and I felt no colder than I had always been. I knew we should not be picked up that night; or even perhaps the next day. So as darkness came on and the stars increased until they were shining so brightly that I could see the reflection of the largest of them brokenly tossed like bits of phosphorescence in the sea, I did as I had always done on a long trip to Germany. I foreshortened the range of my thoughts. I determined not to think beyond the next hour, when the watch would be changed.

Being in that dinghy, that night, not knowing where we were or where we were going, all of us a little scared but all of us too scared to show it, was rather like having an operation. It smoothed the complications of your life completely. Before the operation the complication from all sorts of causes, small and large, income tax, unanswered letters, people you hated, people who hurt you, bills, something your wife said about your behaviour, seemed sometimes to get your life into an awful mess. Many things looked like small catastrophes. It was a catastrophe if you were late at the office, or if you couldn't pay a bill. Then suddenly you had to have your operation. The little catastrophes were cancelled out. All your life up to the moment of lying on the stretcher dissolved away, smoothed and empty of all its futilities and little fears. All that mattered was that you came through.

My attitude on the dinghy that night became like that. Before the moment we had taken off, now more than a day ago, and had flown out towards the snows of Europe, there was little of my life that seemed to matter. You hear of people cast away in open boats who dream sadly of their loved ones at home. But I didn't dream of anyone. I felt detached and in a way free. The trouble with my wife— whether we could make a go of it or whether we really hated each other or whether it was simply the strain of the war— no longer mattered. All my life was centred into a yellow circle floating without a direction on a dark sea.

It must have been about midnight when we saw, in what we thought was the east, light fires breaking the sky in horizon level. They were orange in colour and intermittent, like stabs of Morse. We knew that it was light flak somewhere on a coast, but which coast didn't really trouble us. The light of that fire, too far away to be heard or reflected in the dark sea, comforted us enormously.

We watched it for more than two hours before it died away. Looking up from the place where the fire had been and into the sky itself, I realized that the stars had gone. I remember how the sudden absence of all light, first the far-off flak, then the stars, produced an effect of awful loneliness. It must then have been about three o'clock. During the time we were watching the flak we had talked a little, talking of where we thought it was. Now, one by one, we gave up talking. Even Ossy gave up talking, and once again there was no sound except the slapping of the sea against the dinghy.

But about an hour later there was a new sound. It was the sound of the wind rising and skimming viciously off the face of the sea, slicing up glassy splinters of spray. And there was now a new feeling in the air with the rising of the wind.

It was the feeling of ice in the air.

VII

When day broke, about eight o'clock, we were all very cold. Our beards stood out from our faces and under the bristles the skin was shrunk. Mac, who was very big, looked least cold of all; but the face of Allison, thin and quite bloodless, had something of the grey-whiteness of broken edges of foam that split into parallel bars the whole face of the sea. This grey-whiteness made Allison's eyes almost black and they sank deep into his head. In the same way the sea between the bars of foam had a glassy blackness too.

The wind was blowing at about forty miles an hour and driving us fairly fast before it. The sky was a grey mass of ten-tenths cloud, so thick that it never seemed to move in the wind. Because there was no sun I could not tell if the wind had changed. I knew only that it drove at your face with an edge of raw ice that seemed to split the skin away.

Because of this coldness Ellis changed his plans.

"It's rum now and something to eat at midday. Instead of the other way round."

As we each took a tot of rum Ellis went on talking.

"We'll paddle as we did yesterday. But it's too bloody cold to sit still when you're not paddling. So you'll all do exercises to keep warm. Chest-slapping and knee-slapping and any other damn thing. It's going to get colder and you've got to keep your circulation."

He now gave us, after the rum, a Horlicks tablet each.

"And now any suggestions?"

"It's a sure bloody thing we won't get to Newcastle at this rate," Ossy said.

"You're a genius," Ellis said.

"Couldn't we fix a sail, Skip?" Ossy said. "Rip up a parachute, or even use a whole chute?"

"How are you going to hold your sail?" Ellis said. "With hay-rakes or something?"

All of us except Allison made suggestions, but they were not very good. Allison alone did not speak. He was always quiet, but now he seemed inwardly quiet. He had scarcely any flesh on his face and his lips were blue as if bruised with cold.

"O.K., then," Ellis said. "We carry on as we did yesterday. Ossy and Ed start paddling. The rest do exercises. How are your hands?" he said to me.

"O.K.," I said. I could not feel them except in moments when they seemed to burn again with far-off pain.

"All right," he said. "Time us again. A quarter of an hour paddling. And if the sea gets worse there'll have to be relays of bailing too."

When Ossy and Ed started paddling I saw why Ellis had talked of bailing. The dinghy moved fast and irregularly; it was hard to synchronize the motions of the two paddles when the sea was rough. We were very buoyant on the sharp waves and sometimes the crests hit us sideways, rocking us violently. We began to ship water. It slapped about in the well of the dinghy among our seven pairs of feet. It hit us in the more violent moments on the thighs and even as far up as our waists. We were so cold that the waves of spray did not shock us and except when they hit our faces we did not feel them. Nevertheless I began to be very glad of the covers Ellis had put on my hands.

Soon all of us were doing something: Ossy and Ed paddling; Thompson and Ellis bailing out the water, Thompson with a biscuit tin, Ellis with a small tobacco tin. They threw the water forward with the wind. While these four were working Mac and Allison did exercises, beating their knees and chests with their hands. Mac still looked very like the Michelin tyre advertisement, huge, clumsy, unsinkable. To him the exercises were a great joke. He beat his knees in dance time, drumming his hands on them. It kept all of us except Allison in good spirits. But I began to feel more and more that Allison was not there with us. He slapped his knees and chest with his hands, trying to keep time with Mac, but there was no change in his face. It remained vacant and deathly; the dark eyes seemed driven even deeper into the head. It began to look more and more like a face in which something had killed the capacity for feeling.

We went on like this all morning, changing about, two exercising, two paddling, two bailing out. The wind did not rise much and sometimes there were moments when it combed the sea flat and dark. The waves, short and unbroken for a few moments, then looked even more ominous. Then with a frisk of the wind they rose into fresh bars of foam.

It was about midday when I saw the face of the sea combed down into that level darkness for a longer time than usual. The darkness travelled across it from the east, thickening as it came. Then as I watched, it became lighter. It became grey and vaporous, and then for a time grey and solid. This greyness stood for a moment a mile or two away from us, on the sea, and then the wind seemed to fan it to pieces. These millions of little pieces became white and skimmed rapidly over the dark water, and in a moment we could not see for snow.

The first thing the snow did was to shut out the vastness of the empty sea. It closed round us, and we were blinded. The area of visible sea was so small that we might have been on a pond. In a way it was comforting.

Those who were paddling went on paddling and those who were bailing went on bailing the now snow-thickened water. We did not speak much. The snow came flat across the sea and when you opened your mouth it drove into it. I bent my head against it and watched the snow covering my hands. For the last hour they had begun to feel jumpy and swollen and God knew what state they were in.

It went on snowing like that for more than an hour, the flakes, big and wet and transparent as they fell. They covered the outer curve of the dinghy, on the windward side, with a thick wet crust of white. They covered our bent backs in the same way, so that we looked as if we were wearing white furs down to our waists, and they thickened to a yellow colour the sloppy water in the dinghy.

All the time Allison was the only one who sat upright. At first I thought he was being clever; because he did not bend his back the snow collected only on his shoulders. That seemed a good idea. Then, whenever I looked up at him, I was struck by the fact that whether he was paddling or bailing his attitude was the same. He sat stiff, bolt upright, staring through the snow. His hands plunged down at his side automatically, digging a paddle into the water, or scooping the water out of the dinghy and bailing it away. His eyes, reflecting the snow, were not dark. They were cold and colourless. He looked terribly thin and terribly tired, and yet not aware of being tired. I felt he had simply got into an automatic state, working against the sea and the snow, and that he did not really know what he was doing. Still more I felt that he did not care.

I knew the rest of us cared very much. After the first comfortable shut-in feeling of the snow had passed we felt desperate. I hated the snow now more than the sea. It shut out all hope that Air-Sea Rescue would ever see us now. I knew that it might snow all day and I knew that after it, towards sunset, it would freeze. If it snowed all day, killing all chances of rescue, and then froze all night, we should be in a terrible state the next morning, our third day.

The thought of this depressed me, for a time, very much. It was now about half-past twelve. The time seemed crucial. Unless it stopped snowing very soon, so that coastal stations could send out patrols in the early afternoon, we must face another night in the dinghy. I knew that all of us, with the exception of Allison, felt this. We were very tired and cold and stiff from not stretching our bodies, and the snow, whirling and thick and wet, seemed to tangle us up into a circle from which we were never going to get out.

In such moments as this Ellis did the right thing. He had driven us rather hard all morning, getting us out of small depressed moments by saying: "Come on, we've got to keep going. Come on," or with a dry joke, "No fish and chips for Ossy if we don't keep going. It's tough tit for Ossy if he doesn't get his fish and chips." He knew just when he could drive us no longer. Now he let up.

"O.K.," he said. "Give it a rest."

"Holy Moses," Mac said. "I used to love snow. Honest, I used to love the bloody stuff."

Even Mac looked tired. The snow had collected on his big head, giving him the look of an old man with white hair.

"Jesus," he said. "I'll never feel the same way about snow again."

"What time do you make it?" Ellis said to me.

"Twelve forty-five coming up to six—now," I said.

"O.K.," he said. "Set your watches."

While we set our watches, synchronizing them, calling out the figures, Ellis got out the rum, the chocolate and the biscuits. Afterwards I looked back and knew it was not so much the food, as Ellis's order to synchronize the watches, that made me feel better at that moment. Time was our link with the outside world. From setting our watches together we got a sense of unity.

Ellis gave out the chocolate and the biscuits, in the same ration as before.

"Everybody all right? Ossy?"

"I'm a bloody snowball, if that's anything," Ossy said.

"Good old Ossy."

Ellis looked at each of us in turn. "All right, Ally?" he said.

Allison nodded. He still sat bolt upright and he still did not speak.

Ellis did not speak either until it was time to tot out the rum. He used the silver bottom of an ordinary pocket-flask for the rum and this, about a third full, was our ration. He always left himself till last, but this time he did not drink. "God, I always hate the stuff. It tastes like warm rubber," he said.

"Drink it, Ally," he said.

Allison held out his hand. I could see that the fingers were so cold that, like my own after the burning, they would not flex. I saw Ellis bend them and fold them, like a baby's, over the tot. I saw the hand remained outstretched, stiff in the falling snow, until finally Allison raised it slowly to his lips. I think we all expected to see that cup fall out of Allison's hands, and we were all relieved and glad when at last Ellis reached over and took it away.

As we sat there, rocking up and down, there was a slight lessening of the snow. Through the thinning flakes we could see, soon, a little more of the sea. No sooner could I see more of it than I hated it more. I hated the long troughs and the barbarous slits of foam between them and the snow driving, curling and then flat, like white tracer above. I hated the ugliness and emptiness of it and above all the fact of its being there.

VIII

That afternoon a strange thing happened. By two o'clock the snow grew thinner and drew back into a grey mist that receded over the face of the sea. As it cleared away altogether the sky cleared too, breaking in a southerly direction to light patches of watery yellow which spread under the wind and became spaces of bright blue. Across these spaces the sun poured in musty shafts and the inner edges of cloud were whiter than the snow had been. Far off, below them, we saw pools of light on the sea.

We were now paddling roughly in a straight line away from the sun. We were all, with the exception of Allison, quite cheerful. There was something tremendously hopeful about this breaking up of the sky after snow.

Allison alone sat there as if nothing had happened. He had not spoken since morning. He still looked terribly cold and tired and yet as if he did not know he was tired.

Suddenly he spoke.

"Very lights," he said.

"Hell!" Mac said. "Where?"

"Look," Allison said.

He was pointing straight before us. The sky had not broken much to the north and the cloud there was very low.

"I don't see a bloody thing," Mac said.

"Christ, if it is," Ossy said. "Christ, if it is."

We were all very excited. The paddling and bailing stopped, and we rocked in the water.

"Where did you see this?" Ellis said.

"There," Allison said. He was still pointing, but his eyes were as empty as they had always been.

"You're sure they were Very lights?"

"I saw them."

"How long were they burning?"

"They just lit up and went out."

"But where? Where exactly?"

"You see the dark bit of cloud under there? They came out of that."

We all looked at that point for a long time. I stared until my eyeballs seemed to smart with hot smoke again.

"Ally, boy," Mac said. "You must have awful good eyesight."

"What would Very lights be doing at this time of day?" Ed said.

"I can't think," Ellis said. "Probably Air-Sea Rescue. It's possible. They'd always be looking."

"A kite wouldn't be dropping them unless it saw something."

"It might. Funny things happen."

"Hell they do," Mac said.

"You couldn't expect even Air-Sea Rescue to see us in this muck," I said.

Ossy and Ed began to paddle again. As we went forward we still kept our eyes on the dark patch of cloud, but nothing happened. Nor did Allison speak again; nor had any of us the heart to say we thought him mistaken.

For a time we hadn't the heart for much at all. The situation in the dinghy now looked messy and discouraging. The melting snow was sloppy in the bottom, a dirty yellow colour; there were too many feet. It was still very cold and when we tried to do exercises—I could only beat my elbows against my sides—we knocked clumsily against each other. We had done that before, in the morning, and once or twice it had seemed mildly funny. Now it was more irritating than the snow, the cold and the disappointment of Allison's false alarm.

All this time the sky was breaking up. In the west and south, through wide blue lakes of cloud, white shafts of sun fell as bright and cold as chromium on the sea. These shiny edges of sunlight sometimes produced a hallucination. They looked in the distances like very white cliffs, jagged and unbelievably real. Staring at them, it was easy to understand why Allison had seen a Very light in a cloud.

So we paddled until three o'clock; and I knew it was hopeless. We had another hour of daylight: the worst of the day. The sea, with the sun breaking on it, looked terribly empty; but with the darkness on it we should at least have nothing to look for. Ellis, as always, was very good at this moment. His face was red and fresh and his eyes, bright blue, did not look very tired. He had managed somehow to keep neater than the rest of us. You felt he had kept back enormous reserves of energy and hope and that he hadn't even begun to think of the worst. And now he suddenly urged us to sing. "Come on, a sing-song before tea, chaps," he said. "Come on."

So we began singing. We first sang "Shenandoah" and "Billy Boy." Then we sang other songs, bits of jazz, and "Daisy, Daisy," and then we came back to "Shenandoah." We sang low and easy and there was no resonance about it because of the wind. But it was a good thing to sing because you could sing the disappointment out of yourself and it kept you from thinking. We must have gone on singing for nearly an hour and the only one of us who didn't sing much was Allison. From time to time I saw his mouth moving. It simply moved up and down, rather slowly, erratically, out of tune. Whatever he was singing did not belong to us. He was very pale and the cavity of his mouth looked blue and his eyes were distant and dark as if they were still staring at those Very lights in the distant cloud.

"Flying Officer X" (H. E. Bates)

It must have been about four o'clock when he fell into the dinghy. The sea pitched us upward and Allison fell forward on his face. He fell loosely and his head struck the feet crowded in the bottom of the dinghy, which rocked violently with the fall.

Ellis and Mac pulled him upright again. His face was dirty with snow water and his eyes were wide open. Ellis began to rub his hands. The veins on the back of them were big and blue, the colour of his lips, and he began to make a choking noise in his throat. His body was awkward and heavy in the well of the dinghy and it was hard to prevent him from slipping down again. The dinghy rocked badly and I thought we might capsize.

"Put him between my knees," I said. "I can hold him like that."

They propped him up and I locked his body with my knees, keeping it from falling. I held my bandaged hands against his face and he made a little bubbling noise with his mouth, not loud, but as if he was going to be gently sick.

As I held him like that and as we bumped about in the dinghy, badly balanced, swinging and rocking like one of those crazy boats at a fun fair, I looked at the sky.

The sun had suddenly gone down. Already above the sunset the sky was clear and green and I could feel the frost in the air.

IX

I held Allison's body with my knees all that night and his face with my damaged hands. My legs are long and gradually the feeling went out of them. But once I had got into that position it was too complicated to move.

As darkness came down ice began to form like thin rough glass on the outer sides of the dinghy, where the snow had first settled and thawed. Frost seemed to tighten up the rubber, which cracked off the ice as it moved with the waves. It was bitterly cold, very clear and brittle, without much wind. The sky was very clear too and there was a splintering brightness in the stars.

At intervals of about an hour we gave Allison drinks of rum. At these moments he did not speak. He would make the gentle, bubbling noise with his lips and then leave his mouth open, so that a little of the rum ran out again. I would shut his mouth with my hand. Sometimes I put my unbandaged wrists on his face and it was as cold as stone.

All that night, in between these times, I thought a lot. The cold seemed to clear my brain. All the feeling had gone from my hands and from my legs and thighs, and my head seemed almost the only part of me alive. For the first time I thought of what might be happening, or what might yet happen, at home. I thought of base, where they would be wondering about us. I could see the mess ante-room: the long cream room with the fire at one end, the pictures of Stirlings on the walls, the chaps playing cards, someone drumming to a Duke Ellington record on the lid of the radio. I wondered if they had given us up. I wondered too about the papers. If they had already said anything about us it could only be in the dead phrase: one of our aircraft is missing. Hearing it, did anyone think about it again? We had been drifting for two days on the sea and for a long time we had been on fire in the air. If we didn't come back no one would ever know. If we did come back the boys at the station would be glad, and perhaps the papers would give us a line in a bottom corner. I didn't feel very bitter but that night, as I sat there, holding Allison with my burnt hands, I saw the whole thing very clearly. We had been doing things that no one had ever done before. Almost every week you read of aircraft on fire in the air. You read it in the papers and then you turned over and read the sports news. You heard it on the radio and the next moment you heard a dance band. You sat eating in restaurants and read casually of men floating for days in dinghies. God, I was hungry. I began to think of food, sickly and ravenously, and then put it out of my mind. You read and heard of these things, and they stopped having meaning. Well, they had meaning for me now. I suddenly realized that what we were doing was a new experience in the world. Until our time no one had ever been on fire in the air. Until our time there had never been so many people to hear of such things and then to forget them again.

I wanted to speak. Where my stomach should have been there was a distended bladder of air. I pressed Allison's head against it. I must have moved sharply, not thinking, and he groaned.

"Ally?" I said. "Are you all right, Ally?"

He did not answer. Ellis gave him a little more rum and then I held his mouth closed again.

I looked at the stars and went on thinking. The stars were very frosty and brittle and green. One of them grew bright enough to be reflected, broken up, in the black water. Did my wife care? This, I thought, is a nice moment to reason it out. Neither of us had wanted to have children. We hadn't really wanted much at all except a flat, a lot of small social show, and a good time. Looking back, I felt we were pretty despicable. We had really been attracted by a mutual selfishness. And then we got to hating each other because the selfishness of one threatened the selfishness of another. A selfishness that surrenders is unselfishness. Neither of us would surrender. We were too selfish to have children; we were too selfish to trouble about obligations. Finally, we were too selfish to want each other.

All this, it seemed, had happened a long time ago. Life in the dinghy had gone on a thousand years. I had never had the use of my hands, and I had never eaten anything but chocolate and biscuit and rum. Curious that they were luxuries. I had never sat anywhere except on the edge of that dinghy, with the sea beating me up and down, the ice cracking on the sides, and my feet in freezing water. I had never done anything except hold Allison with my hands and knees. And now I had held him so long that we seemed frozen together.

Every time we gave Allison the rum that night, I smelled it for a long time in the air, thick and sweet. Once it ran down out of his open mouth over my wrists and very slowly, so as not to disturb him, I raised my wrists and licked it off. My lips were sore with salt and, because it was not like drinking from a cup, the rum burnt the cracks in them. I was cold too and moving my hands was like moving some part of Allison's body, not my own.

Then once more the rum ran out of Allison's mouth and poured over my hands, and suddenly I thought it strange that he could not hold it. I waited for Ellis to crawl back across the dinghy and sit down. Then I tried to find Allison's hands. They were loose and heavy at his sides. I tried to move his head, so that I could speak to him. His face was white in the starlight. I bent down at last and touched it with my own.

Ally, I thought. Jesus, Ally. Jesus, Jesus.

His mouth was stiff and open and his face was colder than the frost could ever make it.

X

I held him for the rest of that night, not telling even Ellis he was dead. It was then about three o'clock. I felt that it was not the frost or the sea or the wind that had killed him. He had been dead for a long time. He had been dead ever since he walked out of the bombed house with the child in his arms.

The death of Allison made me feel very small. Until morning, when the others knew, it did not depress me. For the rest of the night, in the darkness, with the frost terribly vicious in the hours up to seven o'clock, my jacket stiff with ice where the spray had frozen and the ice thin and crackling in the well of the dinghy, I felt it was a personal thing between myself and Allison. I had got myself into the war because, at first, it was an escape from my wife. It was an escape from the wrong way of doing the toast in the morning, the way she spilled powder on her dressing-gown, the silly songs she sang in the bathroom. It was an escape from little things that I magnified by selfishness into big things. I think I wanted to show her, too, that I was capable of some sort of bravery; as if I had any idea what that was.

Now, whatever I had done seemed small beside what Allison had done. I remember how Allison and his wife had wanted the baby, how it had come after Allison had joined up, how its responsibilities excited them. I saw now what he must have felt when he walked out of the bombed house with all his excitement, his joy and his responsibilities compressed into a piece of dead flesh in his hands. I understood why he had been dead a long time.

Just before seven o'clock, when it became light enough for

us to see each other, I called Ellis and told him Allison was dead. The thing was a great shock to the rest of us and I saw a look of terror on Ossy's face. Then Ellis and Mac took Allison and laid him, as best they could, in the bottom of the dinghy. None of us felt like saying much and it was Mac who covered Allison's face with his handkerchief, which fluttered and threatened to blow away in the wind.

"It's tough tit, Ally boy. It's tough tit," he said.

I felt very lonely.

XI

The wind blew away the handkerchief about ten minutes later, leaving the face bare and staring up at us. The handkerchief floated on the sea and floated away fast on bars of foam that were coming up stronger now with the morning wind. We stared for a moment at the disappearing handkerchief, because it was a more living thing than Allison's face lying in the sloppy yellow ice-water in the dinghy, and then Thompson, who never spoke much unless he had something real to say, suggested we should wrap him in his parachute.

"At least we can cover him with it," he said.

So while Ed and Ossy paddled and Thompson bailed what water he could and I sat there helpless, trying to get some flexibility into the arms cramped by holding Allison all night, Mac and Ellis wrapped the body roughly, as best they could, in the parachute. Mac lifted the body in his arms while Ellis and Thompson bailed ice and water from the dinghy, and then Ellis spread the parachute. Together they wrapped Allison in it like a mummy.

"Christ, why didn't we think of this before?" Ellis said. "It would have kept him warm. I blame myself."

"He died a long time ago," I said.

"He what?"

"You couldn't have done anything," I said.

Soon they finished wrapping him in the parachute and he seemed to cover almost all the space in the dinghy, so that we had nowhere to put our feet and we kept pushing them against him. The sun was up now, pale yellow in a flat sky, but it was still freezing. The sea seemed to be going past at a tremendous pace, black and white and rough, as if we were travelling with a current or a tide.

I could see that Ossy and Ed Walker were terribly dejected. We were all pale and tired, with bluish dark eyes, and stubby beards which seemed to have sucked all the flesh from our cheek-bones. But Ossy and Ed, partly through the intense cold, much more through the shock of Allison's death, seemed to have sunk into that vacant and silent state in which Allison himself had been on the previous afternoon. They were staring flatly at the sea.

"O.K., chaps," Ellis said, "breakfast now."

He began to ration out the biscuits and the chocolate. One piece of chocolate had a piece of white paper round it. As Ellis unwrapped it the wind tore it overboard. It too, like the handkerchief, went away at great speed, as if we were travelling on a tide.

Suddenly Ellis stopped in the act of holding a piece of chocolate to my mouth. I opened my mouth ready to bite it. So we both sat transfixed, I with my mouth open, Ellis holding the chocolate about three inches away.

"You see it?" he said. "You see it? You see?"

"Looks like a floating elephant," Mac said.

"It's a buoy!" Ellis said. "Don't you see, it's a buoy!"

"Holy Moses," Mac said.

"Paddle!" Ellis said. "For Christ's sake, paddle! All of you, paddle."

I made a violent grab at the chocolate with my mouth, partly biting it and Ellis's finger before it was snatched away. Ellis swore and we all laughed like hell. The sight of that buoy, rocking about half a mile westwards, like a drunken elephant, encouraged us into a light-hearted frenzy, in which at intervals we laughed again for no reason at all.

"We're going in with the tide," I said. "I've been watching it."

"Paddle like hell!" Ellis said. "Straight for the buoy. Paddle!"

I paddled with my mind. They said afterwards that I paddled also with my hands. The buoy seemed to go past us, two or three minutes later, at a devil of a speed, though it was we who were travelling. The wind had freshened with the sun and we seemed to bounce on the waves, shipping water. But we had forgotten about bailing now. We had forgotten almost about the body of Allison, rolling slightly in the white parachute in the dirty sea-water at our feet. We had forgotten about everything except frantically paddling with the tide.

It was likely that we should have seen land a long time before this, except that it was without cliffs and was a low line of sand unlit by sun. In the far distance there was a slight haze which turned to blue and amber as the sun rose. Then across the mist and the colour the line of land broke like a long wave of brown.

Ten minutes later there was hardly any need to paddle at all. The tide was taking us in fast, in a calmer stretch of water, towards a flat, wide beach of sand. Beyond it there was no town. There were only telegraph wires stretching up and down the empty coast, and soon we were so near that I could see where the snow had beaten and frozen on the black poles, in white strips on the seaward side.

I looked at my watch as we floated in, not paddling now, on the tide. It was about eight o'clock and we had been, as far as I could tell, nearly sixty hours in the dinghy.

Then as we came in, and the exhilaration of beating in towards the coast on that fast tide began to lessen, I became aware of things. I became aware of my hands. They were swollen from lack of attention and stiff from holding Allison. I became aware of hunger. The hollowness of my stomach filled at intervals with the sickness of hunger and then emptied again. I became aware again of Allison, wrapped in the parachute, once very white, now dirty with sea-water and the excited marks of our feet, and I became aware, in one clear moment before the dinghy struck the sand, of Ellis and Mac and Ed and Thompson and all that they now meant to me. I became aware of Ossy, standing in the dinghy like a crazy person, waving his spanner.

When the dinghy hit the sand and would go no further I jumped overboard. There was no feeling of impact as my legs struck the shore. They seemed hollow and dead. They folded under me as if made of straw and I fell on my face on the wet sand of the beach, helpless, and lay there like a fool.

And as I lay there, the sand wet and cold and yet good on my face, I became aware of a final thing. We had been out a long way, and through a great deal together. We had been through fire and water, death and frost, and had come home.

And soon we should go out again.

The Air Scout

F. Britten Austin

A large level meadow bit squarely into the edge of the
woodland. The centre of the space, enclosed on three sides
by trees as by a wall, was an empty stretch of turf, browned
by much traffic and littered with the scraps of paper which
are the inevitable deposit of any congregation of human
beings. The left-hand side was occupied by a neat row of
slate-grey motor-lorries. The right showed an equally neat
array of tents and sheds over which hung a faint film of
wood-smoke. At regular intervals along the third side a
series of placards was affixed to the tree-trunks, each
exhibiting a conspicuous number like stands at a cattle-
show. The stands, however, were vacant. In front of the
sheds on the right stood a little group of men in khaki, and
near them two men in shirt and trousers were busy at a
portable forge, whence issued the film of smoke. The
hammer-strokes of these men were visible and evidently
delivered with force, yet, curiously enough, at a little
distance they appeared to fall in silence. A vast noise that
came from beyond the wood swallowed all other sounds.
The drowsy air of the hot noon trembled with concussions
so rapid that they merged into one deep-throated, deafening
roar. The field was the aeroplane depot of the army. The
roar was the roar of the battle which that army was fighting.

Despite the apparent nearness of the strife, there was little of military spectacle about the depot. At the corner of the wood a squadron of dismounted troopers stood by their horses. A little farther back along the rough lane which led into the field, a gun mounted on a motor-lorry stuck its nose perpendicularly into the air. Three or four men sat on the lorry in easy attitudes, and one stood up, glasses to his eyes, scanning the blue sky. The group of khaki-clad men paid no more attention to them than they did to the battle din which swelled over the woodland. They were absorbed in contemplation of a large, curious-looking bush which stood a few yards in front of them.

A closer look at that bush revealed that it was artificial. It was, in fact, a largish shed whose walls and roof were composed of green boughs. Men were busy within it, and a shaft of sunlight that penetrated the leaves fell in a patch of gold upon some yellow fabric. The object thus illuminated was the wing of a small, single-seater monoplane.

A little apart from the other members of the group a slightly-built young fellow, garbed for the ascent, stood in earnest colloquy with a tall, lean staff-officer. Behind them the others conversed in tones just loud enough to be heard in the incessant roar. They were discussing the disaster of the dawn.

The blow of the enemy had been terrible. The army had been smitten in its eyes. It was now only a blind giant striking at an adversary whose vision was unimpaired. The entire air-squadron of the force, rising from its harbourage at the break of day, had been suddenly assailed by a superior fleet that dropped out of the clouds upon them. Watchers from below had seen short lightning-flashes stabbing the grey mist, had heard a sharp outbreak of firing, had seen phantom aeroplanes rising, circling, swooping, colliding in the thin cloud, had seen the machines one after another tumble and dive, lapped by flames, in a sickening rush to earth. Not theirs alone now lay, crumpled and contorted masses of scrap-iron, over the countryside, but of theirs none had escaped. The enemy held command of the air. The rear of their battle-line was a picture that his scouts could report upon at leisure. What lay at the rear of his? None knew, but the vehemence of his fire told that he was pressing his advantage. The presentiment of defeat lay heavy on the little group as they disputed on the blame to be allotted for the catastrophe.

The staff-officer tugged impatiently at his little grey moustache. His teeth champed at a bit of grass that was no longer there. In his anxiety he had not noticed that it had fallen from his mouth.

"I wish those chaps would be quick," he said. "The general is most anxious to have that flank cleared up."

"They are being quick, sir," replied the aviator, with a smile.

His keen, thoughtful face showed that he was not indifferent to the urgency of the situation, but his calm mouth told of nerves that nothing could shake. Within that green bower lay the one hope of the army—its lightest and swiftest monoplane, damaged in landing the day before, now being repaired as fast as skilled hands could do the work.

"You quite understand, don't you?" said the staff-officer, repeating himself for the tenth time. "The general thinks that a movement is in progress against our right flank. A screen is extending there which he cannot penetrate. If they are moving a large force round us he can detach the Sixth Division to hold them, and with a massed attack he'll crumple up their left centre, which they must have weakened. He'll repeat Salamanca, that's what he said. I don't know what happened at Salamanca," he concluded, irritably; "but anyway, he daren't move a man till he's sure. I wish your chaps would get finished." He looked up into the air above him with a circling glance. "How many have they got now?"

"Four, I make it," replied the aviator, equably. "They had ten yesterday. Five were smashed up this morning. One got winged an hour ago."

At that moment a dirty and perspiring man came out of the bower and, approaching them, saluted.

"Ready, sir," he said.

"Right; get her out, then," said the aviator. "No—wait!" His gaze had gone up to the sky. "There he comes again."

"Confound it!" said the staff-officer, staring upwards also.

High in the air an aeroplane was coming towards them,

parallel with their own battle-line. In the swollen roar of the conflict, the hum of its engine was inaudible. It seemed to drift onward leisurely enough, sinking slightly as it approached, but well above effective gun-fire; tiny white dots of smoke that sprang into the air below it were a proof of that. Slowly, as though making a careful examination, it passed overhead. Suddenly it turned and dropped still lower, coming back towards them. Something had awakened suspicion in the men up there. The reason for that artificial bush became apparent. The staff-officer gazed at the aeroplane, now rapidly enlarging itself in his vision, as though mesmerized. Anxiety for that precious machine under the leaves paralysed him.

The aviator had turned to look at the gun on the motor-lorry. The group about it sat in quiet expectation. Its muzzle moved gently, came a little out of the perpendicular. The aviator looked up again at the machine drifting overhead. He heard a sudden heavy detonation on his left, and almost simultaneously he saw a bright flash appear in the dark body of the aeroplane. The machine lurched, toppled, dived, and, falling rapidly, turned bottom-up in the air. A couple of dark figures fell out and raced it in its rush to the ground. A long minute later it struck the centre of the field. Flames burst out of a shapeless wreck. The aviator did not heed it. He ran towards the bower.

"Quick!" he cried. "Get her out!"

Torn down by twenty pairs of eager hands, the bower fell apart. The little monoplane was run out, and lay like a dragonfly resting lightly on the earth.

The aviator climbed into his seat between the wings, sent a glance from the compass to the map held open in its frame, saw that the message-bags were ready to his hand, and tested the strap of the field-glasses hanging from his neck with a sharp tug.

He was ready. In front of him two soldier mechanics stood holding the long blades of the tractor screw. Over there beyond the wood, the uproar of the battle mounted in violent paroxysms, each of which surpassed its predecessor. The tall staff-officer approached and held out his hand.

"Good-bye—and good luck," he said. "And, for Heaven's sake, let us know what's happening on that flank. Don't wait to get back—drop the message." He looked at his watch. "It's now twelve. If we don't know something within an hour it's all over with our chance. Can you manage it?"

"I'll try, sir," said the aviator, checking the hour with a glance at his own clock.

The staff-officer turned an anxious pair of eyes upward for a swift look into the sky, seemed about to make a remark, and then obviously refrained. "Good luck!" was all he could trust himself to say.

The aviator smiled and nodded cheerfully. Then he ejaculated a sharp order to the mechanics. They flung the blades of the tractor into revolution. The machine, emitting a series of rifle-like reports, commenced to run across the field. The tractor became a blur.

The woodland appeared to rush towards him, and then suddenly dropped away in a diagonal underneath. His eyes on the dial of the barograph, the aviator warped the machine round and set the planes to an acute angle of elevation. Confident in the power of his engine, he mounted steeply in a spiral. The record on the dial rose with every second—a hundred feet—two hundred—four hundred. In two and a half minutes he had risen one thousand feet. He cast a swift look below him. He was still over the field, had a glimpse of a group of tiny figures clustered in front of the sheds. The rim of the horizon came up, the earth fell into a great concavity. It was like looking down into a vast bowl containing woods and fields and flattened hills. From the bowl clouds of yellow-grey dust arose like smoke, and out of the dust came a multiplicity of heavy crashes that detached themselves from a background of unceasing clatter mingled with one long, rolling, thunderous roar.

It was but a hasty glance the aviator threw below him. Still mounting, his eyes searched the blue air on a level with himself, above him. The enemy's three machines—where were they? Far off to his left a dark speck hung in the sky. He watched it intently as his machine climbed. It was a biplane. It appeared to be drifting away from him, engaged in a reconnaissance of their left flank, he decided. At any rate, as yet they seemed not to have perceived him. The others were not visible. He shot a glance at the barograph—three thousand feet. He had been climbing for five and a half minutes. Almost immediately he saw a trail of smoke ascending with incredible velocity in the air a little below him to his right. The trail finished abruptly in a vivid flash, a burst of white smoke, and a violent detonation. The monoplane rocked from side to side in the sudden disturbance of the air, but continued to climb. A second later a similar trail ended in an explosion at a level with him on his left. He saw a gash appear suddenly in the fabric of one of his planes and the needle of the barograph switch back fifty feet with a jerk. Then the altitude record mounted again steadily—three thousand two hundred and fifty—three thousand five hundred—four thousand. The noise of the battle diminished as he rose, dropping to a point where it was all but obscured by the roar of his own engine. Below him the smoke trails leaped up at him and burst viciously in vain.

Four thousand five hundred feet—he glanced at the hostile biplane to his left and saw that it hung larger in the sky. Even in the moment for which he watched it, it dilated. It was approaching at top speed. He was discovered, pursued. Instantly he turned off to his right and raced across the battle-field in the direction of the threatening hostile flank. As he did so, he perceived another aeroplane rising from the enemy's lines. It climbed swiftly in bold swoops and then shot off towards him on a great upward slant. Two!—where was the third? He failed to discover it, and held on his course.

His direction was at an angle across the battle-field, which took him towards the enemy's left flank rather than to their own right. As he sped over it, he looked down upon a broad, miles-long belt of yellow-grey dust that rose raggedly into the air and was spotted with an innumerable multitude of white puffs that renewed themselves as fast as they were dissipated. In many places these puffs congregated thickly and, as they broke, linked themselves with others until they floated like little narrow clouds in the air below him. As he looked down into the great concavity of the earth he seemed to be over some enormous smoking fissure in a crater whose circumference was the horizon. The rumble and roar which ascended from it assisted the illusion. Tiny sparks of flame darted and flickered in the fumes of that inferno, and here and there flashed a number of glittering points, the reflection of the sun from advancing bayonets. To distinguish men was impossible, but in occasional rifts in the dust curtain he could make out brown patches of varying size, and, over to his left on the enemy's side, similar though darker patches.

He could permit himself no sustained scrutiny of the scene below him, for the management of the machine began to claim all his attention. Even at that great height above the battle, the air on that windless day, shaken and riven by the unceasing concussions of the massed artillery of two armies, was full of flaws. The needle of the barograph flickered, oscillating violently in leaps to and fro. The monoplane, tilted dangerously, now on one side, now on the other, in eddies of the tortured atmosphere, slid downward dizzily ere it could be brought up to climb a bank of air. It needed strong arms at the controls, a quick brain and nerves of perfect tone to keep her upon the appointed course. Glancing back, the aviator saw that the flight of the nearer of the two hostile machines, the one which had risen from the enemy's lines and was now approaching him on his left, was similarly erratic.

An overpowering heat, as from a vast open furnace, arose from the battle-field below. It was the heat from thousands of explosions, renewed incessantly and sustained over many hours. Stifling gusts blew on to the aviator's face, carrying with them a peculiar smell of burning cloth. With these gusts the roar of the battle seemed to leap up to him. The air was oppressive, despite the speed at which he clove it, highly charged with electricity, heavy with the menace of a storm. Yet no cloud broke the monotony of the blue sky. The machine, racing onward, was now crossing the battle-lines of the enemy's left flank.

Suddenly he heard a faint rattle behind him. The hostile aeroplane, realizing that it had failed to head him off, was firing furiously. He felt the machine shiver under a quick succession of hard raps. Instinctively, he pressed upon his accelerator, and, with a touch on the warping lever, the machine shot forward and upward at terrific speed. The raps ceased. He turned his head and saw his enemy rapidly diminish in size behind him; saw that the other aeroplane, the one he had seen first, had fallen far in rear. A confident smile came on the tight lips of the aviator. He could outpace them both.

He was now above the enemy's left flank—a little to the right of the spot that the Commander-in-Chief had designated as the objective of his possible attack. The scout switched off his engine and commenced to drop along a slant towards the centre of the enemy's position. With the sudden silencing of his engine the roar of the battle came up at him in a crash and stayed there. He glanced at the time—twelve-thirteen—and gave himself a limit of two minutes in which to reconnoitre. For the moment he ignored his adversaries in the air. As he gazed down through the transparent panel between his feet, his glasses to his eyes, the ground that slid away from under him appeared to be subjected to a constantly increasing magnification. Fields, houses, roads grew momentarily more distinct. Without taking his gaze from the scene below him, the aviator checked the drop of his machine and drove forward. Quickly his trained eye took in the details of the ground, the position and approximate numbers of the men that he saw massed in dark patches here and there. Over a long stretch of the position the enemy's line was obviously thinner. The country behind it was empty of troops. The general's intuition was correct. The enemy had weakened his left centre. Point number one was settled. Now what had he done with the troops he had withdrawn?

As the aviator turned his machine to reconnoitre in the new direction, he was surprised to see the hostile aeroplane between him and his objective. Absorbed in his scrutiny of the ground, he had all but forgotten it. It was slightly higher than himself and about half a mile distant. He could not carry out his reconnaissance without coming into a fatal proximity to its machine-gun, and he could not return directly over the battle-lines without passing between the crossed fires of this and the other machine now drawing close. Even as the realization of his position flashed on him, a narrow slit appeared in one of his planes. The nearer of his foes was already firing.

Quicker than thought he turned and raced off into the country behind the battle. A plan, the only one with a possible chance of success, had sprung into his mind. He had no intention of failing in this all-important mission of his. But first he must get out of the range of that deadly machine-gun. He dared not rise across it at barely half a mile range. At full speed he raced away, inclining his machine downwards. The hostile aeroplane followed, depressing her course likewise, to get him into the zone of fire or to force him to the ground. The scout's speedometer registered one hundred miles an hour. Beneath his feet he had glimpses of trees and houses and fields flitting past in a stream where salient features prolonged themselves into long blurred lines. They looked oddly large after the altitude at which he had been contemplating them. He threw a glance over his shoulder at his pursuers. The nearer was now rather more than a mile away. The other had apparently given up the chase. The clock stood at twelve-sixteen and a half. In less than two minutes he had distanced his adversary by nearly a mile. He had therefore a superiority in speed of about twenty-five miles per hour. He did not consciously deduce this result. His trained mind, working with incomputable swiftness under the stimulant of imminent danger gave him the result like an intuition. His plan presented itself to him completely formed. At this distance he could risk the danger-zone of the machine-gun for the few moments he would be in it. He swerved his machine upward and climbed steeply. In a minute the other aeroplane was level with him, beneath him. The scout rose along a slant, slowing down his engine until his pace was almost exactly equal to that of the machine below. Both rose steadily.

The battle-din ceased altogether behind him. He flew in the seeming silence of the roar of his own engine and the deeper bass of the other engine, just audible, below. He bent forward over his map and picked out his approximate position. Then he noted a village some twenty miles in rear of the battle and drew an imaginary line from it southwestward to the enemy's left flank. That village was to serve as turning-point. He should reach it, he calculated, at twelve-twenty-nine. The barograph indicated three thousand feet, and still rising.

Twelve-twenty-seven—the scout bent his eyes on the

ground. A couple of minutes later a handful of white cottages flitted past as he looked down between his feet. His enemy could not be seen. The body of the monoplane hid him as he flew below and slightly in rear, but the roar of his engine, louder than the scout's own, could just be heard.

Now was the time. The scout turned off abruptly at a tangent along the line he had marked out for himself, and drove his engine at its fastest. The speedometer-needle oscillated over a hundred and one miles an hour. He calculated that he had approximately twenty miles to go ere he reached the patch of country he wished to explore. He should reach the commencement of the enemy's left flank at twelve-forty-one, and be able to spend six minutes in flying over five miles of ground, and then have a couple of minutes in hand. To the trained intellect behind his keen eyes six minutes was amply sufficient. Having run along the left flank, it was simplicity itself to turn to the right and glide down into his own lines. There seemed nothing to stop him. The pursuing machine was being quickly left behind. The slow biplane now far off to his right could not possibly arrive in time. The sky in front was clear of any menace.

Again he began to draw close to the great belt of dust-cloud which stretched far to his right, and again the din of battle began to overpower the roar of his engine. Directly ahead was a dark mass of woodland. It was thence that the enemy's screen around the right flank of the scout's army commenced. He swerved slightly to the left, behind it. The hour was a second or two over twelve-forty.

Below him was a network of country roads, and from four strands of that network, which ran in an approximately parallel direction, coincident with his own course, arose long, dense clouds of dust. It was the dust of marching columns. The scout shot a glance back at his pursuer, assured himself that it was five or six miles in rear, and slowed down his engine as he entered upon a long gradual descent over the route of those marching columns.

For mile after mile on those four roads the dust-cloud continued. The scout checked off the distances by villages on his map. Adding the length of the four clouds together, he estimated that about twenty miles of road was occupied by the marching force. It was a whole army corps, then, that

was endeavouring to turn their flank. In the open fields
between the roads he could distinguish small bodies of
cavalry advancing in the same direction. The mass on the
roads was certainly infantry, broken here and there by long
columns of artillery. The low, dense clouds of dust kicked
up by the tramp of thousands of feet were cut into short
sections where the guns and wagons of the batteries rolled
onward. From a rough calculation of those intersected
clouds he decided that four brigades of artillery were on the
march. He had descended now to two thousand feet, and he
kept at that height as he roared over the plodding columns.
Behind him his pursuer had lessened the distance between
them, and was getting dangerously close. The biplane on his
right was also approaching. Nevertheless, the scout held on
his way comfortably. There was nothing to prevent him
carrying out his plan.

He was already well beyond the prolongation of his own
army's line of battle when he reached the head of the
marching infantry. Contrary to his expectation, however,
they were not wheeling to the right. They continued straight
on, marching away from the battle, it seemed. The scout was
puzzled for a moment. He searched the ground in front of
him for more troops. It was apparently empty. Then, from a
fold in the landscape considerably ahead, he saw another,
smaller, dust-cloud arise. At his highest speed he raced
towards it, overtook it in less than a minute. Below him a
cavalry brigade, accompanied by two batteries of horse
artillery, was trotting sharply forward. What was their
objective? He scanned the country in front of them intently.
Some three miles ahead of the cavalry was a wooded hill.
He picked it out on the map; saw instantly that it com-
manded the main avenue of retreat of his own army. The
enemy's plan was clear. He would occupy it with the cavalry
and the two batteries until the infantry got up. The threatened army, then attacked in flank and rear, would find its
retreat cut off. If the scout's commander was aiming to
repeat Salamanca, the enemy was endeavouring to repeat
Jackson's march at Chancellorsville. The danger was pressing. The scout reckoned that within half an hour the hostile
cavalry would be in possession of that hill. In an hour the
infantry would begin to come up in support. Where was the

Sixth Division that he had been told would check the flank movement of the enemy? He searched for it, saw a brown mass about two miles from the wooded hill. Its cavalry might get there in a quarter of an hour by a rapid dash. He had then a quarter of an hour to deliver his message and get the division set in motion. The hour was twelve-forty-eight.

He wheeled towards his own line and commenced a downward glide at a gentle angle. Then, taking his hands from the controls, he rapidly wrote down a clear, concise statement of the case in his report-book. Even if he did not reach earth, his message might. He glanced up to see that his indefatigable pursuer was now swooping down to cut him off. Moments were precious. He ripped out the page, thrust it into the weighted message-bag, and tied it up. Then he started his engine again, aiming for the brown mass of the Sixth Division.

Something made him look to his left. He was startled to see a large biplane rushing up at him from the direction of the wooded hill. It had evidently descended to effect some repairs and had lain hidden far behind his own line. He recognized it at once. It was by far the swiftest and most powerful machine possessed by either army. On his present course a few seconds would bring him within range of its machine-gun. To his right the other machine was rapidly growing larger. In front the slow biplane had sailed over the battlelines, and was heading straight for him. The three machines were converging on him. The scout saw that he would either be forced away from the battle or destroyed, his message undelivered in either case.

He swerved his machine and climbed. If only he could get above the Sixth Division for an instant he would throw over the message-bag, chancing its being picked up. To do this it was necessary to get higher. On his present or a lower level he would be riddled with machine-gun bullets. His adversaries on either hand rose also, but he got the lead of them.

As they rose in circles he watched for his opportunity when both should be turned from him. The moment came. He seized it and dived, with his engine running at full speed. The earth rushed upwards, its features enlarging themselves as though they swelled to burst. The brown mass of the Sixth Division spaced itself out into battalions, squadrons, below him, in front. They were exactly underneath. He flung out the message-bag with something like a prayer in his heart. On either hand his adversaries were swooping down upon him. He thought he heard the rattle of their machine-guns, but in the roar of his own engine he could not be sure.

Down and still down the three machines rushed. Suddenly he noticed the slow biplane in front—on an even lower level than himself. It was very close. He saw the pale dot of the face of the man behind the gun. If he swerved he would be under its fire in a moment. If he kept on his course he must crash into it. His decision was instant. He held on. One thought dominated him as he dived straight at it. Had his message been picked up? If not . . . He saw the gleaming backs of the outstretched planes almost under him. He set his teeth for the impact. A second more—the wide stretch of yellow canvas suddenly jerked to the left and crumpled in a blinding flash. He had not touched. He swerved to the right with all his force in the tiniest fraction of a second and shot past something that fell, flaming. A shell from below had hit the biplane almost at the moment of collision.

He had a confused sense of other shells exploding in the air. A battery below was seizing its chance to get the enemy's aircraft in a cluster, regardless of the danger to him. He continued his rush downward, feeling rather than knowing that the other two machines were in close pursuit. If he could only be certain that his message had been picked up!

He flung a glance back over his shoulder. The powerful biplane that had risen from behind the wooded hill was close upon him. Why did they not fire? He felt himself a target; was surprised not to see the gash of bullets on his machine. The explanation flashed on him. The gun had jammed. The biplane came at him as though it were itself a projectile. Its crew had desperately resolved to ram him, to sacrifice themselves rather than to allow him to bring his precious information to the ground. They were almost upon him. He swerved and dodged. The biplane shot past.

Immediately he saw the other machine close upon him— saw a spurt of fire from the muzzle of its gun. He dived. A belt of trees rushed up at him, fearfully close. Their dark foliage seemed to break into puffs of black smoke over his eyes. He swerved instinctively, and saw a meadow burst through the dark smoke, fly skyward in a mist of blood. With a last desperate effort he banked. His hands slid from the controls—everything swam. He was vaguely conscious of a heavy impact from underneath—

Something was burning his throat—he opened his eyes, gazed into a man's face close to his. Consciousness came back in a rush. He pushed away the brandy-flask that was being pressed against his teeth and struggled to his feet. Strong arms supported him. Several men were round him, looking at him. He was close to a road, and along that road he thought he saw batteries of artillery galloping at full speed. He was not certain of their reality. They passed like phantoms in his vision, wavering up and down . . . He wanted to do something—to ask something—what was it? He all but fixed the elusive thought—and lost it. His hand felt for the duplicate report-book in his pocket—his desire was connected with that. The report-book had gone. Then a fragment of his intangible preoccupation floated, visible as it were, in his brain. He clutched at it.

"What—what guns are those?" he asked, thickly.

"Divisional artillery—Sixth Division," came the reply. "All right, we got your message."

The scout put his hand to his brow and then, dropping it, stared at it stupidly. It was red.

"All right," said the voice. "You're hit—but not seriously. Lie down."

The scout collected all his faculties in an attempt to bring out one more thought from the obscurity which filled his brain.

"What—what time—now?" he asked.

"Just one o'clock." The voice appeared to recede to an enormous distance, although he felt the speaker's face close to his. "They're in time—don't worry. Lie down. The ambulances are coming in a minute or two."

The scout stood, obstinately.

"The—the other—machines?"

"Bagged 'em both. You came down beautifully—like a kite." The voice sounded from worlds away.

The aviator put his hand to his head.

"In time!" He breathed the words rather than spoke them. They came like the sigh of a man utterly spent.

The man who had been supporting him turned round with a jump and focused his binoculars on the wooded hill. A crowd of white puffs was breaking out in the air above it.

The scout, left unattended, swayed with hands stretched out like a blind man. The field whirled round and round suddenly with a fearful rapidity and then rushed up and struck him.

The man with the binoculars ignored his prone body.

"Beat 'em on the post!" he shouted, in joyous excitement. "By Heaven! Beat 'em on the post!"

The Summons Comes for Mr. Standfast

John Buchan

I slept for one and three-quarter hours that night, and when I awoke I seemed to emerge from deeps of slumber which had lasted for days. That happens sometimes after heavy fatigue and great mental strain. Even a short sleep sets up a barrier between past and present which has to be elaborately broken down before you can link on with what has happened before. As my wits groped at the job some drops of rain splashed on my face through the broken roof. That hurried me out-of-doors. It was just after dawn and the sky was piled with thick clouds, while a wet wind blew up from the south-west. The long-prayed-for break in the weather seemed to have come at last. A deluge of rain was what I wanted, something to soak the earth and turn the roads into water-courses and clog the enemy transport, something above all to blind the enemy's eyes . . . For I remembered what a preposterous bluff it all had been, and what a piteous broken handful stood between the Germans and their goal. If they knew, if they only knew, they would brush us aside like flies.

As I shaved I looked back on the events of yesterday as on something that had happened long ago. I seemed to judge them impersonally, and I concluded that it had been a pretty good fight. A scratch force, half of it dog-tired and half of it untrained, had held up at least a couple of fresh divisions . . . But we couldn't do it again, and there were still some hours before us of desperate peril. When had the Corps said that the French would arrive? . . . I was on the point of shouting for Hamilton to get Wake to ring up Corps Headquarters, when I remembered that Wake was dead. I had liked him and greatly admired him, but the recollection gave me scarcely a pang. We were all dying, and he had only gone on a stage ahead.

There was no morning *strafe,* such as had been our usual fortune in the past week. I went out-of-doors and found a noiseless world under the lowering sky. The rain had stopped falling, the wind of dawn had lessened, and I feared that the storm would be delayed. I wanted it at once to help us through the next hours of tension. Was it in six hours that the French were coming? No, it must be four. It couldn't be more than four, unless somebody had made an infernal muddle. I wondered why everything was so quiet. It would be breakfast time on both sides, but there seemed no stir of man's presence in that ugly strip half a mile off. Only far back in the German hinterland I seemed to hear the rumour of traffic.

An unslept and unshaven figure stood beside me which revealed itself as Archie Roylance.

"Been up all night," he said cheerfully, lighting a cigarette. "No, I haven't had breakfast. The skipper thought we'd better get another anti-aircraft battery up this way, and I was superintendin' the job. He's afraid of the Hun gettin' over your lines and spying out the nakedness of the land. For, you know, we're uncommon naked, sir. Also," and Archie's face became grave, "the Hun's pourin' divisions down on this sector. As I judge, he's blowin' up for a thunderin' big drive on both sides of the river. Our lads yesterday said all the country back of Peronne was lousy with new troops. And he's gettin' his big guns forward, too. You haven't been troubled with them yet, but he has got the roads mended and the devil of a lot of new light railways, and any moment we'll have the five-point-nines sayin' Good mornin' . . . Pray Heaven you get relieved in time, sir. I take it there's not much risk of another push this mornin'?"

"I don't think so. The Boche took a nasty knock yesterday, and he must fancy we're pretty strong after that counter-attack. I don't think he'll strike till he can work both sides of the river, and that'll take time to prepare. That's what his fresh divisions are for . . . But remember, he can attack now, if he likes. If he knew how weak we were he's strong enough to send us all to glory in the next three hours. It's just that knowledge that you fellows have got to prevent him getting. If a single Hun plane crosses our lines and returns, we're wholly and utterly done. You've given us splendid help since the show began, Archie. For God's sake keep it up to the finish and put every machine you can spare in this sector."

"We're doin' our best," he said. "We got some more fightin' scouts down from the north, and we're keepin' our eyes skinned. But you know as well as I do, sir, that it's never an ab-so-lute certainty. If the Hun sent over a squadron we might beat 'em all down but one, and that one might do the trick. It's a matter of luck. The Hun's got the wind up all right in the air just now and I don't blame the poor devil. But I'm inclined to think we haven't had the pick of his push here. Jennings says he's doin' good work in Flanders, and they reckon there's the deuce of a thrust comin' there pretty soon. I think we can manage the kind of footler he's been sendin' over here lately, but if Lensch or some lad like that were to choose to turn up I wouldn't say what might happen. The air's a big lottery," and Archie turned a dirty face skyward where two of our planes were moving very high towards the east.

The mention of Lensch brought Peter to my mind, and I asked if he had gone back.

"He won't go," said Archie, "and we haven't the heart to make him. He's very happy, and plays about with the Gladas single-seater. He's always speakin' about you, sir, and it'd break his heart if we shifted him."

I asked about his health, and was told that he didn't seem to have much pain.

"But he's a bit queer," and Archie shook a sage head. "One of the reasons why he won't budge is because he says God has some work for him to do. He's quite serious about it, and ever since he got the notion he has perked up amazin'. He's always askin' about Lensch, too—not vindictive-like, you understand, but quite friendly. Seems to take a sort of proprietary interest in him. I told him Lensch had had a far longer spell of first-class fightin' than anybody else and was bound by the law of averages to be downed soon, and he was quite sad about it."

I had no time to worry about Peter. Archie and I swallowed breakfast and I had a pow-wow with my brigadiers. By this time I had got through to Corps HQ and got news of the French. It was worse than I expected. General Péguy would arrive about ten o'clock, but his men couldn't take over till well after midday. The Corps gave me their whereabouts and I found it on the map. They had a long way to cover yet, and then there would be the slow business of relieving. I looked at my watch. There were still six hours before us when the Boche might knock us to blazes, six hours of maddening anxiety . . . Lefroy announced that all was quiet on the front, and that the new wiring at the Bois de la Bruyère had been completed. Patrols had reported that during the night a fresh German division seemed to have relieved that which we had punished so stoutly yesterday. I asked him if he could stick it out against another attack. "No," he said without hesitation. "We're too few and too shaky on our pins to stand any more. I've only a man to every three yards." That impressed me, for Lefroy was usually the most devil-may-care optimist.

"Curse it, there's the sun," I heard Archie cry. It was true, for the clouds were rolling back and the centre of the heavens was a patch of blue. The storm was coming—I could smell it in the air—but probably it wouldn't break till the evening. Where, I wondered, would we be by that time?

It was now nine o'clock, and I was keeping tight hold of myself, for I saw that I was going to have hell for the next hours. I am a pretty stolid fellow in some ways, but I have always found patience and standing still the most difficult job to tackle, and my nerves were all tattered from the long strain of the retreat. I went up to the line and saw the battalion commanders. Everything was unwholesomely quiet there. Then I came back to my headquarters to study the reports that were coming in from the air patrols. They all said the same thing—abnormal activity in the German back areas. Things seemed to be shaping for a new 21st of

March, and, if our luck were out, my poor little remnant would have to take the shock. I telephoned to the Corps and found them as nervous as me. I gave them the details of my strength and heard an agonized whistle at the other end of the line. I was rather glad I had companions in the same purgatory.

I found I couldn't sit still. If there had been any work to do I would have buried myself in it, but there was none. Only this fearsome job of waiting. I hardly ever feel cold, but now my blood seemed to be getting thin, and I astonished my staff by putting on a British Warm and buttoning up the collar. Round that derelict farm I ranged like a hungry wolf, cold at the feet, queasy in the stomach, and mortally edgy in my mind.

Then suddenly the cloud lifted from me, and the blood seemed to run naturally into my veins. I experienced the change of mood which a man feels sometimes when his whole being is fined down and clarified by long endurance. The fight of yesterday revealed itself as something rather splendid. What risks we had run and how gallantly we had met them! My heart warmed as I thought of that old division of mine, those ragged veterans that were never beaten as long as breath was left them. And the Americans and the boys from the machine-gun school and all the oddments we had commandeered! And old Blenkiron raging like a good-tempered lion! It was against reason that such fortitude shouldn't win out. We had snarled round and bitten the Boche so badly that he wanted no more for a little. He would come again, but presently we should be relieved and the gallant blue-coats, fresh as paint and burning for revenge, would be there to worry him.

I had no new facts on which to base my optimism, only a changed point of view. And with it came a recollection of other things. Wake's death had left me numb before, but now the thought of it gave me a sharp pang. He was the first of our little confederacy to go. But what an ending he had made, and how happy he had been in that mad time when he had come down from his pedestal and become one of the crowd! He had found himself at the last, and who could grudge him such happiness? If the best were to be taken, he

227

would be chosen first, for he was a big man, before whom I uncovered my head. The thought of him made me very humble. I had never had his troubles to face, but he had come clean through them, and reached a courage which was for ever beyond me. He was the Faithful among us pilgrims, who had finished his journey before the rest. Mary had foreseen it. "There is a price to be paid," she had said—"the best of us."

And at the thought of Mary a flight of warmth and happy hopes seemed to settle in my mind. I was looking again beyond the war to that peace which she and I would some day inherit. I had a vision of a green English landscape, with its far-flung scents of wood and meadow and garden . . . And that face of all my dreams, with the eyes so childlike and brave and honest, as if they, too, saw beyond the dark to a radiant country. A line of old song, which had been a favourite of my father's, sang itself in my ears:

> "There's an eye that ever weeps and a fair face will be fain
> "When I ride through Annan Water wi' my bonny bands
>   again!"

We were standing by the crumbling rails of what had once been the farm sheepfold. I looked at Archie and he smiled back at me, for he saw that my face had changed. Then he turned his eyes to the billowing clouds.

I felt my arm clutched.

"Look there!" said a fierce voice, and his glasses were turned upward.

I looked, and far up in the sky saw a thing like a wedge of wild geese flying towards us from the enemy's country. I made out the small dots which composed it, and my glasses told me they were planes. But only Archie's practised eye knew that they were the enemy.

"Boche?" I asked.

"Boche," he said. "My God, we're for it now."

My heart had sunk like a stone, but I was fairly cool. I looked at my watch and saw that it was ten minutes to eleven.

"How many?"

"Five," said Archie. "Or there may be six—not more."

"Listen!" I said. "Get on to your headquarters. Tell them it's all up with us if a single plane gets back. Let them get well over the line, the deeper in the better, and tell them to send up every machine they possess and down them all. Tell them it's life or death. Not one single plane goes back. Quick!"

Archie disappeared, and as he went out anti-aircraft guns broke out. The formation above opened and zigzagged, but they were too high to be in much danger. But they were not too high to see that which we must keep hidden or perish.

The roar of our batteries died down as the invaders passed westwards. As I watched their progress they seemed to be dropping lower. Then they rose again and a bank of cloud concealed them.

I had a horrid certainty that they must beat us, that some at any rate would get back. They had seen our thin lines and the roads behind us empty of supports. They would see, as they advanced, the blue columns of the French coming up from the south-west, and they would return and tell the enemy that a blow now would open the road to Amiens and the sea. He had plenty of strength for it, and presently he would have overwhelming strength. It only needed a spear-point to burst the jerry-built dam and let the flood through . . . They would return in twenty minutes, and by noon we would be broken. Unless—unless the miracle of miracles happened, and they never returned.

Archie reported that his skipper would do his damnedest and that our machines were now going up. "We've a chance, sir," he said, "a good sportin' chance." It was a new Archie, with a hard voice, a lean face, and very old eyes.

Behind the jagged walls of the farm buildings was a knoll which had once formed part of the highroad. I went up there alone, for I didn't want anybody near me. I wanted a view-point, and I wanted quiet, for I had a grim time before me. From that knoll I had a big prospect of country. I looked east to our lines on which an occasional shell was falling, and where I could hear the chatter of machine-guns. West there was peace, for the woods closed down on the landscape. Up to the north, I remember, there was a big glare as from a burning dump, and heavy guns seemed to be at work in the Ancre valley. Down in the south there was the dull murmur of a great battle. But just around me, in the gap, the deadliest place of all, there was an odd quiet. I could pick out clearly the different sounds. Somebody down at the farm had made a joke and there was a short burst of laughter. I envied the humorist his composure. There was a clatter and jingle from a battery changing position. On the road a tractor was jolting along—I could hear its driver shout and the screech of its unoiled axle.

My eyes were glued to my glasses, but they shook in my hands so that I could scarcely see. I bit my lip to steady myself, but they still wavered. From time to time I glanced at my wrist-watch. Eight minutes gone—ten—seventeen. If only the planes would come into sight! Even the certainty of failure would be better than this harrowing doubt. They should be back by now unless they had swung north across the salient, or unless the miracle of miracles—

Then came the distant yapping of an anti-aircraft gun, caught up the next second by others, while smoke patches studded the distant blue of the sky. The clouds were banking in mid-heaven, but to the west there was a big clear space now woolly with shrapnel bursts. I counted them mechanically—one—three—five—nine—with despair beginning to take the place of my anxiety. My hands were steady now, and through the glasses I saw the enemy.

Five attenuated shapes rode high above the bombardment, now sharp against the blue, now lost in a film of vapour. They were coming back, serenely, contemptuously, having seen all they wanted.

The quiet had gone now and the din was monstrous. Anti-aircraft guns, singly and in groups, were firing from every side. As I watched it seemed a futile waste of ammunition. The enemy didn't give a tinker's curse for it . . . But surely there was one down. I could only count four now. No, there was the fifth coming out of a cloud. In ten minutes they would be all over the line. I fairly stamped in my vexation. Those guns were no more use than a sick headache. Oh, where in God's name were our own planes?

At that moment they came, streaking down into sight, four fighting-scouts with the sun glinting on their wings and burnishing their metal cowls. I saw clearly the rings of red, white, and blue. Before their downward drive the enemy instantly spread out.

I was watching with bare eyes now, and I wanted companionship, for the time of waiting was over. Automatically I must have run down the knoll, for the next I knew I was staring at the heavens with Archie by my side. The combatants seemed to couple instinctively. Diving, wheeling, climbing, a pair would drop out of the mêlée or disappear behind a cloud. Even at that height I could hear the methodical rat-tat-tat of the machine-guns. Then there was a sudden flare and wisp of smoke. A plane sank, turning and twisting, to earth.

"Hun!" said Archie, who had his glasses on it.

Almost immediately another followed. This time the pilot recovered himself, while still a thousand feet from the ground, and started gliding for the enemy lines. Then he wavered, plunged sickeningly, and fell headlong into the wood behind La Bruyère.

Farther east, almost over the front trenches, a two-seater Albatross and a British pilot were having a desperate tussle. The bombardment had stopped, and from where we stood every movement could be followed. First one, then another, climbed uppermost and dived back, swooped out and wheeled in again, so that the two planes seemed to clear each other only by inches. Then it looked as if they closed and interlocked. I expected to see both go crashing, when suddenly the wings of one seemed to shrivel up, and the machine dropped like a stone.

"Hun," said Archie. "That makes three. Oh, good lads! Good lads!"

Then I saw something which took away my breath. Sloping down in wide circles came a German machine, and, following, a little behind and a little above, a British. It was the first surrender in mid-air I had seen. In my amazement I watched the couple right down to the ground, till the enemy landed in a big meadow across the highroad and our own man in a field nearer the river.

When I looked back into the sky, it was bare. North, south, east, and west, there was not a sign of aircraft, British or German.

A violent trembling took me. Archie was sweeping the

heavens with his glasses and muttering to himself. Where was the fifth man? He must have fought his way through, and it was too late.

But was it? From the toe of a great rolling cloud-bank a flame shot earthwards, followed by a V-shaped trail of smoke. British or Boche? British or Boche? I didn't wait long for an answer. For, riding over the far end of the cloud, came two of our fighting scouts.

I tried to be cool, and snapped my glasses into their case, though the reaction made me want to shout. Archie turned to me with a nervous smile and a quivering mouth. "I think we have won on the post," he said.

He reached out a hand for mine, his eyes still on the sky, and I was grasping it when it was torn away. He was staring upward with a white face.

We were looking at the sixth enemy plane.

It had been behind the others and much lower, and was making straight at a great speed for the east. The glasses showed me a different type of machine with short wings, which looked menacing as a hawk in a covey of grouse. It was under the cloud bank, and above, satisfied, easing down after their fight, and unwitting of this enemy, rode the two British craft.

A neighbouring anti-aircraft gun broke out into a sudden burst, and I thanked Heaven for its inspiration. Curious as to this new development, the two British turned, caught sight of the Boche, and dived for him.

What happened in the next minutes I cannot tell. The three seemed to be mixed up in a dog-fight, so that I could not distinguish friend from foe. My hands no longer trembled; I was too desperate. The patter of machine-guns came down to us, and then one of the three broke clear and began to climb. The others strained to follow, but in a second he had risen beyond their fire, for he had easily the pace of them. Was it the Hun?

Archie's dry lips were talking.

"It's Lensch," he said.

"How d'you know?" I gasped angrily.

"Can't mistake him. Look at the way he slipped out as he banked. That's his patent trick."

In that agonizing moment hope died in me. I was

perfectly calm now, for the time for anxiety had gone. Farther and farther drifted the British pilots behind, while Lensch in the completeness of his triumph looped more than once as if to cry an insulting farewell. In less than three minutes he would be safe inside his own lines, and he carried the knowledge which for us was death.

Someone was bawling in my ear, and pointing upward. It was Archie and his face was wild. I looked and gasped— seized my glasses and looked again.

A second before Lensch had been alone: now there were two machines.

I heard Archie's voice. "My God, it's the Gladas—the little Gladas." His fingers were digging into my arm and his face was against my shoulder. And then his excitement sobered into an awe which choked his speech, as he stammered—"It's old—"

But I did not need him to tell me the name, for I had divined it when I first saw the new plane drop from the clouds. I had that queer sense that comes sometimes to a man that a friend is present when he cannot see him. Somewhere up in the void two heroes were fighting their last battle—and one of them had a crippled leg.

I had never any doubt about the result, though Archie told me later that he went crazy with suspense. Lensch was not aware of his opponent till he was almost upon him, and I wonder if by any freak of instinct he recognized his greatest antagonist. He never fired a shot, nor did Peter . . . I saw the German twist and side-slip as if to baffle the fate descending upon him. I saw Peter veer over vertically and I knew that the end had come. He was there to make certain of victory and he took the only way . . . The machines closed, there was a crash which I felt though I could not hear it, and next second both were hurtling down, over and over, to the earth.

They fell in the river just short of the enemy lines, but I did not see them, for my eyes were blinded and I was on my knees.

After that it was all a dream. I found myself being embraced by a French General of Division, and saw the first companies of the cheerful blue-coats whom I had longed for. With them came the rain, and it was under a weeping April sky that early in the night I marched what was left of my division away from the battle-field. The enemy guns were starting to speak behind us, but I did not heed them. I knew that now there were warders at the gate, and I believed that by the grace of God that gate was barred for ever.

They took Peter from the wreckage with scarcely a scar except his twisted leg. Death had smoothed out some of the age in him, and left his face much as I remembered it long ago in the Mashonaland hills. In his pocket was his old battered *Pilgrim's Progress*. It lies before me as I write, and beside it—for I was his only legatee—the little case which came to him weeks later, containing the highest honour that can be bestowed upon a soldier of Britain.

It was from the *Pilgrim's Progress* that I read next morning, when in the lee of an apple-orchard Mary and Blenkiron and I stood in the soft spring rain beside his grave. And what I read was the tale of the end not of Mr. Standfast, whom he had singled out for his counterpart, but of Mr. Valiant-for-Truth whom he had not hoped to emulate. I set down the words as a salute and a farewell:

"Then said he, 'I am going to my Father's; and though with great difficulty I am got hither, yet now I do not repent me of all the trouble I have been at to arrive where I am. My sword I give to him that shall succeed me in my pilgrimage, and my courage and skill to him that can get it. My marks and scars I carry with me, to be a witness for me that I have fought His battles who now will be my rewarder.'

"So he passed over, and all the trumpets sounded for him on the other side."